HARD ROAD TO HEAVEN

Center Point
Large Print

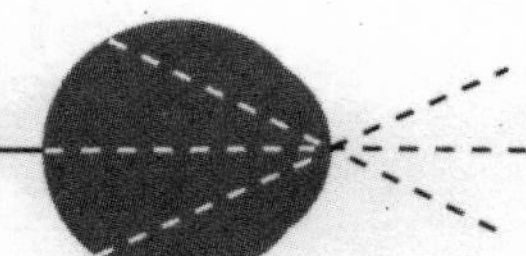

This Large Print Book carries the Seal of Approval of N.A.V.H.

HARD ROAD TO HEAVEN

MARK HENRY

CENTER POINT PUBLISHING
THORNDIKE, MAINE

This Center Point Large Print edition
is published in the year 2005 by arrangement with
Pinnacle, an imprint of Kensington Books.

The text of this Large Print edition is unabridged. In other aspects, this book may vary from the original edition. Printed in Thailand. Set in 16-point Times New Roman type.

ISBN 1-58547-658-7

Library of Congress Cataloging-in-Publication Data

Henry, Mark, 1962-
Hard road to heaven / Mark Henry.--Center Point large print ed.
p. cm.
ISBN 1-58547-658-7 (lib. bdg. : alk. paper)
1. Tracking and trailing--Fiction. 2. Montana--Fiction. 3. Large type books. I. Title.

PS3608.E574H37 2005
813'.6--dc22

2005009292

For Ty, who provided the tinder,
And Victoria, who gave me the spark

Acknowledgements

Many thanks to mentors Henry Chappell and Jimmy Butts for their critique and comment; and to Tyson Bundy for reading just because he wanted to see what happened next.

I am indebted to my agent, Robin Rue for her tireless work on my behalf and Gary Goldstein—an editor who understands the written word and the West.

Most especially, I'd like to thank my fellow gun-toters and trackers—all of whom added in one way or another to this story.

PROLOGUE

Boston
August, 1910

Angela Kenworth's mother was dead-set against her having any adventure that required the wearing of britches.

". . . a great Western adventure!" her father's telegram had promised. *". . . suggest you bring at least two pair of canvas trousers."*

"Young lady, adventure is nothing more than the lie your memory tells you about hardship you've been forced to endure. I stand resolute on this matter."

Mother fastened the buckle on Angela's leather valise with an air of staunch finality, lest any britches find their way inside.

When Mother stood resolute on anything, it did no good to argue. "I will not permit a young woman associated with me or this family to be seen in Montana dressed like a rough boy. Pants have no place on a proper lady when it comes to adventuring."

Mother swelled up like a deviled toad when Kitty, the Irish housekeeper, quietly agreed, observing that she herself had had many fine adventures without her pants. The woman was no smarter than a stick and if she hadn't been such a gifted cook, Mother would have long since given her the sack.

“I shall always despise your father for dragging you out to that dreadful place,” Mother said, driving poor Kitty from the room with a withering stare. As if the fact that she chose to live two thousand miles from her husband wasn’t already enough to show how resolute she stood in her feelings for the man. “You long for adventure, Angela, but believe you me, all you will get is rough men and red savages.”

“Honestly, Mother,” Angela said, running an ebony brush through thick auburn hair. “It’s the twentieth century. Everyone west of the Mississippi River isn’t still mired in the 1800s battling Indians and dueling in the streets at high noon.”

Mother waved her off with an exasperated gasp and went in search of Kitty to check on breakfast. Angela picked up her father’s telegram. She had it memorized, but read it again anyway. “Mother, you’ll get the vapors if you don’t calm down,” she sighed softly to herself. “Red savages in this day and age?”

Mother’s resolution on the matter not withstanding, civilization had even come to places like Montana.

CHAPTER 1

Montana
August 18, 1910

Six days after the train groaned away from Boston's North Station, seventeen-year-old Angela Kenworth showed some resolution of her own and tossed two gray linen traveling skirts out the window of a swaying, horse-drawn coach.

Evidently, her father's idea of adventure had little to do with comfort. It was miserably hot inside the jigging vehicle that seemed to spend more time on two wheels than four. Angela leaned her head back against the smooth, maroon leather upholstery and tugged at the knees of her new canvas britches, regretting the loss of the airy skirts. The snug pants caused her to sweat profusely, confining and pinching in countless unmentionable places. Unable to do anything about it, she consoled herself with the fact that she was no longer confined to the elegant prison of her home in Boston.

Outside, what her father had described as rolling green hills of pine and hemlock had been reduced to charred rock and ruined black snags. Every few minutes the coach rolled over a scab of burned ground, some hundreds of feet across. Mountains of the Bitterroot range peeked up through a brown haze all around her, emerald isles above a sea of greasy smoke.

Her father hadn't mentioned the fires, and she had yet to see him so she could ask about them. A tall, strapping German fellow with soap-scrubbed skin had met them at the station in Saltese and introduced himself as Fritz Mueller, her father's representative. He had white-blond hair, sun-bronzed skin, and chiseled features that made Mother's representative, Betty Donahue, trip on her skirts to fawn over him.

Betty drooped beside Angela, fanning her face with a lace handkerchief. She was a fleshy woman, prone to copious sweating even in cooler weather. Beads of perspiration pasted blond curls to her high forehead and glistened over a moist upper lip. She had a dark, if somewhat alluring, smile of a stain at the scooping neckline of her robin's-egg dress. Mother considered Betty her spy, but at twenty-four the flighty woman was only a few years older than her charge and not much more mature than her five-year-old son, Shad, who sat at her knee playing with a toy wooden horse. Betty did a marvelously irreverent impersonation of Mother by plugging one nostril while she spoke.

"I despise the fact that you've dragged me out to this godforsaken wilderness." Betty's put-on whine harmonized perfectly with the chattering coach wheels. She used the hankie to dab at the sweat that sparkled like a beaded necklace and pooled into a clear jewel at the center of her abundant bosom.

"What does *despise* mean?" Shad said, wiping his forehead, without looking up from the toy horse. He had blond hair like Betty, and shared her tendency to wilt in the heat. Mother had thrown her weight in on the matter of his traveling clothes as well, and he wore an absurdly frilly white shirt with ruffled cuffs, brown knickers, and white knee socks that made him look like a sweaty little George Washington out for a visit to Montana.

Betty let her own brogue slip back while she continued to press the lace against her cleavage, though all the sweat had long since been dabbed away.

"*Despise* describes the way you feel about turnips, dear." She spoke to her son, but kept a hungry gaze on the handsome young German across from Angela. Betty's late husband had been a fisherman out of Gloucester who was lost at sea. She was heavily in the market for another, and the bosom dabbing was her not-so-subtle method of advertisement.

Shad curled his freckled nose and rolled his toy horse across the leather seat between him and the gentleman. "I despise turnips," he said.

"Mr. Mueller, how much further to my father's mining operation?" Angela asked, as much to rescue the poor man from Betty's heaving flirtations as for any desire to have a short journey.

"One half of one hour," the young man said in a clipped accent. "Please to call me . . ."

A sharp crack outside the coach cut him off, and he cocked his head to one side, listening. Panic seized his blue eyes, and he tore his gaze away from Betty to stare down at his chest. A crimson bloom spread rapidly across the pressed fabric of his shirt.

He blinked, opened and closed his mouth like a fish out of water, gasping for air. “I am shot.” A thin sheen of blood covered his perfect teeth.

Angela heard the driver’s shrill whistle, and fell back against her seat as the horses leaped forward into a frantic gallop along the tilted, hillside road.

“Oh, Dear Lord!” Betty put the hankie to her open mouth and gaped, wide-eyed, at the bleeding man. Angela turned to look out her window, and got a glimpse of approaching riders emerging from a cloud of dust behind them. She heard the German groan. His cool hand yanked back surprisingly hard on her shoulder. If not for the blood and the dazed look in Mueller’s pale eyes, she would have thought this was all part of her father’s idea of an adventure.

“Please, don’t, Miss Kenworth,” Mueller said through clenched teeth. Pink spittle foamed at the corner of his tight lips.

An arrow whistled through the same window and lodged in the wall directly above Mueller with a reverberating thud. Shrieking whoops echoed amid rifle shots and the *thwack* of more arrows outside the coach. A shadow flew past Angela’s window as the burly man riding shotgun tumbled from his perch.

The coach careened wildly as it picked up speed, bouncing over rocks and ruts. Shad clutched his toy horse, his eyes locked on the German’s glistening red shirt. A crackling wheeze racked the poor man’s body at each ragged breath.

Mueller pressed a hand over his wound. It seemed to help some—just enough for him to speak.

"Not much time," he groaned, risking a weary glance out his window. "These highwaymen . . . seek money . . . still dangerous. I promise . . . keep you safe. Please . . ." He held a hand out to a cowering Betty to pull her and her son across the coach, leaving the seat next to Angela vacant. Mueller's wheezing grew worse by the moment, his voice little more than a whispered croak. "Behind you . . . in seat . . . is knob. Push . . ." Mueller's eyes clouded, fluttering in a vain effort to remain conscious.

He was drowning in his own blood.

Angela's mind raced while she groped in the crease of smooth leather where the bench met the backrest. It was a tight fit, even for her small hand, and made more difficult by the jigging coach.

This was all impossible. A bone-numbing scream pierced the window as surely as any arrow and made her blood go cold.

Indians.

"I can't find anything." Angela's voice rattled with the coach. She was almost in tears. Searching frantically, her hand finally closed around a cool metal knob. She gave it a push and the leather padding next to her tilted up and forward toward Betty to reveal a hidden compartment the size of a small coffin.

Another bullet smashed into the paneling next to Mueller. Splinters of yellow wood shot across the crimson mess that covered the front of his shirt and oozed between his fingers. He didn't have enough energy to flinch.

"Your father uses . . . to hide precious cargo." Mueller rasped. "Today, you are such cargo."

Angela looked at the dark box and then up at Betty's pleading eyes. "But there's only room for one. I can't . . ."

"No time . . . to argue . . ." The German pulled a black pistol from his waistband and stared resolutely out the window. His breath was shallow, his face sickeningly pale. It seemed a struggle for the once-powerful man to hold the heavy weapon.

"They are upon us." His voice was no more than a whisper now—hardly audible above the melee. "It is your father's place . . . to decide . . ."

A volley of gunfire shattered the air. Betty flinched at each report, and Shad pressed his hands against his ears. Above them, the driver gave a muffled yelp and the coach began to slow.

A chorus of hoofbeats grew louder and drowned out the coach wheels amid the yelping shouts of approaching riders. Angela looked again at Betty's panic-stricken face.

She refused to believe this was happening. "I don't care what my fa . . ."

Mueller's head lolled forward: chin on bloody chest. He was beyond arguing.

The shooting stopped.

"Shad, honey," Angela whispered. She turned the trembling boy's face away from the gore-covered

German. “I need you to lie down in here and be very quiet.” Her voice was higher than normal, tight and overflowing with urgency.

Shad looked up at his mother and sucked his bottom lip. The tips of his small fingers pressed white as he clutched his toy horse.

“Hurry, sweetie,” Betty said. Her eyes were awash, and her tremulous chest now heaved with terror and grief.

Harsh voices milled outside the slowing coach, mingling with the protestations and snorts of horses jerked to a stop.

Angela looked down at Shad in the compartment. “Quiet now. No matter what you hear.”

The shadow of men on horseback flashed past the window. Moments later, heavy footfalls approached.

The seat snapped shut over little Shad Donahue with a resounding click at the same instant the doors flew open. Rough hands dragged the women from their seats on opposite sides of the coach. After the dimly lit interior, the blazing daylight combined with the shock of their circumstances proved blinding and Angela saw only a dark silhouette. Brutish men with stinking breath pawed at her body and threatened to yank her arms from their sockets.

She struggled against her captors, but bit her lip to keep from screaming.

Betty had no such compunction, and her mournful wails rocked the carriage between them.

CHAPTER 2

Montana
August 19

Except for the spot where the blue-eyed mare kicked him above the left knee, Trap O'Shannon woke feeling reasonably pain-free for someone who'd spent most of his forty-eight years sleeping on the ground. He pulled a thin cotton sheet up around his bare shoulders to ward off the morning chill, and tried to nestle deeper into the feather mattress. A twenty-year-old knife wound, puckered and white, decorated the tan flesh over his left shoulder. The injury had gone all the way to the bone, and it troubled him from time to time, particularly if the weather turned cold. Trap was getting to the age where he babied it a little.

Maggie had insisted on three windows in the bedroom when they built their small log home in the shadow of the Bitterroots. Ever a practical man, Trap was sure two windows would be enough, but like most times, he'd let his wife have her way. This summer had proven hotter that normal, and he'd ended up glad she'd cajoled him into that particular luxury. The night before had been so hot, they'd left all the windows open to try and catch a little of the smoky cross-breeze. It seemed a better choice to choke to death on cool, smoky air than bake in confined hot air with the smoke settled out of it.

It would be miserable again when the sun finally poked over the mountain east of O'Shannon's two-room cabin. Most of the fires had slept with the night, and though their smell still lingered, the air was slightly less congested. The cool shadows out the side window, nearest Trap, were green instead of gray, and he managed to take in a full breath of air without coughing. The day would be another scorcher, but with morning's chilly breath still lingering in the cabin, he was happy to have a warm bed and an even warmer wife to sidle up against.

Maggie was still asleep, facing away from him, her airy cotton gown bunched above her hips. Her knees were drawn up toward her belly. One bronze arm ran down in front of her, hand resting between her thighs, the other flung back above her head in careless abandon. Even as she slept, there was something feral about this woman that moved Trap like nothing else. She was still the same fierce creature he'd met when she was only fourteen—older now, with a little more meat on her bones—but just as wild.

Maggie had always been hot-natured. Even in winter conditions that left Trap's teeth chattering, she'd preferred to keep the tent wall rolled up a hair or the window cracked enough to ensure a steady draft.

Her side of the sheet was pushed down to a crumpled pile at her feet, and though the night's chill still lingered in the air, thick tresses of long, black hair sweated to the pillow ticking. She breathed the heavy breaths of exhausted sleep, belly rising and falling deeply with the slow, even rhythm of her soft purr.

They'd been up well past three in the morning playing midwife to the newest spotted mare while she gave birth to her first foal. It was a difficult delivery. Trap knew horses and he was no quitter, but twice, he'd sworn the mare was done for and started for his gun.

Maggie was a different story. A horse was not just important to the Nez Percé culture. It represented the culture itself, and saving one was worth all efforts. She'd refused to give up.

Prayers and mournful songs, helped heavenward by smoke from a bundle of burning sweetgrass from her medicine bag, had filled the dry night air.

The gods Maggie prayed to were a lot like Trap's father's God, who said somewhere or another in His Bible that a good deal of work had to be sprinkled in with your praying.

Maggie had prayed and sang and prayed some more, eventually working her small hand into the birth canal. As much communication as manipulation, whatever magic she'd done had worked.

Just before three A.M., two tiny hooves and a brown nose appeared under the mare's tail. She gave a moaning push and a dandy, spotted mule colt came sloshing out with a gush and a plop into the smoky world.

The coming of a new foal was always a magical event, and the O'Shannons had lingered for a time without talking, arm in arm, marveling at the beauty of it. Once the new baby was nursing well, they'd come inside and collapsed.

Now, Trap coughed quietly and rested a hand on the soft skin above his wife's hip where it melted into her belly. He wasn't sure of the time, but the smoke hanging lazily in the shaft of window light told him the fires were awake again. His grumbling stomach said it was late morning. He didn't care. He wasn't in the Army anymore. Wriggling closer, he nestled against the furnace of Maggie's body. His face buried in the dense tangle of her hair, Trap took a deep breath, drawing in the earthy aroma of ritual sweet-grass smoke that lingered there with the thousand other assorted Maggie-smells that held him together like glue.

He reckoned serenely to himself how retirement—or at least this change in job—had a lot of things going for it.

Maggie stirred. Though she faced away from him, Trap could tell she'd opened her eyes.

"You make coffee?" she said, the rhythm of her breath remaining slow and constant. "I can't smell any coffee."

For three decades, Maggie Sundown O'Shannon of the Wallowa Nez Percé had proven herself a devoted wife and mother, but since moving to their small home-stead, Trap had spoiled her a little by making their morning coffee himself.

Trap snuggled closer and nuzzled the half-moon bite scar on the side of her neck, just below her ear. "Why would I want coffee when I can drink in the smell of my wife?"

Maggie's lips smacked as she woke up slowly. She stretched her head back with a groan, rubbing her thick hair against Trap's cheek. Bits of hay from the ordeal with the mare the night before still hid among the strands. "This old woman's smell will not warm and wake you like some good, hot coffee."

"Oh, I don't know, old woman. I think your smells are waking me just fine." He pressed closer to her, his breath heavy against her ear.

Slowly, she rolled over to face him. "Mmm, I can tell."

She didn't bother with her gown—a fact that Trap considered a promising sign. Fully awake now, she slid a leg over the top of his, drawing him closer with the crook of her heel. Soft, familiar fingers brushed a wisp of salt-and-pepper hair out of his face. He sighed when she touched him on the end of his nose.

"It's not too hot yet." She winked. "I still want coffee, but I suppose it can wait a . . ."

Maggie stopped suddenly, and rose up on one elbow to look toward the east window.

"What is it?" Trap had learned over time to trust his wife's instincts even above his own.

"The horses," she said softly, craning her neck toward the window. She caressed Trap's shoulder over the puckered knife scar. "Our new mother is speaking."

"To who?"

"A visitor." Maggie withdrew her hand, letting it slide

teasingly down his bare chest, stopping at his belly. "Someone's coming on a horse she doesn't know."

Trap threw back the sheet and gave his wife's bare rump a frustrated swat.

"It better be someone important. I hate to leave this behind."

Maggie snorted, but left the sheet where it was.

"Tell them we're not buying then, and come back to bed with me before the day heats up."

Trap heard the horses nicker, and scrambled to his feet. No matter where they went, there were always a sizable number of folks who didn't take too kindly to Indians, or him being married to one. It was a funny notion, considering his own lineage, but he had his father's thick shadow of a beard and smallish nose. That was enough to pass for white among most folks. Nobody had said anything to him yet about Maggie, no more than a buzzing whisper or two at the store, but the feelings were there and he knew it, seething and simmering just below the surface. He'd learned over the years to take no chances when it came to uninvited visitors.

Hopping up and down, half-naked, on one foot, he tried to pull his britches up without falling back on the bed. Maggie chuckled at his little dance. The teasing sparkle of mischief in her dark eyes didn't help matters at all.

"You don't look like an old man right now." She pulled her battered Winchester off the pegs on the wall beside her while she watched. The fact she could shoot the little .44-40 better than most men had added to Trap's confidence on more than one occasion.

He winked back at his wife. He'd be hard pressed to find anything more beautiful than his stocky little bride bathed in the yellow swath of window light, holding a rifle and wearing her thin cotton gown—the hem of which had now fallen down to her knees, to Trap's chagrin. Britches finally buttoned, he abandoned the idea of a shirt and yanked up his canvas suspenders. Clopping hoofbeats passed the front door on their way to the barn. He craned his head toward the open window, listening for a moment.

"Two horses." He scooped up the long rifle that leaned against the wall on his side of the bed. Apart from the bed and a clay washbasin on a chest of drawers, the two rifles were the only furnishing in the room.

Maggie held up two fingers and nodded, agreeing with his assessment.

"I've a mind to shoot whoever I find out there," he said, giving his wife one last dispirited look before he stepped into the front room and eased open the heavy wooden door.

The bright light of morning hit Trap in the eyes like a punch in the beak, a sharp contrast to the cool atmosphere inside the cabin. He squinted to watch the tail of a tall sorrel round the corner in back of his log barn across the stump-strewn yard.

"Help you?" He kept the gun inside the shadow of the doorway, out of sight but within easy reach. There was a hard, uninviting edge to his voice. Maggie watched with her rifle through the east window of the bedroom.

It was already hot outside. So hot it seemed if a man looked at the same spot of parched grass too long, a flame would jump up to meet him. The smell of burning pine pitch hung heavy in the thickening air. Soon the cabin would be hot as well—much too hot to suit Maggie. Trap let the frustration slip out in his voice.

"What can I do for you?" he yelled toward the barn.

"Pa?" A horse snorted and the hollow thump of hooves grew louder as two riders wheeled and came trotting around the barn to the front porch. The O'Shannons' son, Blake, rode a red-freckled leopard Appaloosa they'd given him the year before. A lanky sorrel gelding followed. The sight of the man riding it brought tears to Trap's eyes.

Blake O'Shannon trotted his blocky, pink-nosed gelding up to his father and dismounted. At twenty-four, he stood ramrod strait and just under six feet tall—a trait he'd inherited from his mother's Nez Percé side of the family, along with her black-coffee eyes and the thick head of hair that he kept short, above his ears. He took off a gray, flat-brimmed hat and leather gloves to shake Trap's hand. A shiny silver star decorated the left breast of his light blue shirt. The badge was something Trap hadn't seen before. He gave his son a curious look, but didn't mention it.

"Look who I brought to see you." The young man beamed.

"Ky Roman." The elder O'Shannon shook his head

and rubbed the rest of the sleep out of his twinkling eyes. "Lord have mercy, I haven't seen you since . . . How long has it been?" There was much hand-clasping and backslapping between words.

"Twelve years, give or take," the tall man said with a wide, easy grin. He wore a brown bowler hat and a natty pinstripe suit of matching color. "It was before I left for Cuba."

"Thought you'd be surprised." Blake looked quizzically at his father. "What were you doing in the house at this time of day? You feeling sick?"

The front door to the house fairly exploded off its hinges and a barefooted Maggie ran out to give her son a crushing hug that knocked the hat out of his hands. Though they saw him several times a month, an only son could never visit enough to suit her. Once she released her son, she smiled at Ky and took his hand with both of hers, kissing him softly on the cheeks. Blake ducked his head, kicking at the dirt with the toe of his boot when he saw his mother still wore her nightgown and realized his father had no shirt on.

Roman noticed his embarrassment, and nudged the young man's shoulder. "You think this is bad, kid, you should have seen them when they were youngsters."

Maggie narrowed her eyes and shook a bronze finger at Ky. "You were a youngster yourself if I remember, Hezekiah." She sighed softly, pushing a stray lock of hair out of her face. "Is Irene with you?"

Roman shook his head. "I fear she had a lengthy list of commitments to her women's group back home. She did tell me to say hello to you, and warned me to bring back all your news."

Maggie let her head tilt to one side, her eyes glistening. "I do miss her. How is she these days?"

"Beautiful and pious as ever. She still drags me to church every time the doors open whether I need it or not."

"I'm sure she knows what's best," Maggie said, patting the back of Roman's hand.

He chuckled. "So is she."

Maggie sighed, smoothing the front of her thin gown. "I suppose I should go and put on some clothes. Welcome to our home, Hezekiah Roman."

She turned to go back in the house, then stopped to ponder her son's face for a moment. "Something serious vexes this boy," she said over her shoulder to Trap. Her hand held Blake's cheek for a time, then slipped slowly off as she walked to the front door.

Trap watched her disappear into the cooler interior of the cabin, and hoped he was the only one who noticed the teasing wink she gave him before the door swung shut.

"How are you getting along, Ky?" O'Shannon leaned his rifle against the log wall and gave his friend a proper looking over. He'd grown a bit older in the space of twelve years. They both had.

Roman was made for the Army, with piercing gray eyes and a no-nonsense military bearing that made him look a decade older than his peers. Had he not been in command, the rest of the unit would have still respected him as their elder even though he was only five years older than Trap. The mainstay of his mystique came from the creed by which he lived.

"When it comes to what's right, gentlemen, never pause—Proceed," he'd often tell his men. When the lines got fuzzy to everyone else, Captain Ky Roman always seemed able to tell the difference.

He'd trimmed back his already tame mustache so it was no more than a whisper of the one he used to wear; just a thin silver line under his hawkish nose to match the silver in his hair. The added gray and the extra pound or two around his middle only added to his natural surety, and gave him the dignified air of an honest politician—if there was such a thing. There was an aura—Maggie called it a smell—that fairly flowed from Roman's presence. He was the kind of man other men naturally trusted and followed.

"You hear Geronimo passed over last year?" Roman asked.

Trap took a deep breath and pensively toed the dirt. *"Goyathlay."* He whispered the warrior's Apache name reverently. Of course he'd heard about the death of their old adversary. It was big news across the entire country. Still, it came at him hard every time he thought about it. Trap had wished the ruthless, old killer dead dozens of times—cursed the ground he'd walked on. Then, he'd seen a photograph of the deflated war leader posing in some kind of Plains Indian feather getup like some sort of sideshow attraction. All the starch was completely gone from the once-proud man.

Now, each time Trap heard the name Geronimo, he could no longer think of the times they'd skirmished in the sweltering deserts and mountain country of the fierce Chiricahua. He could only ponder on the dispirited eyes of the withered old man in the photographs. It was better for some people to die in battle, but Trap tried to keep such thoughts out of his mind. He was, after all, an old warrior himself.

"Heard you got sick with the Rough Riders." Trap leaned against a rough-cut porch pillar and used it to scratch his back while he spoke. He was already beginning to sweat, even without a shirt.

Roman shrugged. "A lot of us did. Turned out to be fortuitous I went, though. Roosevelt has more energy than anyone I ever saw. Bowl right over you if you let him, but he's a friendly sort and got to know some of us quite well. It never hurts to have a friend in the White House. Old Teedie got me the marshal's appointment in Arizona after he got elected."

"I heard. Sure appreciate you helping Blake get on as a tracker with the federal boys up here. He's a good man, but with his mama and me as his breeding stock, a fellow needs a little extra boost to get a good job in these parts." Trap thumped the badge on Blake's chest with a forefinger. "What's this all about anyway? Since when they let you pin on the star?"

The fact that anyone with as much Indian blood as Blake O'Shannon would be allowed to wear a badge when he was barred from a good many establishments in Montana was a little hard for Trap to believe.

Tracking for the marshals was one thing. Everyone expected an Indian to know how to track. Pinning a badge on one, that was another matter.

"I deputized him, Trap," said Roman.

O'Shannon brimmed with a thousand things he wanted to ask his old commander, but bit his tongue knowing the man would get to most of them in his precise, methodical way. Instead of quizzing the captain, he turned an eye back toward his son.

"You all right? You know your mama. If she says you're vexed, you best just go on ahead and consider yourself vexed."

"Big things going on, Pa." Blake was not normally the fidgeting sort of person, but he twisted the stained cowhide gloves back and forth in his hands. "Think I might be in over my head here."

"Sounds serious." Trap scooped up the rifle and took a deep breath. All his life, he'd preferred to be busy while he worked important things through in his head. Digging a ditch, sharpening a knife, or feeding horses; it didn't matter. His brain worked better when it was lubricated with a fair amount of elbow grease. "Follow me, boys, and let's talk. I got a new mama out here who deserves a little grain."

While the scoop of oats hissed into a wooden feed bunk, Ky Roman put his boot on the bottom rail of the fence and leaned across the top.

"Truth is, Trap, I'd intended to come look in on you next week when my business was done in Spokane. Blake knew I was there and sent word yesterday for help. Shortly after I got his call, I received a wire from President Taft."

"*The* President Taft?" Trap bent to step between the fence rails, and began to rub the spotted mule colt while its mother munched oats. He'd met a number of important men in his life and was not easily impressed; though it was a curious thing such an important man would be calling on Ky in Spokane.

Blake said, "A girl named Angela Kenworth was kidnapped off the NPR right-of-way yesterday afternoon." He seemed to glow with nervous energy, and the spotted mare gave him an anxious snort. Blake noticed, and stepped away from the fence completely to keep from spooking the horse and agitating his father.

Trap calmed the new mother with a reassuring pat on the shoulder. He said to Blake, "Your mama was right. You are vexed at that. I feel bad about the girl, son, but you've tracked bad men before."

Blake looked at Roman, then back at his father. "From the looks of things, it was Indians that got her."

Trap let the odd news slide by. It was a modern world. Indians didn't do this sort of thing anymore. "This girl any relation to Peter Kenworth of the PK Gold and Timber Company?"

"His seventeen-year-old daughter," Roman said through his teeth, his chin on the top rail. "She was on her way to visit him from Boston where she lives with her mother. Her party was bushwhacked west of Saltese right at the junction with Goblin Creek. Most everyone else was killed and the Kenworth girl's gone missing.

The kidnappers did leave behind her little finger."

"Still wearing a ruby ring," Blake added, staring blankly at the nursing colt.

"I heard there was still some renegades operating out of the Sierra Madre." Trap picked up each of the mule colt's feet, rubbing and tapping them to help gentle it for future shoeing. "We got us some deserted places up here in Montana, but none as bad as Mexico." His brow now furrowed deeply in thought. "Any place up here where a body could sell a white woman in this day and age?"

"Not that I know of." Blake shook his head. "But they only took the one. There was another woman in the party. Whoever did this used her something awful, then killed her. If they were looking to sell women, why only take one and murder the other?"

The two older men looked at each other; then Trap took a deep breath. There were certain aspects of life a father hoped he never had to pass along to the next generation. "I don't know, son. Could be a whole lot of reasons. Maybe one of them fought harder and hurt their manly pride? The Kenworth girl could be dead already somewhere else and you just haven't found the body yet." He shrugged. *"Quién sabe?"* Who knows?

Blake said, "We found a five-year-old boy hiding, but everyone else is dead. They were butchered, Pa . . ." The young lawman's eyes turned glassy for a moment. He gave his head a shake to clear his thoughts. "Anyhow, the kid hid out in a secret compartment under the seat where Kenworth hides gold he's bringing out from the mines."

Blake described the bloody scene to his father. He told him of finding the frightened blond boy, wide-eyed and catatonic, hiding in the dark box under the leather seat, the ammonia smell of urine and the buzzing drone of the green flies the only thing to give away his location.

"Looks like his mama was the woman they killed."

"Does he say it was Indians done it?" Trap straddled the mule colt and rubbed its long ears while it nuzzled the mare's flank.

"No, but there's arrows everywhere, and I counted at least two different sets of moccasin tracks along with a lot of boot prints. The bodies were carved up something fierce. Pa, when was the last time you heard of an Indian raiding party?"

Trap shrugged but said nothing.

Blake looked up toward the house to make sure his mother wasn't coming. "That's right. Nobody uses a bow anymore. I don't know much about Flathead or Blackfoot arrows or any of the Montana tribes."

He turned to focus on his father. "I could be dead wrong about this . . ." He paused, looking over at Roman.

"Blake says the arrows are made of salt cedar, which I assume doesn't grow up here," Ky said. His eyes groaned with fatigue. "I think he ought to be one who could recognize the track left by an Apache moccasin. Don't you?"

Trap stood up and climbed back through the fence, rubbing the sore spot over his knee. "How many people know about this?"

"Old Chauncey Skidmore found the bodies while he was making his deliveries."

"Everyone from here to Bozeman then." Trap bounced a closed fist on the top fence rail while he thought. The dry-goods salesman was a renowned tongue-wagger. The telephone was making a general appearance around western Montana, but there were still only two surefire ways to spread information: telegraph and tell-Chauncey.

"Since it happened on railroad right-of-way, there's been a lot of folks see it," Blake said. "Heck, they're ridin' by on flatcars to have free peeks at the show."

"True." Roman nodded. "But I doubt anybody around here could tell the difference between an Apache arrow and a quill pen."

"They don't have to." Trap chewed on the inside of his cheek while he chewed on the situation. "Most of these folks couldn't tell Geronimo and Chief Joseph apart if you stood 'em both side by side. They'll see a bunch of arrows and feel free to take their leave to exercise a hate for all Indians. They won't need to take the time to focus on any tribe in particular."

Maggie came out with three empty cups, a pot of coffee, and a sweating glass of lemonade. "I got some cold water from the springhouse for your lemonade, Ky. I'll have fry bread in a minute," she said, wearing a smile and a fresh calico dress that stopped just past her knees. Her hair was pulled back in a thick ponytail that hung to her waist.

Ky took the glass and nodded his approval.

"Clay never did get you to start drinking the hard stuff, did he?" Trap said sipping at his coffee. It was hot and black like Maggie's eyes.

"Nope." Roman winked, used to the teasing about his odd Mormon ways, and raised his glass of lemonade in salute.

"How is Kenworth weighing in on all this?" Trap wondered out loud. "I've heard tell he's got his own private army."

Roman held the cool glass up next to his temple and closed his eyes while he spoke. "He does, but most of them are out fighting fires to protect his timber investments. He's the one that called President Taft—him or his wife. She comes from old money and has a lot of connections with the party. From what I understand, she was against the girl's coming here at all." The marshal shuddered. "Lizbeth Kenworth may be a small woman, but she's as imperious as Queen Victoria. I believe I'd shoot myself if I were married to her. At any rate, the Kenworths are understandably scared. Peter knew of my service during the campaigns, and when it looked like Apaches were involved, he asked the president to have me look into it. Blake was one step ahead of him. He knew I was over in Spokane on business and eventually on my way to surprise you."

"I needed you both," said Blake. "Both the deputies are down in Billings. My marshal and Judge Straby are back in Washington, D.C., doing some politicking. Marshal Roman has the official clout I need to deal with the locals, and you're the best tracker I know. Besides that, you both know Apaches."

Trap smirked and looked over at his wife, who stood silently by his side.

"Son, I *am* Apache—half one at least. Since my dear mama was your grandma, that gives you a considerable amount of expertise on the subject yourself. And all the hazards that go along with it."

"That's why we need Mr. Roman. Kenworth doesn't trust us redskins. There's more out there," Blake said. "But I'm not sure what it all means. I think you two should have a look for yourselves." He turned to look at his mother, filling in the details she'd missed, without getting too graphic about the murders and the condition of the little Donahue boy.

"I'm worried about you out here by yourself if Papa comes with me," Blake told her. "Most men are out working on all the fires, but people with grudges are getting mighty worked up about Indians right now. I heard an old Salish man just about got himself lynched between here and Missoula last night trying to get his loose dog back from a neighbor's house. Quite a few of these folks still remember the Nez Percé war."

"So do I," Maggie said simply.

Trap snaked an arm around his wife's shoulder and gave her a squeeze. "He's right, Mag. Why don't I take you over to Trissy Bloom's place in Taft and the two of you can work on that quilt you started?"

"I'll bring my rifle." Maggie took the empty cups and strode for the house.

"Of course." O'Shannon picked up his own gun.

The men watched her walk away.

"She's pretty as ever. You remember the time . . . ?" Ky looked at Blake, who toed at the dirt again. "Never mind. I won't embarrass you, boy. You're one lucky man, O'Shannon."

"I know." Trap shook Ky's hand. "It's sure enough good to see you. Even under these circumstances. It does put me in a mind of old times."

"Me too, *Denihii*." Roman used Trap's Apache name. "Me too. All things considered, I'm glad for a chance to ride with you again."

"All right then." Trap looked at his son. "I need to get dressed and get your mama over to the Blooms' place."

"Kenworth's already greased the skids with the railroad so they'll give us all the cooperation we want," Roman said. "Just put your mule in a boxcar when you take Maggie, and then ride back from Taft to meet us after you get her settled in at her friends. You got somebody to feed your stock?"

Trap nodded. "I'll turn 'em out into the pasture and they should be set for a while. I'll stop in with Old Man Rosenbaum on the way into town and ask him to give a look now and then in case the fires come this way. Folks around here feel pretty much the same way about him as they do about us."

"Good enough." The young deputy put his hat and gloves back on. A relaxed smile returned to his face and he breathed easier now that his father had taken up his cause. "I'm going to get Marshal Roman some better work clothes, so we should get there about the same time. I got a jailer standing guard on the place, but he's not much, so I want to hurry. Let's say three hours at Goblin Creek. It's about a mile before you start up that long hill from the valley."

Trap patted his son on the back, then gave his old captain a halfhearted salute. Roman returned it with a grin.

"That was a poor excuse for a salute, O'Shannon—but you never did stand much on protocol." The man's eyes sparkled and he took Trap's hand again. "Twelve years gives us a lot of catching up to do, my old friend."

"That it does, Captain." Trap said. "That it does."

The two visitors had mounted their horses and trotted through the jack pines by the time Trap made it from the barn to the cabin. Maggie met him as she came out the front door with a large clay bowl covered with a cup-towel.

"I got this butter out of the springhouse when I went to get Ky's lemonade. I was hoping Blake might stay for fry bread."

"Sorry, Maggie. He had to push on." Trap started through the door, but his wife rocked sideways to block him with a hip.

"I know. This is all bad." Her face tensed. "Very bad. I was almost ready for you to go fight the fires, but now I think this trail will take you from me for a longer time.

I don't like it, but I know you have to go—for Blake's sake. I see they gave him a badge now." Maggie pursed her lips, then let out a slow sigh. She held the bowl of butter against her waist and ran the fingers of her free hand along the stubble on Trap's jaw. "You're getting a little gaunt, Husband—like a hungry wolf."

Her face relaxed and her eyes became moist and bottomless. "I have grown used to having you underfoot, you know. We may be apart for a while. . . . I noticed when I got the butter that the springhouse is very cool at this time of day."

"The springhouse is always coo . . ." Trap's eyebrows shot up. "It *is* nice and cool in there, ain't it?" He looked off through the smoke where the two men had disappeared. "But we got a lot to do and I gotta meet Blake and Ky in three hours."

"Hurry then." Maggie started through the trees for the earthen cellar. She used her free hand to hike her dress up just below her bottom so she could tease Trap and move faster as she sauntered through the stump row. There was an exaggerated wiggle in her full hips. A lifetime of riding and the miles she walked in the meadows near their new home had blessed her with the firm legs of a woman half her age. Bronze calf muscles flexed as her bare feet padded their way across the dusty, pine-thatched ground.

Trap felt his mouth go dry and he swung his rifle, barrel first, over his shoulder to trot after her. He too couldn't help but think about how long he might be gone. The idea of riding with Ky again after so many years fanned a flame of adventure O'Shannon thought had long since flickered out.

Trap was proud of the man his boy had become. He knew Blake was capable; there was enough of his mother in him to see to that. Watching him work would be pure pleasure. But this business with the badge worried him. An Indian marshal investigating what people saw as an Indian killing could turn into a real powder keg.

On the other hand, women like Maggie Sundown O'Shannon only came along about every other lifetime and he'd spent enough time away from her already. He had to go; there was no question about that. It was his duty. But having to ride off from Maggie, adventure or not, left a pit in his stomach that even a romp in the springhouse wasn't likely to cure.

CHAPTER 3

Where his son was a tall spruce, Patrick "Trap" O'Shannon was more of a broad oak. Thick arms and shoulders branched from a tree-trunk chest planted squarely over stout, if somewhat stubby, legs. He was slightly bowlegged from years in the saddle, but his sure feet gripped the earth through leather moccasins with such ferocity, it seemed he was rooted to the ground. When Trap was very young, his missionary father had told him it didn't matter so much how tall he grew as long as he made certain the inches God gave him counted for something. He often wondered what his father would have thought about the way he'd turned out.

At a shade under five feet eight inches tall, O'Shannon paid special attention to the size of his mount. There had been plenty of tall, well-broke mules in the Army, and an equal number of stub-legged things with backs that could pack a four-poster bed. Hoping to save his knees from riding too long on a wide mule, he'd settled for one of medium height and narrower build. It also happened to be the most sullen beast he'd ever come across.

General Crook had seen the benefit of riding a mule. As a rule Trap agreed, finding most of the hybrids to be surer of foot, smoother to ride, and smarter. But smarter didn't necessarily mean easier to get along with.

This particular mule came to him as a two-year-old by way of what seemed at the time like a shrewd trade. Since then, it had been his companion for many a mile and the last fifteen years. Trap had heard of mules living past forty. Hashkee was too mean to die any time soon and would likely see Trap go to his grave. A wild eye seemed to say that was the plan anyway. Hashkee meant *angry* in Apache, and the mule lived up to its name on a daily basis with pinned ears and a kinked tail at every saddling.

Tomcat-mean, with lightning hooves that had lain to rest one hapless coyote, six dogs, and too many rattlesnakes to count, Hashkee had more bad habits than most of the shavetail mules Trap had dealt with in the

Army. He bit and bucked and on some rides, only knew two directions: backward and straight up.

About the time Trap had decided to put a bullet behind the animal's ear, the two had come to a sort of understanding. Every day, for almost a month, Trap had saddled the sullen mule thinking he'd shoot it by nightfall. Hashkee had seemed to sense his peril, and from that point on gave no more than a halfhearted crow-hop while Trap was aboard. The mule never gave up its bloodlust for dogs, but Trap didn't consider himself much of a dog lover anyway.

What Hashkee lacked in the way of good nature, he made up for with consistency. On one campaign, deep into Mexico, when oats were nowhere to be found, both Trap and his grumpy mount had gone almost a week on a jug of tepid water and a handful of stale tortillas. No matter the adversity, the animal did what was asked of it. Not that there wasn't a certain amount of griping. Hashkee was, after all, a mule. But he'd seen them safely out of many a bad scrape, and that was enough to make up for an ornery disposition.

There was no real love lost between man and beast, but on a mission like this one, the last thing O'Shannon wanted to worry over was his mount.

Leaving Maggie at the Blooms' place was a hard thing, the hardest thing Trap had done in a long time. He felt as if he'd tied a gut to a low limb of the sycamore tree in front of their house and slowly uncoiled his insides the further he rode from his wife. When he was younger, adventure had often curled her beckoning finger and drawn him to the trail. At each separation, the cramp in his heart grew stronger, but the urgency of each campaign pushed the melancholy back to the far reaches of his mind. Over the years, though, he'd discovered Maggie had infinitely more temptations to offer than any adventure and found, to his surprise, he enjoyed the quiet evenings with her as much as any hostile engagement.

The frolic in the springhouse had been more than enjoyable; Maggie was amazing at that sort of thing. Trap's face flushed at the memory of it. The freshness of it burned his cheeks more fiercely than the blazing sun.

He busied his mind on the task at hand and tried not to ponder on the leaving too much, but there was no way to deny the hungry nagging that got deeper with every step the mule took. It was impossible to know how long he'd have to be gone. Once Trap cut sign, he would stay glued to it no matter where it led.

He always planned for a lengthy campaign, but he didn't need much. Three days of oat rations in a canvas nose bag straddled his saddlebags, and a wool bedroll hung across the mule's mutton-withers tied to the pommel of his Mexican-style saddle. An extra wool shirt hid between his two saddle blankets, one of which had a hole cut in it so he could use it for a serape when he had to stand watch on a chilly mountain night. His .45-70 Marlin hung comfortably under the stirrup fender on his right side, butt-stock to the rear so it didn't catch the brush. On his left side, facing forward—away from the cantle of his high-backed saddle—hung a break-top Smith and Wesson Scofield in .45 caliber. There were newer pistols around, double-actions and fancy new auto-loaders, but if Trap was anything, he was faithful. If something worked, he stuck with it.

When he could, Trap eschewed a sidearm during a scrap, preferring his trusty long gun if given time to make a choice. He'd seen too many men he needed to stay down walk away from a pistol wound. Many of them died later, but in a fight, he preferred those he dispatched to go down and stay there. Good men had been killed by good-for-nothing hombres who didn't have the sense to know they were already dead. On the field of battle nothing beat the huge hunk of lead the rifle spit for assuring that sort of thing didn't happen. When the fry-pan-sized bullet hit, a person knew they were done for.

Both the rifle and pistol had their niches, but when a scrap got tight Trap preferred his knife. The blade rested in a simple leather scabbard off his right side, held in place by an antler button on a leather whang. It was relatively short as far as sheath knives went, barely nine inches overall. With a simple stag handle, it was in all ways unremarkable except for what it could do in Trap's capable hands. He'd proven more than once that his knife could work miracles in close combat, and it had the added advantage of never needing to be reloaded.

Hashkee covered the ground quickly, a jarring grudge in his normally smooth mule-gait at having to work on such a sweltering, smoky day. Standing in the flat stirrups designed to be more comfortable on his moccasined feet, Trap squinted into the hazy glare and made out two riders up the narrow valley. At a distance, at least, his eyes still worked the way they did when he was a young man. He was relatively certain it was Blake and Ky, but he hadn't survived these forty-eight years by stumbling into things on easy assumptions. Pointing Hashkee into the shadowed forest and up a steep grade alongside the train tracks, he lost only five more minutes and came in beside his two friends from a small knoll, slightly above them. The sun was to his back.

"Thought I was foolish to look for you to come up the road like a normal human being." Roman shielded his eyes as he watched mule and rider slide down the hill on low haunches among a skittering shower of dirt and pebbles. He held a hand across the pommel of his saddle as the mule came up next to him and released a low growl.

Trap shook the offered hand and shrugged. "These don't sound like normal times, Captain. Fact is, I don't think I remember ever livin' in what a man could call normal times."

"True enough." Ky nodded.

"It gets less and less normal every minute, Pa." Blake's brow creased and he twirled the end of his leather reins.

"How's that?"

"Just got a wire from Mr. Madsen. He's already in

Montana and on his way to see you. Seems someone offered him a job working security for the railroad. He was up in Helena talking with them about it."

"Clay Madsen in Montana?" Trap smiled. He stood in the stirrups with a slow groan and rubbed the small of his back.

"He's on his way to see you."

"I haven't seen either of you boys for twelve years and now I get a full dose of both of you all at once," Roman told Trap, grinning, showing his teeth. "When did you two part company?"

"Almost three years ago," said Trap. "His father died and he went back to Texas to give the family ranch a go. I came north with Maggie—away from the heat." Saddle leather creaked when O'Shannon resumed his seat. He needed to do something so he could digest this new information. "I'd like to get on over to Goblin Creek and take a look if we could, Captain."

Ky tipped the wide brim of the mouse-brown hat that he'd replaced his bowler with.

"Lead on, Blake. Take us to Goblin Creek. We've got work to do." With the same ease that he'd switched hats, Roman went from a visiting guest to commander.

Jailer Joe Casey probably thought he was doing his level best to keep folks away from the bloody carnage that surrounded the stage—but he was old and there was only one of him against an endless tide of gawkers. There weren't that many automobiles in this part of Montana, but a few folks had them. Trap supposed the snaking set of tire tracks leading back down the creek-side road belonged to Peter Kenworth. Other onlookers had been coming in by the wagonload all day long, braving the smoke and heat to set eyes on what was already being called the Goblin Creek Indian Massacre.

Trap shook his head slowly while he took in the scene. No matter the brutality, someone would enjoy looking it over. He'd seen people bring picnic lunches to hangings to gnaw on chicken legs while they watched condemned men dance their last mortal steps at the end of a rope. Trap didn't have a stomach for such things. He'd taken the lives of other men, even looked them in the eye while he did, but he took no joy in it. And he certainly never stood around to admire his own handiwork.

People were softer now, protected from the harshness that used to mark the frontier. He supposed these folks had never been exposed to the real thing, so the green flies and glistening gut piles in front of them seemed more like an imagined illustration from a dime novel than the soulless carcasses of once-living, breathing human beings. Civilization might have come to Montana, but the people were no more civilized for it.

Overwhelmed by so many visitors, Casey had slipped from his role as guard to that of an informal tour guide. He kept the onlookers back a few feet from the bodies, but pointed out this wound and that, gesturing with outstretched arms to share his theories about what had happened. His gray hair blew in thin wisps on the hot breeze and the sun had severely pinked the top of his bare scalp. Trap shook his head in quiet wonderment that a man would be out on such a fiercely cloudless day without his hat.

Scarcely ten yards from the corpses, three women in plain cotton dresses stood, hands to their mouths, in front of a weathered buckboard and tired gray horse. Gaping at the scene before them, one held the hand of a curly-headed toddler, who hung disinterested at his mother's side. He wiped his runny nose on the hem of her dress. Beyond the women two boys, no older than thirteen, stared slack-jawed at the naked, mutilated bodies tied to the coach wheels.

"Get back from there, all of you," Ky growled in a righteous indignation that caused the boys to scamper up the side of the hill, where they disappeared into the jack pines. Casey began to stumble over his own feet, trying to get away himself. The three women snapped out of their stupor, and the young mother suddenly thought it necessary to cover her little boy's eyes with the palm of her hand.

Ky stopped his snorting horse upwind, a scant twenty yards from the bodies. Dismounting, he flipped the leather reins around a scrub of buck brush. Trap and Blake followed, but remained in the saddle.

"I'm ashamed of you folks standing around here like this," Roman told the women as he would a group of small children. He meant to scold harshly, but without particular malice. "Have you no reverence for the dead? Now go on home." He nodded his head with an air of such finality, Joe Casey looked over at Blake, whom he considered his immediate superior.

"Me too, O'Shannon?" The sudden arrival of more lawmen had put Casey on edge, and his shoulders flapped up and down toward his ears with so much nervous energy when he spoke, he'd have taken flight if wings were attached. His face twitched and popped like a pot of simmering oatmeal. Trap had never met Casey, but it was easy to recognize him as the man Blake called Jiggin' Joe.

"No, you stay," Blake snapped, with a considerably harder edge than Ky had used to speak to the gawking townsfolk.

"There was too many of 'em to fend off," Casey whined. "I did the best I could." The twitching man looked ready to burst into tears.

Blake glared and raised a hand to silence him. Turning without another word, the young deputy looked over the bloodbath in front of him and closed his eyes.

Trap gave his son a nod of approval. It was the boy's second time to look at the mess the killers left behind. Trap was glad to see it disgusted him. A second helping of carnage like this shouldn't be any easier to stomach than the first.

Plumes of dust puffed up from Trap's moccasins as they hit the parched ground. What little wind there was had fallen off completely. The brooding smells of blood, death, and fear filled the void it left behind. He tied Hashkee to a twisted scrub so dry, one good pull from the mule would turn it to dust. It really didn't matter. The thin leather reins were no more than a bluff anyway when it came to keeping a one-thousand-pound animal tied. Stepping closer to the coach, Trap was careful to watch where he put his feet. He almost chuckled when he saw what the old fool Casey had done with his hat.

A stout, blond man, obviously muscled by hard work in life, hung like a flaccid doll, tied to a front wheel of the coach. His body was riddled with a half-dozen arrows. Only a trace of blood oozed around the wooden shafts at their entry points. Trap hadn't seen anyone scalped in some time, and the sight of it caused him to go hollow inside. Glistening flies, black and metallic green, crowded around the bloody edge of the white bone circle on top of the dead man's head. Flies were as bad as gawkers, and there always seemed to be some nearby to exploit such a gruesome occasion.

What was left of the man's hair lay in crusted locks against a swollen face. Long cuts ran up, down, and sideways across the puffed skin of his nude body like a scored ham. Whoever tied him to the wheel had been unwilling or unable to lift him any higher, so he sat, arms outstretched to the sides and legs straight out in front of him, like a great, bloated bird coming in for a landing. Casey's tattered hat lay across the man's lap, covering his mutilated groin.

"I kept pukin' every time I looked at what they done to him." Jiggin' Joe hung his head between bobbing shoulders.

Trap leaned over the body, careful to avoid any footprints that might remain unsullied by the curious onlookers that had visited the scene before him.

"Wound on his left side below his heart . . . bullet came out the back there, but the wagon spoke's untouched," Trap mused to himself. "Must've been killed somewhere else." A look inside the coach confirmed his theory.

"They did all this to him after he was dead, didn't they?" Blake stood a step closer to his father.

"Reckon so." Trap pointed at the arrow wounds. "All these are for show. Dead men don't bleed very much. What little bit you see there is likely from the bloating. If it was Indians that done this, they were mighty angry about somethin'. I worked the border nigh on to thirty years. Seen some mighty rough things, but this scalping business has got me puzzled." He took a small notepad and pencil stub from his shirt pocket. Touching the tip of the pencil to his tongue, he began to make sketches while he spoke.

"It's not that Apaches never scalped, mind you, but they generally did it in retaliation for something. In all those years, a lot of the meanest renegades we ever came across didn't even know how to take a scalp. Of course, the rest of this . . . I'm sad to say, I've seen this kind of thing before."

O'Shannon shook his head and groaned while he looked at the young woman tied to the back wheel. It seemed unthinkable that Casey had been moved by the butchered man enough to cover him while he'd left the poor woman so exposed.

Fleshy and pale, her skin had taken on the appearance of soap left too long in the tub. Already a day and a half under the blazing sun, she'd begun to cook. She was tied upside down, her legs lashed crudely to opposite spokes of the large coach wheel. A jagged, half-moon gash along her belly nearly cut her in half and her bowels spilled down the front of her, obscuring her face in an obscene, buzzing mass of flies and stinking entrails. She had no arrow wounds, but she'd been scalped like the man. Bruises the shape of a large hand encircled her trailing wrists. Dried blood from her scalp drenched her face and hair. The dead didn't bruise—or bleed so profusely, even from a head wound. Much of this had been done to her while she was alive.

She was lighter than the man, and her tormentors had been able to lift her a little higher on the wheel. Her head just touched the ground, and her neck bent unnaturally under the weight of her slumping body. Trap had to get down on his hands and knees to examine it more closely. A bullet behind her ear had ended her suffering. The gutting had been for show after her body was tied to the coach wheel. She'd been positioned to make a point.

The driver, apparently overlooked, had been spared from mutilation and lay undisturbed, but every bit as dead as the others, beneath the coach. A fusillade of gunfire and arrows had brought down the four horses and they lay in bloating heaps, still in their traces.

Trap closed his eyes and tried to imagine the bloody scene as it happened. The driver shot, the groans of the butchered man, mixing with the terrified screams of the poor women, the crack of rifle fire, and the wild squeals of the horses. He could smell the gunpowder—hear the laughter of the killers—for they had surely laughed.

The men who did this took great pleasure in their work.

Hoofbeats, loud and hollow, like the thumping of a melon, drummed over the dusty ground and shook Trap from his imaginings. Five riders, dressed in starched clothes for a town visit instead of rugged travel, reined up beside the coach. The youngest of the bunch, barely old enough to coax a whimsical bit of hair from his chin and upper lip, rode a fresh horse. He had trouble controlling the animal at the smell of so much gore.

There was still enough fear in the air that Trap could smell it, even above the smell of death. The animals smelled it too, but he doubted anyone else did. The stench of fear was worse than death. Everyone died, but there were few who deserved to die afraid.

"Tom Ledbetter," Blake whispered under his breath. "I'm sure of it. Rides a big dun. He's got the reputation of a troublemaker. Been in jail a few times for letting his temper get the best of him."

"Reminds me of a scalp hunter I once knew." Trap took a step closer to his son to show some solidarity as well as protect the spot where he thought he'd have some good tracks from further defilement. "Who's he workin' for?"

"Kenworth."

Trap judged the frowning man to stand a shade

under six feet tall. Thick-necked and broad-shouldered, he looked strong as a range bull. Dark eyes raged with an irrepressible anger under the brim of his high-crowned hat. He had a dangerous smell about him that made folks slink out of the way when he came toward them.

Most folks.

"We got a few tracks we need to keep undisturbed, if you don't mind, sir," Trap said, standing his ground as the burly man unhorsed himself and strode forward ahead of his four cronies.

"Well, I do mind, not that it's any of your business, Stubby." Ledbetter tugged his hat lower over angry, deep-set eyes. Muscles twitched along an angular jaw as he clenched his teeth. He continued to walk as if he expected Trap to spring to one side and clear a path. When that didn't happen, he pulled up in a blowing huff. "I'm gonna get one of them arrows for my proof when I have to hang the Indians that did this."

Blake yanked an arrow out of a dead horse and offered it to Ledbetter. "Take this one, and move on. But be careful who you hang. You could end up swinging yourself."

Ledbetter spit on the ground, narrowly missing the dusty toe of Blake's boot. "I was just about to say the same thing to you, Red Bug." This brought a chuckle from the group behind him. "Just wearing that fancy badge don't make you any more white or more of a man." Hand on his gun now, Ledbetter pressed closer.

A purple vein pulsed on the side of the man's thick

neck. Molten hate hung in the dead air around him. His vehemence wasn't for show.

Blake stood his ground, but flipped the arrow so the bloody point faced Ledbetter and pressed against his gut enough to dent the tight cotton shirt. The young lawman held the arrow in his left hand and touched the butt of his pistol with his right.

"Mr. Ledbetter, I don't want this to go the way it's goin', but make no mistake, this is the scene of a crime and I'm not about to let you muck it up."

The big man wrinkled his long nose. The taut muscles in his reddened jaws flexed as he stared hard at Blake, studying him through narrow eyes. His nostrils flared and he took a step back, accepting the bloody arrow with a toss of his head.

Trap moved sideways to take up a position away from Blake. He found himself glad he'd decided to strap on the old Scofield. Ky cleared his throat, rifle in hand, on the other side of the interlopers, and Ledbetter nodded, smacking his jaws. Casey stood a few feet behind Ky with a shotgun, trying to redeem himself from his earlier foolishness. His shoulders still flapped, but not enough to keep the scattergun from providing a worry for Ledbetter and his men.

"I see how this is gonna be." Ledbetter stared daggers at Trap. "I shoulda known when I saw you wearin' the moccasins. Bein' shod like that, you got red nigger blood in you; I'd bet my life on it." He wheeled, striding defiantly over to his dun, and swung easily into the saddle for a man of his bulk. The bloody arrow was still in his hand, and he used it to drive home his point as he spoke to Blake.

"You just keep pokin' about in the blood and gut piles, boy. We'll see to catchin' the savages that did this. Mark me good, though, you best watch your own hair. I've seen Indians scalp other Indians as quick as they would a white man."

Ledbetter turned his big dun on its haunches and loped away, spanking it on the rump with the arrow. The greenhorn on the frisky mount whirled three times before he got it pointed the right direction and galloped off after his compatriots.

Blake and Trap let them leave without a word. Taunts and threats didn't do much for men like Ledbetter. He was a problem that would require seeing to sooner or later, but he'd chosen later. Neither O'Shannon saw any reason to provoke a showdown at a moment when time was of the essence.

"Got a moccasin track over here and some horse prints as well," Ky said when the riders were out of earshot. After the initial examination of the bodies, he'd moved to the perimeter, leaving the close work to Trap. Roman was a pious man and the sight of the woman's nude body troubled him. Trap was certain of that. It troubled Trap as well, but not in the same way. Roman had always been more bashful.

Trap studied the dusty ground at the base of the butchered man, then around the pile of bloating horses. Many sorts of tracks stitched the area around the bodies, most of them from Jiggin' Joe and the other onlookers; but few of them had taken time to look at the horses. A careful study of the blood-soaked dust around the bloated animals let Trap narrow the number of possible tracks to six: two moccasins and four boots. Blake had taken the time to make some decent sketches on his first trip to the site. Comparing what he had with the sketches brought the number down to five. The tracks Ky found allowed them to discard a set of hobnails that probably belonged to one of the gawking boys who'd disappeared into the trees.

"Except for the boot tracks, it sure looks like Indians are the ones behind this," Ky mused, looking across the parched hills in the direction of the hoofprints. Kenworth's place was up Goblin Creek to the north. The tracks led south. "But I suppose most Indians wear boots nowadays."

Trap grunted in agreement. "And some white men wear moccasins. But it looks like you sure hit the mark, son. The person that left this track doesn't land on his heels like a white man. Look here at the heavy toe on this one. Your grandma sewed moccasins just like this. They're Apache all right—a mite new-looking, though, to be this far from home."

"What to you make of this, Pa?" Blake squatted next to a clump of bunchgrass.

Trap found signs of struggle in the twists of yellow grass and dusty stones. A splash of blood cut a black line across a tuft of bent stem, too far away to come from the bodies beside the coach. The dry bunchgrass had been pressed into the dirt by a twisting heel.

"I'll bet one of them clipped the Kenworth girl's finger right here." Trap laid his hand across two long scuff marks in the dirt, turning so he didn't cast a shadow and obscure any sign. The dusty earth was almost too hot to touch. He made a mental note of the size and shape of the girl's track. "See where her feet went out from under her. She likely fainted."

Ky squatted down beside his friend and looked him in the eye. "I pray to God she fainted before she saw what they did to her companions."

Blake brought up an arrow he'd pulled from the coach wall and ran a finger along sparse fletching. "Trade point, salt cedar shaft. Looks like an Apache arrow to me."

"It does." Trap kept his hand on the ground, as if he were gaining information from the feel of the hot earth. "I've seen a passel of Apache arrows in my day, but I never thought I'd see one up here in Montana in nineteen and ten. Not with blood on it anyhow."

Ky took off his hat and wiped his face with a white handkerchief. "Doesn't it seem like an awfully big coincidence that the last three members of our scout-tracker unit are all in this little part of God's vineyard at precisely the right time to track a bunch of renegade Apache?"

"I don't believe in coincidence and neither do you, Captain. This whole thing is a puzzlement to be sure. In the old days this is somthin' you'd pray over and I'd consult Maggie about." Trap thought of his old friend Clay and smiled. "And Madsen would seek the arms of an understanding woman to chase the whole thing out of his mind."

"We have to consider the possibility of ambush." Roman let his gaze wander along the hazy hills above them.

"I'd say we should count on it," Trap said.

"Ambush or not, the Kenworth girl's out there and someone has to go after her," Roman said, stating the obvious.

The wind shifted a bit, giving Trap a whiff of the nearby corpses, and yanked him back to grim reality. "All right, Captain." He looked across the road at Jiggin' Joe, who stood drooling and useless, trying to hide from the hard gaze of the other three men. Trap suddenly felt the need to put as much distance as he could between himself and so much incompetence. "We should get on with it."

"Blake," the marshal said, returning the hat to his head. "Have your man lay these poor souls to rest. I doubt he'd be much use to us on the trail."

Trap grabbed the wide horn on his saddle and started to swing up, then stopped. He turned and looked at Blake, thinking. "The sign all points south, toward the Idaho line. With the captain's permission, I'd like you to go back and look in on your mama. I want her to try and talk with the boy. He survived all this and if he's got a story to tell, she's the one who can get him to tell it. If we've got an ambush ahead, it would sure help to know what he saw. You pie-aye back to us as soon as you can with Mr. Madsen. We'll leave a good solid trail for you to follow. I don't know if these renegades will stay to the mountains or not, but there are a couple of little burgs over into Idaho we should probably check."

"Yes, sir." Blake nodded. "Be careful."

"You do the same and make fast tracks. I got a feeling these killers are headed for the High Lonesome. If they do, we'll need you and Clay both to ferret them out."

Blake's Appaloosa kicked up dust as he wheeled to lope off toward Taft.

Trap turned his attention back to Ky. "Shall we go, Captain?"

"You got a fine son there, O'Shannon." A hot breath of breeze caught and tugged at Ky's gray hair. His smile seemed out of place in amidst the surrounding. "Takes after his mother."

"I hope so." Trap watched Blake disappear into the distorted waves of heat that rose up from the scorched ground. He tried not to think about the carnage thirty feet away. The possibility of ambush was almost certain, and he needed to focus all his instincts on what lay ahead.

Trap turned the mule and trotted over to take up the kidnappers' trail. From the corner of his eye, he saw Joe Casey retrieve his bloody hat from the butchered man's lap and return it to his sunburned head.

CHAPTER 4

Fire Camp

Blue smoke curled like a faded silk ribbon on the heavy green thatch of towering cedars. Giant trees slouched under the weight of the desolation they'd seen. Beneath the layer of smoke, the flint-hard odor of scorched earth pressed two dozen bleary-eyed men to the blackened ground like an unseen hand. The sharp smell of burned cedar stung their bloodshot eyes and pinched at their raw noses.

Granite Creek gurgled over clean melon-sized rocks, just a few feet away from the men. It was cool and clear in contrast to the superheated oppressiveness of the gray air, but the parched men had to rely on the warm water in their canteens for moisture. Fires in the mountains had rendered most of the smaller streams undrinkable. Flowing over the charcoaled skeletons of thousands of burned trees transformed the water into lye strong enough to make soap—or eat a hole in a man's gut.

For now, the sound of the stream was all they had to cool them. The surviving trees gave some measure of shade; the heat of an August sun ate its way through and threatened to boil the good sense out of the already blistered men. Warm water and juice from their rations of canned tomatoes were in good supply to wash down a plentiful diet of bacon and pancakes, but the heat put a tight fist around the men's stomachs and kept their appetites small.

Rather than eating, the exhausted men were content to lounge here and there on dirty blankets across from blackened snags and the few remaining cedars at the far edge of the firebreak. Many of these trees were large enough that four grown men could stand in a circle and not reach around the trunk. The last night and most of the day was spent working the wide firebreak so the ranger could set a back-burn and stop one of the largest wildfires in its tracks.

The work was much like building a road; they scraped and chopped and grubbed anything that might burn in a wide swath over a mile long. Further up the valley, Granite Creek joined a larger stream that no one seemed to know the name of and helped keep the distance manageable. Once the firebreak was completed, the men had used torches to set a back-burn ahead of the prevailing wind to burn any flammable material and starve the oncoming fire when it arrived.

It had worked, and apart from a few spots where popping embers shot across the wide break, the backfire had stayed on the far side. When the wildfire approached, it had no fuel and sputtered to a stop before it reached the break. The fire boss, Ranger Horace Zelinski, posted fireguards for the jumping embers and they were extinguished immediately.

The blaze of the day contained, the break provided a safe haven for the beleaguered men. Most of them used the time to sleep, stretched out where they had fallen, exhausted on the dust and sand of the forest floor, blackened blankets pulled over soot-covered faces to hide them from the bright haze of light.

Four of the crew sat in the shade of one of the largest cedars, playing cards on a grimy blanket. A somber mood hung above the little group and mingled with the smoke. Their voices were a buzzing whisper, drowned out from the others by the gurgling creek.

Daniel Rainwater, a nineteen-year-old Flathead Indian with perfect white teeth, crossed his long legs under him at the edge of the dusty blanket. His poker face was a constant grin, gleaming like a crescent moon. His friend Joseph sat to his right. The same age as Rainwater, Joseph was shorter by a hand and kept his own teeth hidden behind a closed mouth. Daniel knew his friend cared little for cards, but played because *he* did.

Rainwater also knew he was taking advantage, but the knowledge that the tough-minded Joseph was nearby allowed him to push things—to take chances he wouldn't otherwise take—like playing cards with the likes of the two men across the blanket.

Ox Monroe was easily six and a half feet of mean bone, knife scar, and fire-hardened muscle. He sported two gold front teeth that snapped together like scissors when he was angry or frustrated. The giant sported a twisting green tattoo of a serpent that started at his neck and ran down the front of his filthy shirt before it crawled out and ended in a large fanged mouth on his thick forearm. Everyone assumed he'd been a sailor, but he never said anything to confirm the rumors.

Monroe's companion, Roan Taggart, was a big man in his own right, but next to Ox, he was almost dwarfed. An odd scar, pale and pinched, covered the left side of his face from chin to shriveled ear. It pulled the skin tight around a squinty left eye and ran down behind his hat before disappearing beneath the frayed collar of his dingy shirt. A remnant of a nasty burn. Premature flecks of white hair had invaded Taggart's red beard and earned him the nickname Roan at an early age. In his late forties, there was hardly any red left. A constant diet of bacon and canned tomatoes disagreed with his belly and made him prone to violent eruptions of gas that made the unscarred portion of his face go red. He blew often, and when he did, everyone else sought a safe haven upwind. Two of the crew had worked fires up on the Yellowstone, and commented on how Roan's sulfurous additions to the air reminded them of the place.

The buzz throughout the fire camp was that Monroe and Taggart had escaped from a prison in Colorado. The fire season was bad enough that every able body was needed, and if the authorities knew anything, they didn't mention it.

Both of the big men wore pistols openly on thick leather belts at their sides, but they fingered long-handled bowie knives while they played. Rainwater knew playing cards with such men was not so dangerous as winning at cards with them, but the brash young Flathead couldn't help himself.

Big Ox clicked his gold teeth in silent frustration, a sure sign he had a bad hand. Roan fiddled with the rawhide whang on his knife sheath. He wasn't holding anything worthwhile either.

Joseph had won slightly more than he'd lost, but Daniel couldn't seem to make a mistake. If he held a pair and threw in three, he'd draw a full house. If he threw back four, he'd pull back a straight or at the very least three of a kind. As the young Indian's smile spread, the mood across the blanket grew as dark as the blackened landscape across the firebreak.

Roan let go of his knife handle long enough to deal the next hand.

Monroe swept his cards up in a beefy paw. "If you ain't a son of a whore," he said, glaring across the blanket at Rainwater as if he'd been the one to give him the bad hand. His voice was rough and punctuated with a gritty cough.

Daniel shrugged, but his smile only dimmed a little. At two bits a hand, he was almost seven dollars ahead and no amount of talk could chase away his happiness. He threw back three. The white crescent of teeth was unwavering as he studied his new cards and rearranged them to his liking.

Roan drew two, passed a voluminous cloud of rotten-egg gas, and then folded. Joseph folded as well, leaving the game to Rainwater and Monroe.

Big Ox waved away Roan's addition to the smoky air and gave his cards a satisfied grunt. He smiled like he'd just swallowed someone's prize poodle and fanned three jacks on the blanket. His cards in the open, Monroe's heavy brow furrowed over seething eyes that dared the young Indian to best him. He'd stopped clicking his gold teeth, but thick fingers tapped the hilt of the long knife at his side.

Daniel shrugged, smiled, and tossed down a straight flush, queen high.

Monroe shot a withering look across the blanket. His dark eyes boiled like storm clouds that might at any moment shoot thunderbolts and consume what was left of the forest and Rainwater along with it.

"You thievin' little nit." The giant man grabbed the greasewood handle of his long knife. The blade hissed up an inch from the sheath. But he didn't draw it completely.

Joseph's hand already rested on his own blade.

Daniel Rainwater didn't move. Instead, he smiled his toothy smile. "Nothing harmed, Big Ox. We'll just play for fun."

Ox was already up on one knee, his mood as scorched as the twisted trees across the burn. "It ain't gonna be no fun what I aim to do with your hide, young buck. I ain't one to lay down and take a cheatin'." Monroe glanced down at Joseph and let loose a rumbling chuckle, which Roan Taggart joined. "You best keep that sticker hid, nigger. You'll both be stompin' your own guts before you skin it and I'll already have your hair."

Rainwater let his eyes slide sideways to his friend.

Nothing moved on Joseph but his nostrils, which always flared before he did battle. The big man didn't scare him, but Rainwater's own stomach churned. Not that he was afraid to die. He was enough of a warrior to accept that day when it came. He didn't want Joseph to die on his account—especially over a card game. Using both hands, he pushed the pile of money across the blanket, being careful not to lean so far that Monroe could reach him. Joseph would certainly strike if that happened, and Daniel wanted to prevent it if he could.

The big man jerked the blanket back toward him with a growl, upsetting the money and the cards. Most of the money was in coins, but the lone bill floated down between them in the still air. "I don't want the stinkin' money. I aim to take what's mine outta your red nigger hide."

Roan Taggart nudged his partner with an elbow and gave a sideways nod toward their grizzly bear of a fire boss, Horace Zelinski, who stood on a burnt knoll above them, giving the little group what everyone on the crew called "the eye." Beside him stood a white man in the khaki wool uniform of the United States Army. On the Army officer's right stood the thickest black man Daniel had ever seen. Dressed much the same as the white officer, the Negro trooper's muscles strained at the wool uniform blouse. If he'd taken a step sideways in front of the fire boss and the officer, the trooper would have blocked both men from view.

Zelinski was shorter than Monroe by a head, not even as tall as Taggart. Compared to the broad Negro trooper he was willow-wand skinny, but the thunderous bark that emanated from his fearless chest seemed capable of felling trees. Some of the men who'd worked with him before swore in hushed tones they'd seen Zelinski bark at a fire only to have it turn away from his wrath.

Brimming over with a puritanical work ethic, the forty-year-old forest ranger was the senior man in the newly created Nez Percé National Forest and he took his charge seriously. He held himself to a strict set of standards and didn't tolerate shirkers or troublemakers of any sort.

Rainwater relaxed slowly when he saw this man who seemed to him to be as much a force of nature as the wind or rain, or the fire itself.

"Everything all right down there, men?"

Monroe met the ranger's icy stare and turned his head away, as a big bear might do when a bigger bear came in to challenge his territory. Zelinski had strong medicine, and even a stiff-necked man like Big Ox Monroe was smart enough to take note of it.

"Everthing's jake with us, Boss." Instead of resheathing his knife, Monroe snatched up a can of tomatoes and used it to punch two holes in the top, looking at Rainwater with a threatening sneer while the thick steel blade slid easily through the tin lid. Waving to the fire boss, he threw the can to his lips and sucked out the juice. The liquid cut pink ditches in the black-sooted stubble as it dribbled from the corners of Monroe's crooked mouth.

"How about it, Rainwater? Everything all right?" The

fire boss had the ability to stare down several men at one time, and Daniel couldn't tell if he was focused in on him or Monroe.

"We just finished a card game, Mr. Zelinski."

"Good enough then," the ranger barked. His eyes never left Monroe while he spoke. "Rainwater, the Department of the Army has sent us reinforcements from the 25th Infantry. Would you be so kind as to show Corporal Rollins here a good place this side of the firebreak to set up their camp?" Zelinski gestured toward the black trooper who eclipsed the sky behind him.

Both Indian boys scrambled to their feet. "Yes, sir," Daniel said.

The order given and understood, Zelinski turned and walked away with the white officer.

Monroe wiped his mouth on the sleeve of his filthy shirt and belched. He kept his voice low so the huge trooper on the knoll above them couldn't hear. "If you Injuns wasn't bad enough. Now we got to sleep on the same mountainside as a bunch of . . ."

Corporal Rollins slid down the embankment toward them and held out an enormous paw. "Bandy Rollins is my name." He smiled through a row of white teeth on a face wide enough to match the rest of him.

Monroe ignored the offered hand and turned to face Rainwater. "The boss man saved your hide just now, to be sure, boy. But have a care. Even he ain't everwhere all the time." The big man cleaned his knife on the front of his thigh, then drew the gleaming blade through the air in front of his own grizzled throat. "You're a dead Injun and don't even know it. Next fire, when everyone's busy watchin' their own hides, you should be right careful. Folks can't be expected to watch over you all the time." He turned back to his can of tomatoes.

Rainwater started to walk away and Taggart put out his hand. "Leave the money." The stench that surrounded him stirred when he spoke and made the young Indian cough.

He smiled and gave the smelly, pink-faced man a nod. "I'd planned to."

"That was a close one," Rainwater said when they were across the grove and clear of Big Ox. He stuck a hand out at Corporal Bandy Rollins. "Daniel Rainwater of the Flathead Nation. This is my cousin, Joseph." Joseph shook the corporal's hand.

"I'm Bandy Rollins, Company G, 25th Infantry. The Army sent us over from Spokane. Most of us is camped over at Avery, but we been assigned to help you boys fight fires." He cast his eyes around the clearing. "Though it looks like you done got 'em licked."

Daniel chuckled and glanced at his cousin. "We got it done here, but there's always another one over the next mountain. You ever fought fires before?"

"Can't say as I have, but I'm one heck of a learner. An All Army baseball player I am. People says I'm bull-strong, racehorse-agile, and hound-dog-smart. I reckon me and my men can pick up quick enough on what needs to be done."

"You a baseball player, huh?" Daniel slapped the black trooper on his broad back. "I saw a baseball game once over in Kallispell. Looked like it would be fun enough."

"From what I just saw, you boys should take up the game so you could stay outta trouble. You liable to get in dutch playin' cards with the likes of those yayhoos." Rollins shook his massive head and clucked to himself. "Yes, sir, boys, consortin' with those kind of men will get you kilt for certain. You best show ol' Bandy where you want us to camp. I'll look after you and teach you how to play baseball to boot. No, sir, ain't nobody gonna hurt you with somebody as bull-strong, race-horse-agile, and hound-dog-smart as Corporal Bandy Rollins around."

CHAPTER 5

Doc Bruner's modest whitewashed house doubled as his office. It was exceptionally nice for a loosely knit community like Taft, which got its name when William Howard Taft came through on a campaign tour and chastised the people at the then-unnamed railroad stop for their riotous and wicked ways. The wayward souls didn't repent, but they did name the town after their pious president.

An independent sort who enjoyed the rough-and-tumble life in a wild town like Taft, Bruner was the only doctor between Wallace and Missoula. Accustomed to living alone since his wife quit him for a life in the big city, he had the unkempt look of a bachelor who didn't have a woman to tell him it was time for a haircut, and the relaxed demeanor of a man that wasn't looking to find a woman—or a barber.

Except for the occasional whiff of antiseptic that chased back the smell of baking bread, the doctor's house had a homey feel. It made Blake feel drowsy on such a hot afternoon. He wondered how much of the massacre little Shad Donahue had seen when they'd brought him out of the coach. Blake knew what he'd be like if he'd seen his own mother butchered like the Donahue woman. The thought of it brought a tightness to his chest that threatened to crush him, and he forced himself to think on something else. He couldn't blame the boy; he'd probably go silent himself in such a situation.

A paddle fan, with great, spade-shaped blades of woven palm leaves, twisted in slow, whumping revolutions on the high ceiling. Blake slouched in a padded-leather chair across from his mother and the Donahue boy, and marveled at how cool a little breeze made the room. Doc Bruner sat a few feet away in a chair that matched Blake's. He shook his head at the progress Maggie had made in such a short time.

At first, Shad did nothing to even acknowledge the fact that there was anyone else in the room. He sat cross-legged on the floor and pushed his wooden horse back and forth on the dark hardwood along the edge of a braided-rag throw rug. Without speaking, Maggie knelt down beside him and took the leather pouch from around her neck. She began to hum a soft tune, her chest rising and falling as she breathed deeply. Ignoring the child, she continued her humming while she used a finger to sort through the soft leather bag. When she found what she wanted, she nodded, leaned back against the couch, and pushed her feet straight out in front of her, then smoothed her dress down around her thighs to make a sort of table on her lap. She dropped the pouch in the cradle of cloth and held up a small bone flute, no more than four inches long.

Blake remembered the tiny instrument from his childhood. The sight of it brought back a thousand tender memories of time spent with his mother. For a moment, he thought he could smell the pinnons and cedar smoke of his Arizona youth.

Maggie pressed the bleached white pipe to her lips and let her humming turn into a flute song that trailed softly upward, toward the whispering ceiling fan. It was a light but mournful tune. Happy and sad at the same time, it tugged at the heart and the mind all at once. Maggie had played the same tune after Blake's baby sister had died, then again when she'd prepared to celebrate his father's homecoming after a long absence. It had fit the occasion—both times.

Shad ignored her for a time, rolled his toy horse, and stared at the wooden floor—then, slowly, he began to hum the tune along with her. His fragile voice started softly, but rose gradually to match Maggie's flute song.

He moved the horse more in rhythm with her playing. Then, in a flash of fluid movement that made Blake catch his breath, the boy crawled across the dark wooden floor and climbed into her lap.

Maggie's dark eyes gleamed, but her face remained stoically calm. She played on for a few more minutes, and the lonely little boy put his arms around her neck and buried his face against her soft breast. Blake had done the same thing, countless times, when he was a child in need of comfort. Gently laying the flute on the rug beside her, Maggie wrapped her arms around the boy, pressed him to her, and patted him softly on the back. The flute music gone, she resumed her humming.

"Will Mama come for me?" The boy leaned away from Maggie enough to look up at her.

"No, child, she had to go away."

"The bad men took her away, didn't they?" Shad began to whimper softly. "They killed Mr. Fritz, and made Mama and Angie cry. Then they took them away. Angie made me hide in the coach seat even though Mr. Fritz wanted her to hide there."

Blake knew better than to break the spell by speaking, and was relieved when his mother asked the questions that weighed heavy on his mind.

"Did you see the men who made your mama cry?" Maggie's voice was a soft and comforting blanket that enveloped everyone in the room. She used both thumbs to clear away the tears from the young boy's cheeks. Then she wet her finger on the tip of her tongue and rubbed away a bit of dirt from his chin. Blake recalled struggling during many such spit baths, and supposed all boys had to undergo such indignities from their mothers. Shad didn't seem to mind having someone mother him, and endured the cleaning quietly.

"I couldn't see very good," he finally said. "There was only one little crack in the wood. One of the men was bald-headed. I heard the other men call him Feet or something like that. He's the one that hurt Angie. I saw another man too. He wore a big black cover on his eye like he was blinded. He hurt Mama and dragged her off when Feet gave him permission." The boy coughed to clear a hoarse throat. "The one-eyed man was . . ."

Shad stared at Maggie's face for a moment, then reached out and touched her cheek. He was silent long enough to make Blake's stomach knot in anticipation. Maggie remained relaxed.

Blake's gaze wandered to the ceiling. He counted the revolutions of the paddle fan above him, and got to eighteen before the boy spoke again.

"I mean the one with a patch over his eye . . ."

The boy paused again, but Maggie didn't prod him.

"He was . . . like you." Shad touched her face.

"An Indian?" Maggie's eyes opened wide in genuine interest. "I see. Well, you're safe with us now so you don't need to worry about him."

Shad shook his head and looked over his shoulder at Blake and Doc Bruner. He slowly blinked wide blue eyes as if seeing his surroundings for the first time.

"That's my son." Maggie kept her arms around the boy and used her chin to point to Blake. "He's an Indian too. He's a good man and wants to help us find the men who hurt your mama."

"Can he bring Mama back?"

"No, child, he can't." Blake could see his mother looking up at him as she pulled the little boy even closer. Her eyes brimmed with tears, and she blinked them away while she tried to comfort him.

An hour later, Shad slept on the couch, still whimpering softly with each breath, sometimes cooing the tune Maggie had played on her flute.

"The boy sounds like he could identify at least one of the men, maybe two," Blake whispered.

Maggie looked past the linen curtains on the parlor widow.

"If the kidnappers know that, he is in danger. We have to keep him someplace safe. I want to stay with him. He should have someone to mother him now, and I need to do something so I don't worry so much about you and your father."

Blake fell into thought for a moment, tapping his hat against his thigh. He didn't doubt his mother's ability to care for the boy—or herself for that matter. But that didn't stop him from worrying. Especially since he knew many people in the area shared General Sherman's view when he said he'd seen a good Indian once—a dead Indian. Tom Ledbetter, for instance—to him, an Indian was responsible for any sin or depravity committed by any other Indian. His own people had shared the same logic in the past . . . a lot of people had.

"Come on outta there, squaw, afore we have to come in and get you." A gruff voice crashed through the open front window like a jagged stone and punctuated Blake's worry. Murmured grumbles and demands, too muffled to understand, followed.

The sun drooped low on the horizon, and the streets in front of Doc Bruner's house danced with long orange shadows in the smoke and dust. Blake peered around the edge of the window frame to see a small band of thugs gathering beyond the doctor's sun-bleached rail fence. Some carried clubs. At least one held a pickax. No guns were visible, but Blake had no doubt pistols hid themselves in greasy waistbands.

He turned to his mother. "I think we should try to slip out the back way."

Doc Bruner stepped in from the hallway that led to his office and shook his head. His steady whisper of a voice engendered trust and soothed almost as well as Maggie's. The double-barreled coach gun in his hands helped too.

"There are two more out back to be certain you don't go that way." Bruner peered at Maggie over the top of his wire reading glasses, then at Shad, who still slept on the couch. "Both of you might as well just stay here. I can watch out for them, son. Most of those folks aren't from around here. They don't look very friendly, but I doubt they'd make a move on a doctor's office." He folded the glasses and tucked them into the pocket of his white shirt before focusing his attention on Blake. "Taft is well known around these parts for its abundance of the demon rum. I imagine these men are here fighting the fires and wandered into town for a good drunk. Tommy Ledbetter's with them, though, and that troubles me. I'm sure he's fired 'em up about your Indian mother."

Blake took a deep breath and checked the rounds in his sidearm. He slipped the old Remington back into his holster and studied his mother's passive face. She seemed completely relaxed. The way she always looked when she had walked with him in the deserts near their home back in Arizona and spoke to him of the earth. He struggled to remain calm and feel the way Maggie looked.

"Your grandfather used to say it is better to face a cougar than run from it," Maggie said. "Walk toward it, and the cat will often turn away. If you run, it will *always* give chase and strike you down from behind." Maggie rested an open hand on Blake's chest and looked up at him. "You must get to your father. Tell him what the boy said—especially the part about the Indian with the eye patch—but I don't think we need to sneak out like mice. I only count eight people. If we face them now, we can put an end to this."

Blake cast a worried glance at the doctor. "If this goes bad, keep the boy in here and try to get a message to my father about what he told us. If we can convince them to disperse, bring the boy out to us."

Maggie patted his arm. "It will be fine. You are so much like your father. I've seen him face many men such as these."

• • •

Tom Ledbetter wheeled his tall dun and loped away without so much as a backward glance as Blake pushed open the door. Eight dour men milled around at the edge of the street and glared at Blake and Maggie through bloodshot eyes. Doc Bruner had been right. The group looked like men who'd come to fight the forest fires that had charred the mountains around them for miles. With many of the blazes now under control, the brigades were getting some time off for visits to nearby towns to wet dry throats at the local saloons and spend some of their twenty-five cents an hour on some of the fiery women of western Montana. Though they were soot-covered, bleary-eyed, and exhausted from their labors, Ledbetter had done a good job of working them into a frenzy, no doubt describing the massacre scene in graphic detail. Aggravated by the lack of women, they didn't need much to set them off. They were middle-aged men, and some of them had probably lost relatives to hostile Indians. It had been an easy job for Ledbetter to fan their latent hatred into a terrific burn.

Blake knew these men itched for a fight. Smoldered inside for it. Sodden with whiskey after their back-breaking labor against the fires, most were no doubt frustrated by the fact that Taft and all of western Montana, for that matter, were going through not only a dry summer, but a drought of sporting women as well.

With thousands of firefighters, loggers, and miners to choose from, there just weren't enough women to go around. The sports found they could be a little fussier than normal, and the ugliest, smelliest would-be customers shared the dregs from what was an otherwise unsavory cup to begin with.

"Tell us who done it," a grizzle-faced man with a bobbing goiter shouted from the back of the group—as if Maggie had been a party to the murders.

"You men go on about your business," Blake warned, keeping his hand close to, but not touching, the butt of his revolver. "We want no quarrel with you."

"Well, you got it anyhow, son," a self-appointed leader said matter-of-factly from the front row. He was a tall, cadaverous fellow, mangy and raw from his firefighting, skinny as a fence picket, except for an alcoholic bulge at his belly that made him look as if he'd swallowed a chamber pot. The charred brim of his gray slouch hat hung across his face like an angry brow. "You got a quarrel if you want it or not unless you stand aside from that there squaw." Chamber Pot held a hickory pick handle loosely in his bony, blackened hand.

"We gotta set an example for justice," the Goiter bobbed enthusiastically in the back.

The man in the burned hat patted the pick handle against an open hand and sneered. "You ain't got nothin' against justice, have you, Sheriff?"

"It's Marshal," Blake corrected, knowing as he did that the words weren't going to make any difference. "What you're up to's got nothing to do with justice."

"First I thought you was a greaser with a badge, but

you got an Injun look about you too, now that I think on it." Chamber Pot took a step forward, followed by the other men. "It's no wonder you take up with the squaw."

Blake felt his mother move a step away from him, giving both of them room to maneuver. Once he drew his pistol, there was bound to be bloodshed. Were it not for the fact his mother stood beside him, he would have welcomed it with men of this caliber. He had confidence in his abilities, but one stray bullet could spell disaster.

"Why, bless me if it ain't Maggie Sundown!" A drawling voice punched through the hazy smoke in front of an approaching rider. The southwest sun made a statuesque silhouette of him and his horse against the golden haze. Blake couldn't make out his face, but the stranger had used his mother's maiden name and there was no mistaking that booming Texas voice. It had the disconcerting effect of a cannon shot over the crowd, but just hearing it brought Blake's anxiety level down a notch.

Long shadows rode along the dusty ground in front of Clay Madsen and his muscular bay gelding. When he came out of the sun, it was easier to see the high-crowned silver-belly hat canted rakishly to the left. A drooping mustache as dark as his bay's tail and a neatly trimmed goatee framed his smiling mouth.

"Blake, my boy, how the blazes are you?" Madsen bellowed. He ignored the gathered mob as he trotted his jigging horse through the middle of them, dismounted, and handed the reins to a dismayed man in faded overalls standing beside Chamber Pot.

"Looks like you're havin' a party and forgot to invite me." With his back to the grumbling drunks, he winked at Blake and extended his left hand, keeping both their gun sides free. After a hearty, pump-handle handshake, Clay turned to a flustered Maggie. He gathered her up with both arms and kissed her on the lips with a loud smack.

"It's been too long, Maggie my darlin'," he said, putting her down to straighten her crumpled dress. "Where is that mean little man you married? From the looks of things, these boys are having a bit of luck that he's not anywhere near these parts." The big Texan gave a swaggering smirk as he looked over the situation.

"Working." Maggie managed to regain some of her composure, but still wore an embarrassed grin and flushed cheeks, despite the fact that the men in the street wanted to see her hang.

"Working?" Madsen let his jaw drop. "Mercy, woman, I thought he retired. I'd hoped to spend a little time talking before . . ."

Chamber Pot cleared his throat. His whiskey-slurred speech quivered as he worked his confidence back to the fore. "You best be moving on, mister, if'n you know what's good for you. We got us a sworn duty to bring this Injun here to justice."

Clay frowned, letting his breath out slowly through his nose in a disgusted sigh.

"Fiery darts of the adversary!" he bellowed. "These bastards are annoying, aren't they, Maggie." Their greeting kiss had knocked his hat back some, and he used his left hand to settle it over smoldering gray eyes as he turned to address the group. His voice built like a hot wind as he spoke.

"Beat it, all of you. Mercy, I've seen meaner lynch mobs at my six-year-old niece's birthday party. These fine folks are friends of mine and I'll be go-to-hell if I'm gonna let you damnable fleas get near them." He turned back to Maggie, ignored the mob again, and tipped his hat. "Sorry about the language, dear, but that man with the funny little belly has kindled my ire."

Chamber Pot's slow simmer shot up to a full boil. He fumed, raised the hickory pick handle, and snapped, "You turn around and look at me when I'm talking to you, you high-minded son of a bitch. I can see what you're about, kissin' all over the little red whore. I'm fixin' to . . ."

Clay's long-barreled Colt hissed out of his holster as he wheeled. Advancing on the man with one quick stride, Madsen cut the threatening words short with six inches of cold steel rammed through teeth and against the back of Chamber Pot's throat. The pick handle clattered harmlessly to the dust. Chamber Pot gagged and fell back to join it with a muffled grunt, both hands grasping the gun barrel that protruded from the bleeding gash of his mouth.

With slow deliberation, Clay thumbed back the hammer and spoke to the men around him, his voice barely above a whisper. "You boys best sober up and be on your way. If this nice lady's husband were here, you'd all be lookin' at your innards 'bout now." He let the piercing gaze fall to his trembling victim.

"As for you, you have worse language than I do. This is a respectable woman and I believe she deserves an apology."

"Thorry, ma'am," the deflated man mumbled around a mealy pink drool of broken teeth and blood that dripped from the pistol barrel. His clenched eyes pressed tears of fear from singed lashes.

"I reckon that'll have to do," Clay said, yanking the gun barrel back so a few more teeth caught on the front sight blade on the way out. The man groaned and covered his bleeding mouth with sooty fingers. Clay held the pistol in his relaxed hand and tapped the long barrel against his thigh while he thought. "I expect you'll have revenge burning a hole in your head if I let you go."

Chamber Pot groaned and suddenly smelled as bad as he looked. He shook his head so hard, the charred hat fell off. "No, thir! No, I thwear I don't." He winced when he lisped across the broken teeth. Spittle hung in bloody threads from his grimy chin.

"Just the same," Clay said, rapping him on top of the head with the heavy gun barrel, "I think you'd better sleep on it." He stepped back to survey the rest of the crowd.

"Who's next?" He played the cocked pistol back and forth across the crowd.

No one breathed.

"That's what I thought. Now, that was just a little layin' on of hands. Make for the woods, boys, or we'll have to start havin' a real prayer meetin'."

Two of the would-be vigilantes grabbed their bleeding compatriot and dragged him by the armpits across the dust. The drunk who'd held the bay's reins silently pushed them out toward Clay, as if he wanted to get rid of them without getting too close to the formidable Texan.

Clay lowered the hammer on his sidearm and returned it to the holster. "Much obliged," he said, and smiled as if nothing had happened.

When the mob had slunk into the brown curtain of smoke up the street, Clay turned to Blake. "It's been my experience that if you apply a masterful enough ass-whippin', you can generally take care of a man's thoughts of revenge—for a while at least." He tipped his hat to Maggie again. "Pardon the plain talk, hon. Anyhow, we'd probably do well to saddle on up and scoot, in case there's a back shooter amongst that little mob. What'd you do to rile them up so bad?"

Blake filled him in, while Maggie went in to get Shad. The boy dozed against her shoulder when she brought him out. Doc Bruner stood in the open doorway with his shotgun, smiling at the entertainment he'd seen, and watched up the street for any of the men to return.

"You're right." Clay nodded, removing his hat to let all the new information settle in his brain. "We can't leave the boy here."

"I'll stay with him." Maggie fingered the leather medicine pouch that hung around her neck. "His spirit is sick. He feels safe with me and I can help him."

Blake rubbed his face. Being a deputy was turning out to be a heck of a lot harder than being a tracker. He didn't feel right about leaving his mother. Especially not with drunken mobs roaming around trying to hang her, but he needed to get the information Shad had given them to his father.

"I'll be fine, son," Maggie said. "Really. Ask Mr. Madsen if I can't take care of myself."

"I'm sure as hell scared of her." Clay grimaced. "Sorry again, Maggie dear. If you don't count my sister—and I don't—I haven't been around a decent woman in so long I've forgotten my manners."

Blake blew out a quick breath and spoke before he could change his mind. "Let's get over to the jail. There's a room off the office you can bunk in. They've paroled near everybody in Montana to help with the fires, so it should be empty. It's built for stout, so it should keep folks out as well as in. John Loudermilk is working tonight. He's a good man. I trust him."

"What brings you all the way to Montana, Clay?" Maggie waved good-bye to the doctor. "You know Ky Roman is here as well?"

"I heard. It will be good to see him—and that little wart you call a husband. You should have married me, Maggie. You know that, don't you?"

Blake chuckled. He'd grown up around such talk, and was used to a certain amount of harmless flirtation between his mother and Mr. Madsen. He was the only man alive who could get away with it.

"You came up to steal me away from Trap?"

"Nothing so spectacular. But it is an interesting story." The Texan looked down the street the way the mob had disappeared. "Let's head on over to the jail and I'll tell it to you."

CHAPTER 6

There was something familiar about the smell. Angela wanted to ask Betty about it, but she was busy over by the coach talking to one of the Indians. The sun was right in Angela's eyes, and made it so difficult to see she felt dizzy. Shad was gone or she would have asked him about the smell. He was exceptionally bright for such a young boy.

Angela needed to get to her father's mining operation and couldn't understand why they were stopped. There was really no time for this. Her head ached and she needed to use a bathroom in a bad way. She would have to talk to the driver about all this dawdling. He was an employee of her father and by association, an employee of hers. Father would be expecting them and she didn't want him to worry.

Fritz Mueller opened the coach door and leaned out, smiling widely and ignoring the fact that the Indian talking to Betty had a hand on her shoulder. The handsome young German's voice was hollow and rattled from the dark nothingness of the doorway.

"Come back to the coach, Miss Kenworth . . . and bring your finger with you."

Angela looked down at her feet and saw her little finger lying on the ground. The ruby ring her father had given her was still on it. It would never do to leave the ring behind. Mother would be furious. Angela bent to pick up the finger and caught the smell again.

It was a hard smell, hard enough to hold—and smelling it made her feel heavy, like she couldn't keep her feet. Slowly, the smell turned to a bitter taste, then Betty screamed and the taste turned to pain. Angela gagged and her eyes fluttered . . .

She was so hot, it was hard to breathe. Thick, putrid air closed in around her, and she realized she'd vomited down the front of her clothes. Someone had done a cursory job of cleaning it up, but the smell still lingered. Pain replaced the fog in her head. Slowly, with great effort, she willed her eyes open and remembered where she was.

The metallic taste of blood pushed at her throat. She'd been biting her cheek in her sleep. Sometimes, her brain tricked her into thinking she could still feel her little finger. She couldn't keep from checking each time she woke up from the shock-induced naps that peppered her time in captivity with black dots in her memory. The finger was gone each time; nothing remaining but a tiny nubbin, no bigger than a chicken bone, covered by a bloody, ooze-soaked scrap of cloth. A sickening, gut-wrenching throb started where her finger used to be and rushed up her arm, where it threatened to blow out the top her head before ricocheting back to her arm again at every beat of her heart.

Angela couldn't remember what day it was. She felt a pressing need to use the privy, but it was not yet desperate, and she supposed from that that she'd slept through the night and into another day. She remembered the wilted woman with dirty blond hair and a large mouth taking her to the outhouse the night before. Afterward, she'd tended to Angela's finger, soaking it in salt water and whiskey, before putting on a fresh bandage. Once, Angela had torn off the bandage to be certain the finger was gone. The woman had slapped her on the hand hard enough to make her cry.

"Don't let the air get on that bone. You best keep it covered like I tell you to," the woman had whispered in a throaty, liquor-sodden voice that sounded as desperate as Angela felt. She had a humorless look and a racking cough that turned her face red when it hit her. When she wasn't coughing, she looked as if her whole body was turned down into a deflated frown.

Now, fully awake, Angela sat slumped against the wall with her eyes half open, trying to get rid of the gritty film that covered them, and looked around her dim, smoky prison. Asleep or unconscious, she'd been all but ignored, so she scanned without turning her head.

A bald man sat hunkered in a metal tub across the room, blowing noxious green smoke from a cigar as fat as his stubby fingers. Angela had never seen even the top half of a naked man before—not even her father—and she found herself wondering if it was normal for all men to have such a coarse rug of hair over their shoulders. She'd always supposed that when men went bald, they were pretty much hairless everywhere.

Angela let her head loll back against the rough plank wall. She surveyed the rest of the room to get her mind off the man's hairy back. The room was no more than fifteen feet across, and there was only one door. Beams of light cut through narrow cracks in the rough-cut timber, and Angela felt herself wondering what the cold Montana winter must be like in such a place. Next to the far wall was a sagging double bed, with a sad-looking quilt and two crumpled gray pillows. From the looks of the bedclothes, Angela thought this woman might have once had taste, but the men she entertained probably didn't take the time to care for lace and frills.

A small wooden table squatted beside the bed. A brightly bound notebook with a red linen spine lay beside a chipped porcelain pitcher and basin. She thought maybe the woman kept a diary. Angela had always kept a diary, and supposed a prostitute might find use for such a thing. The book was the only color in the room, and looked out of place in the otherwise drab surroundings. Two chairs that looked wobbly even with no one sitting in them completed the meager furnishings.

"Come see to scrubbin' my back, woman." The bald man's voice was a rough growl.

The same blond woman who'd helped Angela with

her wound sat up from a tangle of quilts on the creaky bed. She wore a sweat-stained bodice, yellowed by time and washes in mineral-laden water, and a cotton petticoat of the same dingy color. Her blond curls stuck in ringlets against the perspiration on her flushed face.

As Angela's head cleared, she recognized the man in the tub as the same man who'd ordered the murder of the stagecoach driver—the same man who'd cut off her finger. She remembered the Indians had called him Feak.

The sweating woman's breasts bulged against the threadbare cotton of her soiled bodice. Angela thought of Betty, and caught a sob. It was hard in her throat like a piece of food that was too big to get down, and brought a sharp pain between her shoulder blades and tears to her eyes.

Feak blew another cloud into the air and coughed while the woman scrubbed his back. "Don't be so damned rough, Moira." He leaned forward in the tub, the white knots of his spine erupting from the hairy mat of his back like mountaintops above the tree line.

"Take off the dirt, not the hide." He spit into a rusty can on the floor beside the tub.

When Moira had pinked his back sufficiently, he leaned back and threw an obscenely pale leg over the side of the metal tub. The top of his boot had rubbed a bald spot in the thick rug of black hair halfway up his calf and made him look like a dog with a bad case of mange.

"I got to be figuring on what to do about that boy."

Feak blew more smoke into the close air. "He mighta seen my face."

"He don't know you from Adam, Lucius." Moira coughed into her sleeve, then dipped her scrubbing brush into the water and worked on his shoulders—lightly, so he shut his eyes.

"Don't matter. Can't be leavin' things unfinished." Angela heard the same cruel rumble in his voice she remembered hearing just before he'd cut off her finger.

Shad was okay! At least for the time being. If that were not the case, Feak wouldn't be worried about him. This fact alone filled Angela with a new sense of hope, and she felt the pain in between her shoulders ease some. Even the throb in her hand quieted with the news.

The door opened and a baby-faced white man sauntered in with the two Indians. He held a half-empty bottle of whiskey by the neck in one hand and a rifle in the other. Feak and the woman must have been used to such intrusions because Angela was the only one who jumped. His name was Scudder, she remembered that much.

"Look who's awake," Scudder slurred, staggering across the room to prod Angela's foot with the toe of his boot. His pouting mouth was turned up into a sickly grin. The few dark hairs that tried to be a mustache were pasted across his pale, carplike lips in stark contrast and made them look like a badly infected wound sewn together with catgut. "She don't look like she's worth ten thousand dollars."

Feak didn't look up from his bath. "Well, she is, so leave her be for now."

Angela sighed quietly when Scudder walked away. He was a young man—maybe four or five years older than her—not too tall, but big around the belly from lots of drinking and with a cruel look in his puffy eyes. Angela had seen the look before in her neighbor's cat when it was toying with a wounded bird. He enjoyed other people's torment. He didn't look too awfully strong, merely mean-hearted. His look was the only thing sharp about him.

A horse snorted outside, then pawed at the ground. The sound of muffled voices carried through the cracked window on the smoky outside air. The door probably led to a back alley so Moira's patrons could come and go unnoticed by their neighbors unless they happened to pass one another in the alley, in which case they were likely to keep such things between themselves. Bumping into someone in an alley behind a prostitute's house is not the kind of thing a person brags about. In any case, Angela knew rescue from this place was unlikely. The Indians or Scudder would be on her before she made it to the door. She felt weak, hardly able to even get to her feet, and knew she wouldn't make it far without collapsing if she did get outside.

Angela tried to sit up to ease the pain in her back and make herself a little more comfortable on the rough pallet of blankets, but realized the need to use the privy was becoming more urgent. The woman had offered her some warm soup earlier, but the smell of it had made her gag. Now she felt hungry, but she was afraid if she had anything to eat, it would only make her situation more critical. At first she'd been glad she was wearing britches instead of a skirt. It made her feel more modest when they'd dragged her around. But now there was no way to accomplish what she had to without taking down her pants, something she would put off as long as she could around these men.

Billy Scudder flopped down backward on one of the two rickety chairs and rested his arms along the backrest. "Turns out you heard right, Feak. There was a kid," he said, yawning wide enough to show a mouth full of whiskey-rotten teeth. "From what I can tell, they got him over at the jail in Taft. Some Injun woman's with him."

"What they want with a Injun woman?" Feak sat straight up in the tub and stared intently at Scudder. For a moment, Angela feared he would stand up.

"She's lookin' after him, I guess. Funny, I ain't never heard of no Injun with an Irish name. Maggie O'Somethin' or other. They got her tryin' to get the boy to talk." Scudder chuckled into his folded arms and nodded toward the two Indians, who idled by the wall. "I reckon me and the boys scared the water right outta him with our doin's yesterday." He spoke as if they had done no more than a harmless prank. He looked across his arms at Angela and chuckled. "Too bad you conked out and missed all the fun."

Angela felt bile rise up in her throat at the thought of what they'd done to Betty.

"See to the screamer," Feak had said. But Scudder and the Indians had argued, reminding their boss he'd promised they could have some fun with her before they rubbed her out. Angela turned her head and tried to vomit on the floor, but her stomach had already voided itself of everything but anger and pain. So much pain. It hit her in the back of the head like a hammer. She drew her wounded hand to her belly, curled up in her filthy quilt, and sobbed.

"What? You got no stomach for such talk?" Billy Scudder sneered. "Neither did your chubby little friend . . ."

Feak snorted. "Shut up, Billy, before you scare her to death. The boss wants her alive."

Moira slumped back on the edge of the bed, her scrub brush dripping suds and dirty water on the sheets. If she cared, she didn't look like it.

"Maggie O'Shannon," Moira droned. "I've heard of her."

The older of the two Indians glared at the far wall intently with his good eye as if he were remembering something from his past. A mottled burn scar furrowed the left side of his face from jawline to forehead. The string of his black felt eye patch ran across a twisted nub of skin where his ear used to be.

"Maggie Sundown of the Wallowa." His voice was pinched and he spit the words more than said them. "Strong medicine, that one. She is the wife of *Denihii*, friend to the one who did this to me." He gestured to his eye and the scarring on his face. "Her power is all that kept me from killing Roman those years ago. She is an evil witch. If she were among my people, we would torture her and hang her from a cottonwood tree for the buzzards. I would very much like to cut out her filthy heart."

"Mercy, Juan Caesar, you got it in bad for that woman." Feak chuckled, then rubbed his face in thought with a wet hand. Moira slouched and let the scrub brush drip more gray suds onto her bed.

Scudder sat upright at the mention of the word *witch*.

"I need you to be ridin' back to Taft tonight, Billy. We gotta do somethin' about this boy, big medicine or no."

"T-t-tonight? Me?" The sneer bled from Scudder's mouth. "Why, come on, Lucius, you just now heard Juan Caesar allow as how he wants to be the one to carve her heart out."

"If Billy is afraid of this witch, then I'll go. I have no fear of an old woman and a pitiful child." The younger of the two Apaches smirked.

Juan Caesar looked at his young companion and shrugged. "Her medicine is real. It is no joke. But she does have a weakness. She keeps her charms in a leather bag around her neck. I believe if she was caught without the bag she would not be as powerful."

Bill Scudder's eyes darted around the room, searching for some way, any way out of this assignment. "I . . . I don't want to go after no witch. I . . . think maybe I should stay here with you. What if someone comes to try and rescue the girl?"

"The A-patch will stay and help me with that."

"Send them to kill the kid." Billy's voice was high and tight as a guitar string. "They know more about this Injun woman anyhow."

Feak's mood went as dark as the cloud of his cigar smoke. "Come here, Billy, so I can be sure you're hearin' me proper."

Slowly, Scudder skulked up to the edge of the tub, a dog waiting, knowing it's about to get kicked, but too afraid or stupid to do anything else.

Without warning, Feak's hand shot out from the tub like a viper curling between Scudder's legs and behind his left thigh so the young man straddled his crooked arm. Billy's eyes went pie-pan round and he swallowed hard, standing perfectly still. The Indians grinned openly.

"It ain't safe for the A-patch to be seen too much." Feak's voice was a whisper, slow and even. "The boss wants us to keep them out of sight. I'm tellin' you to go and take care of the kid. If you can do it without comin' up against this fierce Injun witch, so much the better. Hell, kill her too, I don't care. Cut her heart out so Juan Caesar can chop it into little pieces. Take her medicine pouch and burn it if you have to, cut it off with her Injun neck. But . . . whatever you do, you best be takin' care of that kid so he don't ever talk again."

Feak paused, staring hard at the man, who towered over him while he sat in the tub. "Understand, Billy?"

Scudder nodded. His belly trembled and his breath came in short gasps. He was almost whimpering.

"Thought you would." Feak withdrew his hand

slowly, and Angela was able to see the long skinning knife. A dark trickle of blood mixed with the soapsuds and water along the razor-sharp edge of the blade.

Angela slumped as far as she could to the floor. What chance could she possibly have to survive if these people were bent on hurting each other?

CHAPTER 7

"Ten thousand dollars is a hell of a lot of money." Peter Kenworth slammed a ream of yellow stock certificates on the flat of his desk. The shiny red of his well-fed jowls reflected in the polished cherrywood finish. Kenworth always sounded pinched when he talked about money. One didn't get to be rich by buying other people's lunch at every meal and Peter Kenworth was very rich. Cattle wearing the PK brand ranged over most of five sections of rolling foothills above the Bitterroot Valley. Most years the grass covered these hills and the cattle were fat as ticks, but the spring of 1910 brought unusually hot weather, and what little snow that fell in the high country melted early. Not a drop of rain fell through May, June, or July. August brought only more searing heat—and fire.

Already, acre after acre of PK land had been consumed by the spot fires that dotted the dry, brown hillsides and sent plumes of dark gray smoke up into the darkened sky, only to settle back to turn the once-picturesque Bitterroot Valley into a haze-filled mess of charred stumps, bloated dead cattle, and black, skeletal husks of what used to be his buildings.

As strange as it seemed to some, Peter Kenworth didn't care about the cattle or the vast ranches. He hated the loss of his profit, but mining was his first love. While others enjoyed the wide-open spaces and tree-covered hills, Kenworth longed for the darkness of the mines, the cool breeze that blew from a side shaft when it connected him with the heart of the earth herself. When he went below, Peter felt connected, part of something larger than himself. On top of the ground, with all the big sky in the world above him, he often felt untethered, as if he might float away.

Even with the fires, Kenworth mines near the St. Joe and holdings near Anaconda still brought him a steady income. Not as much as they had in the beginning, but steady nonetheless. A good deal of that he sent to his wife back in Boston. Not that there was any love lost between him and Lizbeth. If circumstances had not conspired against him back at his humble beginnings, he'd have divorced the dictatorial woman long before. As far as he could see, she had only ever given him two things of any value in the twenty-year span of their miserable acquaintance—a grubstake, which he'd paid dearly for over the years, and a daughter, who she'd kept from him and held over his head at every turn. Lizbeth had always hated tight places, and Peter often wondered if his own love for the mines signified something about his strong desire to be as far away from her as possible.

She'd not been able to get through to him on the telephone, but her wire had been bad enough. She was unforgiving and vindictive after he'd informed her of the kidnapping.

"Get her back quickly. Stop. When you do, send her home at once. Stop. My fault for trusting you. Stop. No foolishness will be tolerated. Stop. Lizbeth."

Peter knew it was sheer foolishness with Lizbeth on a dark, humid night in Boston so many years ago that had led to Angela's arrival, but that didn't keep him from doting on his daughter at every opportunity. Lizbeth had tried to keep them apart, but the girl was too much like him—too full of spirit, goaded by her sense of adventure to try out new things. No matter what his wife did, she'd never been able to keep him from getting to know his own daughter.

Now he even doubted himself. He'd vomited when he saw what had happed to the poor Donahue woman. His whole body ached at the thought that they would find Angela somewhere in the nearby woods—his poor, beautiful daughter, disemboweled and naked. Strangely, it was a comfort when one of his men found her finger with the ruby ring still on it. It seemed like a sign that she'd been taken alive. Peter had wrapped the precious little finger in his handkerchief and tucked it safely inside his vest pocket. Even now, the pitiful thing rested in a small wooden box in the lap drawer of his desk.

Tom Ledbetter stood across the spacious wood-paneled room. He held his hat in one hand and an arrow in the other. "We didn't see who shot it, Mr. Kenworth. I have men out now looking for a trail. We plan to track whoever it was at first light."

Kenworth held the rolled note that had been tied around the arrow up to the gaslight again. "I'd gladly pay ten thousand dollars if I knew she was still alive. I'd pay ten times that if I could only be certain."

Ledbetter's face glowed red. He hung his head as if he was about to cry. "I feel downright awful, sir. I know it was my idea to send Mueller to pick the young lady up in the coach. I can't help but think if I'd been the one to go . . . maybe met her myself . . ."

"Then you'd be dead as well and I'd have no one to rely on right now. Stop blaming yourself, Tom. All I care about now is getting her back, not what we all should have or could have done."

"The note seems like the only chance, sir. We take the money to the crossroads and they'll have the girl there. There's not much of a choice for now." Ledbetter shrugged. "They picked a perfect spot. Open land all around so they don't have to fear we'll ambush them. If they're telling the truth, I'll have your daughter back by tomorrow night."

Kenworth collapsed back in the padded chair and rubbed his beleaguered eyes with both hands. The man meant well but, dammit, it wasn't *his* daughter out there with a mutilated finger and who knows what other kind of humiliations. He should never have gone and seen what they'd done to the poor Donahue girl. Now he couldn't close his eyes without envisioning the same treatment for Angela. He spoke into clenched fists—more to himself than to Ledbetter. "And if they aren't?"

Ledbetter's eyes grew dark. His long lips pressed together. He nodded slowly to his employer. "I will take care of this myself, sir. One way or another, I plan to track down these redskins and kill them all whether they bring back your daughter or not. I promise you, they won't have the money for long."

Ledbetter made an imposing figure in the dancing gaslights. Kenworth felt a little better to have such a capable man on his side. "Are you so certain Indians did this?"

Ledbetter held up the arrow and snapped the wooden shaft in half with a beefy thumb. "I'd say this is proof enough."

"I don't know Tom. It's all just too pat. Indians may be cruel, son, but they're not stupid. Why use an arrow unless they wanted us to know they were Indians?"

Ledbetter's jaws convulsed as he ground his teeth together. His vehement hatred for all things Indian was common knowledge in western Montana, but few knew why. "Hell, I don't know what was going through their sick minds. But everything about this massacre stinks of red sweat and treachery."

"Just the same," Kenworth said with a weary sigh, "I think we should talk to that Donahue boy, see what he has to say about it. He had to have seen something."

Ledbetter shrugged. He suddenly seemed preoccupied with something outside the window. "If you say so, Boss. I don't mean no disrespect by this, but it's a waste of time. They say he's not doing much talking."

"You know the lawmen guarding him?" Kenworth snatched a pen from the gray marble holder on the desk and began to scribble a note.

"I do." Ledbetter took a step toward the desk. His eyes twitched and he looked into the gaslight instead of at Kenworth. The muscles along his jaw clenched again as if he were chewing through a difficult thought. "I know you're worried about your daughter, sir, but I hate for you to get your hopes up about this boy. It won't do no good to talk to him. Even if he talks, he's gone crazy. After what he seen them savages do . . . anybody would."

"Nevertheless, I want to talk to him." Kenworth blew on the paper to dry the ink, then folded it lengthwise before sliding it into a tan envelope he produced from the lap draw. He handed the letter to Ledbetter and rested his elbows on the desk, leaning his chin against his hands. "You take that to the deputy and then bring the boy here tonight. I want to talk to him as soon as possible."

Ledbetter nodded, a soft sigh escaping his narrow lips. "They say there's an Indian woman with him. She may not be so eager for us to talk to him if she thinks we can find out the truth."

Kenworth kept his chin against his hands, but let his tired eyes float up to meet Ledbetter. His voice creaked with the weariness of a man twice his age. "Arrange to bring me the boy, Tom. Nobody but the people who have Angela will care if I talk to him or not. There's something not quite right about all this Indian business. How would Indians know my daughter was to be on that coach?" He sighed and closed his eyes. "I just don't buy into it yet."

"What about the things they did to those poor people? You can't believe a white man would do such things as that."

"Oh, Tom, my boy." Kenworth leaned back in his stuffed chair and tried to stretch forty years of tension out of his weary spine. "You shouldn't underestimate what one white man could do to another. Indians don't have the corner on the atrocity market."

CHAPTER 8

The other firefighters looked like woodchucks far below Daniel Rainwater as he swayed in the smoky wind 120 feet up in the lonely top of a ponderosa pine. It had been an easy climb, and Daniel had the best eyesight of anyone he had ever met. He felt a strange need to make the fire boss proud of him, and volunteering as a spotter seemed a good way to make that happen.

Even with the thick haze, Daniel could see for miles. Jagged peaks stuck up from a blotchy patchwork of parched brown and singed black. Rivers of smoke ran in thick streams along the low-lying valleys. Plumes of gunmetal smoke billowed up every mile or so in all directions as far as the eye could see. So many fires burned, he couldn't count them. Taking a deep breath of the relatively cooler air before he clambered back down the swaying tree, Daniel took one last look around. He was supposed to give a report to Mr. Zelinski with the location of the nearest fire so they could march to it. From his vantage point, it didn't look like finding a fire to fight would be a problem. Any direction they walked would give them ample opportunity to do battle with any number of blazes. They were surrounded by fire.

While locating a place to work would be easy, surviving the night might pose a bit of a problem.

After shinnying back down the tree, Daniel let himself drop from a high branch about eight feet off the ground. He landed in a crouch a few feet from his friend Joseph. Zelinski was nowhere in sight, but a dozen other men pressed in closer to hear what Daniel had seen. Big Ox Monroe towered in front of the group. He sneered and clicked his gold teeth when Rainwater looked at him. Roan Taggart leaned against a tree beside him and stared across his pink nose.

"What did you see?" a tall man with soot-streaked blond hair asked. He wasn't much older than Daniel.

Corporal Rollins stood to one side with his oak-tree arms folded across a massive chest. The rest of his men were working a line about half a mile away. There had already been two brawls between colored troops and men egged on by Monroe and Taggart, so Rollins preferred to keep his men working as far away as possible but still get the job done. He watched, but said nothing.

"Where's the boss?" Daniel looked at Joseph. "I need to see him."

"Talking to White," Joseph said.

"Come on," the blond man, whose name was Peterson, pleaded. "How many fires did you see?"

"Who says he saw anything at all," Ox Monroe said from his leaning spot at a nearby tamarack. Though Roan Taggart stank to high heaven from his farting, the air around Ox felt dead as a corpse. "He's probably up there sendin' signals to his red devil friends so they know where to slip in and cut all our throats. I say we send somebody up we can trust and dump the skinny little buck and his friend in the creek where they belong."

A nervous chuckle rolled through the small group. They cast bleary, bloodshot eyes back and forth as if looking for guidance. It didn't pay to ignore Monroe's jokes completely.

"How many fires, Daniel?" Corporal Rollins unfolded massive arms and let a relaxed hand rest on the upright handle of a pickax beside him. He spoke to Rainwater, but sent a pointed smile at Ox Monroe. "Don't listen to Mr. Ox there. He just foolin' with you, I'm sure of it. Ain't you, Mr. Ox?"

Monroe grunted and spit on the ground, but he didn't answer.

"I hope you was just funnin', Mr. Ox." Rollins flipped the pick around and around in a hand the size of a shovel blade the way a smaller man might toss a hammer, catching it by the end of the handle on each full rotation. "I think you and me, we gonna have to wrestle one of these days, Mr. Ox. I think you'd get a kick outta that." He beamed and shook his head slowly back and forth while he spoke. His eyes never left Monroe. "Yes, sir, I just love to wrestle."

"Why don't you wrestle your own self, you ignart tar baby, I got no truck with you." Monroe didn't know it, but Roan Taggart who was always stuck so close he seemed like another appendage, looked around for a place to hide and took a half a step back at the last remark.

Rollins caught the pick by the handle and held it out in front of him as if it were no more than a light twig.

Daniel sighed. His ever-present smile faded away. "I need to talk to the boss, boys. There's too many burns to count. The whole country's on fire and we're in the middle of it."

"Why don't you do that, young buck?" Monroe said with a swagger, his eyes still locked on Rollins.

The corporal nodded slowly, flipping the pick again in one hand. "Yeah, Daniel, why don't you go ahead and tell Mr. Zelinski what you saw while me and Mr. Ox decide the rules to our wrestlin' match."

Monroe scoffed. "Why you always takin' up for the Injun? You're too stupid to see what's goin' on here, ain't you. They must call you niggers buffalo soldiers 'cause you're so thick-skulled."

Rollins let the pick fall to the dust and slowly popped his powerful neck from side to side. His head bowed like a bull on the fight as he spoke. His quiet words cut the air. "I don't know about them others, but the name suits me 'cause I'm 'bout to trample your mangy ass."

The fire boss's thunderous voice rolled through the trees. "Rainwater, get over here and look at this map."

Daniel looked back and forth at the two giants, poised for a fight. Monroe's hand hung above the handle of his knife. Rollins stood with empty hands, his big chest heaving, eyes narrowed.

"Ask Corporal Rollins to come along," Zelinski yelled. "I need to see him as well."

"You best run along like you're told, soldier man." Ox Monroe smirked. "I reckon we'll have to put off this match until later."

"Oh, we'll get to it, Monroe," Rollins said. The relaxed smile returned to his broad jowls. "I'll make certain of that."

Horace Zelinski rubbed at a five-day growth of black beard and stared at a square map held down by four stones on the flat stump in front of him. An enormous gray wolfhound with a head the size of small horse rested on the ground to his right, its shaggy face cocked quizzically to one side. The dog had appeared in camp the week before, wandering in to steal or beg whatever it could find in the way of scraps and fresh water. It was a little gaunt, but other than a singed coat, it looked in excellent health. It couldn't have been roaming the hills for too long. Several men, lonely for their own families, tried to coax the animal over to them with bits of bacon or ham, but it remained aloof to everyone but the fire boss. The dog seemed to sense the leader of the group, and after sniffing the air around the camp padded straight to Horace Zelinski. Ever alert to the moods of its new master, from the time it first went to him the shaggy wolfhound never strayed far from the ranger's side.

The fire boss scratched his own head and then the dog's before he pitched a small book, its pages curled and worn from much reading under the elements, on top of the map. When he stopped scratching to rub his weary, smoke-reddened eyes, the wolfhound whined and nosed at an elbow until he resumed his attentions.

"George," Zelinski sighed, his voice gravelly from shouting orders over countless roaring fires. "We are up against something the patent-leathered bean stackers back in Washington didn't think on when they wrote our little handbook."

George White, Zelinski's second in command, took a swig of water from the canteen on his belt and wiped his mouth with the back of his blackened forearm. At just over thirty years old, his thick hair had gone prematurely gray. Some said it was from trying to live up to the expectations of his mentor and superior in the Forest Service. If it was stress-related, it didn't show in the rest of his demeanor. Where Zelinski's gaze was sharp and hard as fire-tempered steel, White's sky-blue eyes always held a spark of mischief and pure glee. The bulk of the fire crews followed both men out of sheer devotion and respect.

White chuckled. "I used the last few pages in my little book earlier this morning at my constitutional." He winked at young Rainwater, who returned the kind look with a smile.

The Use Book that was intended to guide each forest ranger on his roving patrol over what sometimes amounted to millions of acres was not much use for anything besides kindling backfires.

"Ride as far as the Almighty will let you and get control of the forest fire situation in as much of the mountain country as possible," the handbook taught. *"And as to what you should do first, well, just get up there as soon as possible and put them out."*

By way of strategy, Zelinski and his men were on their own. Luckily for the crew, Zelinski was a man of action who needed little direction from his superiors. Though the Washington bureaucrats who wrote the Use Book gave men like him little in the way of practical instruction, Congress had made fire bosses arguably the most powerful men in the government's employ in 1908 when they passed a law permitting deficit spending to fight fires. Who else could hire as many men as he wanted, requisition as much equipment as he needed, and never worry about the cost? Not even the Army had that kind of authority.

Consequently, the Washington bureaucrats put a great deal of time and forethought into the type of men they hired for such positions. They needed men of high moral character, men who could be trusted with the lives of other men as well as the taxpayers' dollar. They needed men of action. They needed men like Horace Zelinski. The son of a Lutheran minister and Wyoming schoolteacher, Horace was as at home in the woods as he was in front of a congregation. He'd never missed a day of work in his life due to illness, and the word "shirk" was not in his vocabulary. He pushed himself beyond the limits of human endurance, and expected those in his employ to do the same. Firefighting was, after all, just that: a fight. It was a battle against the most destructive force in nature. A devil incarnate sent to destroy his beloved woodlands.

Snow in the high country the previous winter had been sparse, so the streams and rivers flowed at half their usual rate. Every blade of grass and twig was dried to the point of combustion at the tiniest notion of a spark. So dry, the swish of a pretty girl's petticoat walking by might ignite them.

No one knew what started the first fire—summer lightning, sparks from a passing train, a stray cigarette from a wandering cowboy. There were so many separate fires now, all were likely to blame. Hundreds of men had been hired or pressed into service in fighting the fires: from rich cattle barons down to a trainload of vagrants brought in from Spokane. Almost everyone with a backbone was enlisted, not only to save the forests, but to save their towns and their own homes as well.

"What did you see up there, lad?" Zelinski waved Rainwater over to the stump table.

"Too many fires to count, sir. Thirteen plumes of smoke coming up in this valley alone. All the really bad ones look like they're to the south of us." Daniel looked down at the map and tapped it with his finger. “Two big fires over along the back side of Bear Mountain—here.” He pointed to a deep, narrow valley running from the high country and spilling into a wide plain that swept down above the tiny railroad town of Grand Forks, Idaho.

Zelinski’s head snapped toward White, then back at the Indian boy. “Did you say there are two separate fires back there? That’s a mighty narrow valley.”

Rainwater gave a single nod. “I saw two plumes of smoke, one near the mouth of valley and another north, closer to the headwaters of this little creek here.”

The wolfhound gave a startled jerk when Zelinski pounded his fist against the stump. “I’ve got men down there, George.” His voice echoed across the parched clearing. He turned to Rollins. “Corporal, has the Army got any troops nearby that can go assist them?”

Rollins shook his head. “No, sir, not that I know of. Want me to take some of my men and look in on them?”

“No.” Zelinski glared across the shadowed camp toward the base of a huge white pine where Ox Monroe sat napping, his huge paws across his belly. “I’m afraid I need you here for the time being.” The fire boss turned to George White.

“Pete Seaver and his boys are down there, maybe trapped between two fires. George, I need you to take two men with you and get a signal to them. The fires should lay down tonight. Pete might have sent up scouts, but he’s young and inexperienced. I should never have sent him over there in charge of such a young crew. Let's just pray you can get to them in time." Zelinski picked up the map and held it closer to study in the failing light. "It's just over four miles, but you have two sizable mountains to hump before you get there." He traced a line on the map with a blistered finger. "If you cut down here toward the trail to Grand Forks, you should be able to make it well before morning."

George White studied the map for a moment before he handed it back to his boss. "I'll get to him, H. I'll take McGowan and Baker. Be nothing but a short stroll for us."

Zelinski rolled the map and slid it back into a leather tube. "Thank you, gentlemen," he said, buckling the end cap. "Oh, one more thing. Corporal Rollins, you have my permission to stage a wrestling match whenever you see fit. I think it might be good for the morale of the men."

Rollins slapped his great hands together with such relish, Monroe jumped in his sleep clear across the camp.

Firefighting was a war all right, but Horace Zelinski aimed to win it without any casualties. He waved George White on his way, confident he'd picked the correct men to make the journey. Ninety-nine times out of a hundred, White made the same decisions Zelinski would have made himself. The other one percent of the time, it was a coin toss as to who was right.

The big wolfhound nosed at his master's thigh and let out a low, mournful whine, sniffing the air. The ranger scratched his companion on the shaggy head and raised his own face to the smoky breeze.

The wind was shifting around to come in from the south. The dusty green fronds of the great cedar trees seemed to shake with anticipation of things to come. The dog noticed it, as did Zelinski.

Almost imperceptibly, the wind began to build.

CHAPTER 9

"I'm askin' with all due respect." Blake O'Shannon rode abreast of his father's best friend. Clay Madsen had been a fixture in the O'Shannon home for as long as he could remember, and Blake thought of the brash Texan as a much-revered uncle. "All I ever heard you talk about to my father was how you wanted to get back to Texas and work your father's ranch someday."

The trail before them was a bold one, so they kept the horses at an easy dogtrot and tried to eat up ground as fast as they could.

"I did say that. Hell, I even thought it was a fact until I went back and started in doing it." Clay turned up his nose and shrugged. "Found out that the ranchin' way of life is pretty much like bein' a farmer. It's every rancher's dirty little secret. Seems like I was on the ground doing something or another with the hay fields or fences more than I was in the saddle working cattle.

Reckon I always wanted to be a cowboy more than a rancher anyhow. A rancher can't afford to be as lazy as I am."

Madsen's bay had a smooth trot, and he carried on the conversation like he was sitting around the stove swapping stories. The Texan had a kind of easy, hat-thrown-back, feet-up personality and his zest for life jingled as loudly as his spurs.

He leaned across the space between the two horses as if to confide a secret matter to Blake. "Truth be known, I reckon I don't really have the gumption for that kind of hard work. Once you get a taste for man-huntin', everything else is bland as empty piecrust. When the railroad called and said I'd come highly recommended, well, it seemed like my ticket off the ranch." Madsen shrugged. "My sis wanted it all for herself and those mean-hearted little whelps of hers anyhow. She always did resent me coming back to take it over, what with me being the prodigal and all."

"And they didn't say who recommended you to them? The railroad, I mean." Blake was still having a hard time chewing over the fact that arguably the three best trackers in the nation just happened to be in the right spot when marauding Apaches carried away a Boston girl.

"Nope. Just said they needed someone to head up security for the railroad and wanted to offer me the job if I'd come up to Helena. We ain't got one of those telephones out on the ranch yet, so all our correspondence was by letter or telegram."

Madsen let out a rumbling chuckle that caused his horse to cock an ear back and throw him a wary eye. "I should have known something was up when the letter said I came highly recommended. I ain't been highly recommended for anything in my life except maybe a whippin' back in grade school when I popped the gawky kid who called himself a teacher in the ass with a piece of broken quirt." He saw Trap and Ky on the road ahead of them and stood in the saddle, urging his horse a little faster at the sight of his friends. Before letting the bay break into an easy lope, Clay looked over and winked at Blake. "The bully son of a bitch had it comin'. The whippin' was well worth what I paid for it."

It was impossible not to like Clay Madsen.

Ky Roman sat, arms folded loosely across the saddle horn on his lanky sorrel, keeping an eye on the horizon while Trap studied the ground. Both figures seemed to dance in the heat waves that drifted up from the blackened landscape. A scar of burned buffalo grass cut a swath a half mile wide as far as the eye could see to the east, and culminated in a huge gray-white plume of smoke that billowed up from behind a scorched ridge to the west where the fire devoured a stand of lodgepole pine.

Madsen coughed as he reined in the bay next to Trap and Ky. He spit to clear his throat. "I thought Texas was hot. If it weren't for all these pretty mountains, I'd figure you were about to welcome me to Beelzebub's doorstep."

"Not quite yet, but I imagine you know the way." Roman extended his hand with a grin. "Good to see you, Clay. You're looking well."

Madsen tipped his hat. "So are you, Hezekiah. Or, it's Marshal now, isn't it? I hear from young Blake here congratulations are in order."

"Thank you, but it's got nothing to do with me; it's my wife and her good politics."

"Well, whatever it is, they ought to pay you marshals a little more so you can afford the rest of that mustache you're trying to grow. I remember your face hair being a lot more robust than that little shadow of a thing you're wearin' now."

Trap groaned from his stooping and took a step toward his old friend. "I'm glad you're here, Clay Madsen," he said with a genuine grin that turned up not only the corners of his mouth, but caused the apples of his cheeks to glow and his brown eyes to sparkle with more life than Blake had seen in them in a long while. "We could use another good set of eyes on these tracks."

Aside from Clay, none of the men were given to much foofaraw or wordiness. After a quick exchange of pleasantries at their reunion, they were content to let him do the lion's share of the talking.

After a short scout, Trap regained the killers' track on the far side of the burn. The trail headed straight for Grand Forks, a little nubbin of a town not far across the Idaho line through the railroad tunnel and less than a mile away to the southwest. Blake watched the way his father smiled while he studied the trail and listened to his friend go on and on. He thought of the times when it was probably just so—his father watching the ground, Captain Hezekiah Roman scanning for ambush, and Clay Madsen providing the entertainment with his lusty yarns and general love for life on the trail.

After hearing what the others knew about Angela and the massacre, Clay filled them all in on his life in Texas, his father's death, and the telegram from one Mr. Elwood R. Pasqual III, Esquire, of the Northern Pacific Railroad that had asked for his services as a railroad detective.

"I figured it would be a good excuse to take a trip up here to look in on that beautiful wife of yours." Clay twirled his reins while he spoke. "Needed to see if she was ready to get shed of you yet and take up with someone of greater substance and charm."

Trap beamed and shook his head at Blake, like he was just so proud to be back in the company of such a good friend. Another man might have earned a bullet for the same kind of talk, but Blake knew Madsen was more devoted to his father than any man alive.

The Texan slowed his horse along with the rest of the men and looked across the trail at Blake, scratching his goatee. "What the hell kind of a name is Pasqual anyhow?"

Ky stopped his sorrel at a broken water trough by a dried-up spring where dusty trail turned into rutted wagon track. Most anything that would burn looked as if it already had. Everything else had been hewn down with a vengeance in a wide swath along the edge of the tumbled excuse for a town. The dry ground was tilled in such a way that the ramshackle tents and buildings looked as though they were surrounded by a parched, unproductive garden two hundred feet wide. A scorched wooden sign made out of a broken barn door proclaimed in white letters a foot high: FIREFIGHTERS WELCOME AT THE SNAKE PIT.

"They got a constable of sorts here," Blake said. "Least he used to be a constable over in Missoula—he's a railroad agent for the Northern Pacific now. Think he migrated here to make it a little easier to booze on duty." He pointed to the assortment of yellowed canvas tents and shacks of rough-cut timber that made up the settlement of Grand Forks, Idaho. It lay jumbled in the rocky crook of a mountain valley like a pile of unwanted lumber, and was likely filled with the same sorts of vermin, poisonous spiders and snakes. "He's getting' along in years," Blake went on.

"You mean old, like your pa," Clay offered.

Blake nodded. "A mite older."

"Looks like a fire swept through here not long ago," Trap said, shaking off the comment on his age.

Blake crossed his hands on the saddle horn. "Back in July, the whole town near went up in flames. A local sportin' woman robbed one of her patrons and ended up killing him to shut him up. She decided to burn the body to cover her crime and by the time she was done, she'd torched the whole town for good measure."

Madsen whistled low under his breath. "You gotta

watch those mean ones. What'd they do to her?"

"This one got away. No one cared much for the victim, but a lot of good whiskey went up in smoke, so they were prepared to hang her for that. I still got a wanted poster for her back at the office."

"So all this has been rebuilt since July by the good citizens of Grand Forks." Ky said.

"That's a fact." Blake pointed to an odd, boxlike structure high amid the branches of five white pines. The little copse of trees had somehow escaped the July fire. "A few of the local sports put themselves up a new crib up yonder in that tree house. They been doin' a right smart business from what I understand."

Clay slapped his knee and squealed enough to startle his bay. He gazed up at the treetop brothel. "Well, that would be a first for me."

"I doubt that." Ky replied. "We better get on about our business before Madsen goes to climbing trees."

Clay shook his head back and forth mocking the marshal, grinning. If he was offended, he didn't show it.

"I know Constable Steese," Blake offered to the group. "I can go talk to him and see if he's seen or heard of anything."

"Couldn't hurt," Ky said, working out all the possibilities of confrontation in his mind. "Better if we don't ride in all together anyhow."

"True enough," said Clay. "You two badge-toters go and talk to your lawman friend while me and ol' Trap saunter on over to do a little reconnoiter at the Snake Pit." He made an X with hand across his chest. "I promise I won't go swingin' from the branches while you're away, Hezekiah."

Ky looked at Trap, who shrugged.

"It might be worth a try, Captain," O'Shannon said. "If there's a woman there, she's liable to tell him all she knows."

"And some she doesn't," Ky agreed. "One thing you two need to know before you go." He held out a gloved hand toward Blake, who'd ridden his Appy up beside him. The young deputy reached in his shirt pocket and produced a folded leather envelope. He passed it to Roman.

Ky cleared his throat. "By the authority vested in me . . ."

"Ain't this nice." Clay threw an arm around Trap's shoulders as they sat stirrup to stirrup. "He's gonna marry us."

Trap knew what his old captain was up to, and shrugged off his friend's arm.

Ky rolled his eyes and sighed, cutting to the meat of the matter. "I'm making you both my deputies. This isn't my district, so I'm deputizing you for the Judicial District of Arizona. As long as we're here and Blake needs the help, I think it best we're all official. I'm certain President Taft would approve."

Railroad agent and constable when it suited him, Fred Steese was only four days away from his seventy-first birthday. He was out cold in a drunken stupor, and Blake thought the old man might be dead when they first found him sprawled across a sagging cot in the small office next to the whistle stop. When they finally did rouse the old man, they found him stricken with such a bad case of the wheezing croup, it was difficult to understand a word he said.

The thick smoke that hung in the air like dirty quilt batting was hard on the old man. Each time Steese drew a breath to speak had him red-faced and sputtering to catch his breath. The two lawmen thought he might suffocate or burst a blood vessel at every word.

"Lucius," he coughed. "Snake Pit," he spewed. "Bald-faced killers."

The old man pointed a bony finger out the greasy window in the direction of the Snake Pit roadhouse, and broke into a riotous fit of coughing that caused him to pound his fist on the edge of the mattress, and then collapse back on his pillow. His forehead was drenched in beads of sweat.

"Amazing how nothing else matters when you can't get air," Ky said when he put his hat back on outside the constable's makeshift office. The marshal's voice was strained, and it was plain he wanted to get over and check on his friends. "Don't like the sound of this, son. Let's go see what our two partners have gotten themselves into."

CHAPTER 10

The new slab-wood door still oozed sticky amber sap in the heat of the evening. A long wooden frame covered with a canvas roof made up the building called the Snake Pit. Most of the lumber had been fresh cut no more than a few weeks before and thrown together with no time to cure. Every piece warped its own peculiar way, and this gave the frame a twisted, drunken appearance.

Anyone who wanted to get into the place bad enough could just cut through the canvas over the six-foot wooden walls. Several long rows of stitching showed that someone impatient for whiskey had done exactly that. Consequently, management didn't spend too much of it's profit on fancy doors. An establishment like the Snake Pit drew a rowdy clientele that could put them through three broken doors a week.

A crumpled drunk lay slumped in the canvas breezeway, propping open the sticky door. Spraddle-legged and drooling, the man sat with his mouth agape, exposing both of his two bottom teeth. A greasy pall of smoke drifted out on a shaft of yellow light, and mixed above the drunk's head with the brown haze of smoke from the forest fires.

Trap tied his mule to a rusty iron ring on a stump beside Madsen's bay. He had to step around the sprawling man to get through the door. It galled him that he had to go out of his way to get somewhere he didn't particularly want to be in the first place.

His rifle nestled in the crook of his arm, Trap looked over at Clay as they crossed the threshold into the dingy bar. "As you get older do you have more trouble—"

"Peein'?" Clay finished. "Why, yes, I do now that you mention it. I reckon it's just something we have to live with as we get on in our years."

Trap shot a glance back to the entrance, remembering how a conversation with Clay was liable to lead any which direction if it wasn't headed off quickly. "I was going to say with malingerers like that gump there in the doorway. Seems like I have less and less patience with lazy folks."

Clay clapped a hand on his friend's back. "Then go easy on me, my friend, because lest you forget, I'm likely the worst one of that sort you ever came across." Madsen's eyes sparkled in the dim lantern light of the bar. "Now Trap, I aim to order two beers, one for me and another for me. You don't go drinkin' anything. You get mighty mean when you drink."

"I haven't had a drink in years, you know that," Trap said, his eyes trying to adjust to the smoky tavern.

Inside, the Snake Pit was just what the name implied: full of venomous creatures. In the long, thrown-together structure, there was just enough room to get one row of four tables down the left wall. Split pine slabs lay across squat barrels along the other wall. This served double duty as a bar and as a hiding place for the poisonous-looking man wiping dirty glasses with an even dirtier rag. The barkeep recoiled at the new arrivals and eyed them carefully. He stared hard under bushy black brows, and gave the odd assortment of greasy whiskey glasses a squeaky rub.

A short, stout woman with matted red hair, the color of a cigar coal, leaned on both elbows against the table across from the glaring man. A green summer dress clung heavily to a round rump as if she'd sweated through it. Her solid legs were set slightly apart over bare feet, roughened from life on a hard-packed dirt floor. Trap was a tracker. He noticed feet.

A glass, two times as large as the ones served to patrons, sat half-full of whiskey on the bar in front of the woman. If it weren't for the hard-knock life she led, she might have been considered pretty by some—Clay surely would have chosen her in his early years. Trap smiled inside himself when he remembered how his partner used to describe his favorite woman.

"A fine woman is like a fine horse," Madsen was fond of saying. "Fiery of spirit, round of hip, and pretty of face."

This one met at least the first two criteria, and in a dim bar after a couple of drinks, Clay had been known to overlook some things.

The barkeep's head swayed menacingly on the end of a long neck as the woman pushed up from her leaning position over the poor excuse for a bar. He tongued a fleck of something black out of his front teeth and muttered a spate of hissing, unintelligible words. It didn't matter what he did; Clay had his eyes on the woman, and no foolish mumbling from an uppity barkeep was about to make him change his course.

The two had already begun the quiet eye-to-eye dance some folks came by naturally. Trap was never quite at ease around much of anyone, let alone women, and had never been able to muster such communication with anyone but Maggie. Clay was at ease with just about everyone, particularly this sort of woman. Trap had always known him to be fiercely faithful during his married years, but between wives, he'd been at ease with women of varied shapes, sizes, and moralities.

At the far end of the narrow room, three men in soot-covered shirts and ragged britches hunkered around a heavy table of split logs. The moth-eaten head of a mule deer buck hung just behind them on an upright support post. Dusty cobwebs draped from the antler forks to the nappy forehead, and one of the ears was burned to little more than a singed nubbin. If you didn't count the woman in the green dress, the dead deer was the only decoration in the bar.

Under this lone bit of barroom décor, the men sat bleary-eyed and exhausted, going through the motions of a card game. One looked up to give Trap a cursory glance; the others ignored him completely. They seemed no threat, though they might know some useful information.

Trap approached them surely, not quite as forcefully as a lawman might, but his words were direct for an inquisitive stranger.

"Looking for a girl," he said while the men dealt a new hand.

One of the gamblers, an older fellow with an overbite and huge mustache to enhance it, looked up at Trap and nodded, before spitting on the floor. "There's one over yonder, but I wouldn't wait around for her if I was you. Franco, the barkeep, was about to have a go with her when you two came in. He's wicked jealous for a man who runs a sport. Now that your friend's laid claim on her, it's liable to be a little wait. And that's if there ain't a fight."

Trap nodded when he saw the woman had resumed her position leaning against the bar. Clay stood sidled up next to her, elbow to elbow. Franco stood a few feet away, eyeing Clay with dart eyes and a deadly look.

"I meant a particular girl," Trap said.

All three of the men snickered. The bucktoothed spokesman arranged the cards in his hand and spit again. "Well, Cora ain't particular. That's for damn sure." He winked at his friends.

Trap held his breath and chewed on the inside of his cheek. It had been so long since he talked to anyone at length besides Maggie, and much of their communication was unspoken. He felt out of his element with so many words coming out of his mouth. "Have you seen any other girls around here? Maybe earlier today?"

"Sorry, friend." The old man stared at his cards. "We only snuck in from the fires not more than an hour ago. Fact is, we just had time to have a few minutes each with old Cora there and get this game goin' before you came in. Ain't seen nobody but you fellers."

Trap's stomach did a flip at the thought of Cora entertaining all the men in turn. He was grateful Clay was the one doing the talking to her. Convinced the three cardplayers had no useful information, he busied himself studying the cobwebs on the deer head to give Clay time to see what Cora knew. For a time, the two talked in hushed tones. Clay listened intently with his hat thrown back in that boyish way of his, every few moments giving an understanding nod. After a few dragging minutes, he counted some bills out on the bar before a wide-eyed Cora. Trap couldn't hear the conversation, but he saw Franco throw his dirty towel down in disgust. Cora began to cry. Clay patted her on the back and then tilted her head up with his index finger so he could look her in the face. He dabbed at her eyes with his bandanna, kissed the round little woman on the end of her nose. She sniffed, took his bandanna, and kept talking, pointing out the back door. Clay stood up straight at whatever it was she told him and shot an excited look at Trap.

Clay kissed her again, this time on her forehead. He took something from his vest pocket and placed it in her hand, curling her fingers around it and holding her fist in both his beefy hands. She looked up at him, blinking with the wide eyes of a lapdog. Gently releasing her, he turned and shook a finger at the sullen bartender before rejoining Trap.

"Our man's name is Lucius Feak. According to our new friend, he's not above cutting the fingers off a woman." Clay cast a nod over his shoulder as he started for the door. For the first time, Trap saw Cora was waving her good-byes minus the ring and little finger on her right hand.

"She allowed as how Mr. Feak got tired of her a few months ago. He's taken up with a new woman named Moira Gumm—stays with her when he's in town. She's got a little shack a couple of stumps around the mountain, over behind what used to be the old Anheuser Hotel. Her place is one of the few that didn't burn in July." Clay shoved open the rickety door and nodded into the darkness behind the little tavern. "Cora was kind enough to give us directions. I didn't get the impression she likes Miss Moira very much."

Trap looked over his shoulder one last time before stepping into the smoky air. Compared to inside the Snake Pit, it seemed fresh as spring. "Looked to me like you gave her some money, then made her cry."

Clay shrugged, absent his usual chuckle. "She's dumber than a boot sole, Trap. Been used something awful—too many times. I gave her a little tortoise-shell comb I picked up down in Dallas a while back. You'd a thought I gave the poor girl a diamond, the way she looked at me so. Reckon no one ever gave her much but a hard time." Madsen sniffed. "Whenever I meet a woman like her, I can't help but ponder on what she'd be like if I'd found her before she was pushed so hard by whatever it was that pushed her and damaged her so. You ever wonder about things such as that?"

O'Shannon strained to see his old partner in the darkness. "Sorry, Clay, but my mind just don't work that way." Trap could see the big Texan's eyes sparkled with tears in what little light sifted through the cracks in the dry lumber walls and amber tent fabric.

Clay wiped his nose and coughed to clear his throat. "The mean-eyed booger behind the bar was about to help himself to her when we showed up. If I'd had more time, I'd have knocked his head down into his shoulders. Instead, I bought her services for the rest of the night and told him to leave her be. If we have time tonight after we kill Feak and get the Kenworth girl back, I think I'll stop in and check on his behavior. I might have an opportunity to swat him yet."

"I hope we have the chance to get our hands on this Feak character and his men as soon as all that," Trap whispered as they weaved in and out of the charred stump row. The entire settlement of Grand Forks was nothing more than a pile of tents and shacks nestled in the crook of a rock-strewn mountain.

"We'll find out shortly." Clay pointed with an open hand. "From Cora's description, I believe that's Moira's place yonder."

"I'm a little quieter than you in my moccasins. I'll see if I can get up close enough to see how many there are."

Clay nodded and wiped his nose with the back of his hand. "Sorry about that nonsense there. Didn't mean to go all blubbery on you. I reckon I'm gettin' a little emotional in my old age, especially when it comes to the womenfolk."

Trap rested a sure hand on the Texan's shoulder and gave him a wide smile. "You were always emotional when it came to womenfolk. That's why my wife loves you enough to make me crazy."

Clay opened his mouth to say more, but bit his lip instead. He took a deep breath and got back to business. "There's a crack in that south wall a body could throw a cat through. You should be able to get a good look from there. Hopefully, Ky and Blake will see our horses out in front of the Snake Pit. Cora said she'd send them this way." Clay had his pistol out in a relaxed hand.

Trap stooped to a crouch and glided off toward the cobwebs of light spilling out from the cracked walls of the tiny shack Moira Gumm called home. He kept his rifle low, even with his belt, but ready for action. Feak and his men faced hanging for what they did, and were sure to put up a fight.

The cabin walls were thin, and Trap heard muffled voices by the time he was twenty feet away. He couldn't make out words, but there was definitely a man inside and he sounded mighty unhappy.

CHAPTER 11

In front of the Snake Pit, Blake patted Clay Madsen's bay on the shoulder as he dismounted. He tied his own animal to the same hitching ring. The horses groaned quietly and the stout Appaloosa cocked a hind leg up to rest it. Roman stepped down next to him and froze in his tracks. Both men listened intently to the inside of the rough saloon.

The sound of breaking glass chattered through the canvas walls. A pitiful yelp cut the thickness of the night air and caused Blake to shudder. Ky's eyes narrowed at the sound of another whimpering scream. Hackles up, his long neck bowed like a horse ready to charge, the marshal set his jaw.

"One thing is certain," Roman said, striding with deadly purpose toward the open saloon door. "Your father and Madsen aren't alive if they're in there. No woman would cry like that twice if they were." The tall lawman hopped nimbly over the drunken body of the man in the threshold and shoved the door hard enough to loose it from its top hinge.

Blake followed closely on his heels, startled by the thought that something might have happened to his father. What he saw inside stopped him as surely as a stone wall.

Shards of broken glass mingled with puddles of spilled whiskey on the filthy floor. Two men, their yellowed teeth gleaming in amber glow of coal-oil lamps, held a sobbing woman by each arm, facedown across a low wooden bar. Most of her ragged green skirt had been ripped away, and what was left was hiked up in a crumpled wad above her waist. A third man, with dark, raccoonlike circles under his eyes and a bartender's apron, administered cruel blows to the bare skin of her buttocks with a leather razor strop.

The poor woman's face was toward the door, and Blake could see her eyes clenched shut in fear and anticipation of the next blow.

The bartender stopped when he saw the two newcomers. His dark eyes blazed and the veins in his forehead bulged as he screamed at them in a high-pitched gurgle. The thick strop hung poised in air. His face was flushed from the exertion from his beating. "Go out of here or you will be the next." He had a thick Italian accent.

A maniacal growl erupted from somewhere deep within Hezekiah Roman, and he scooped up a tall wooden stool from beside the bar. Advancing on the team of men holding the woman, he never looked around.

The only other man in the place sat with his chair tipped back watching the show. Blake drew his pistol and gave him an eye to get an idea of his intentions. The grizzled man raised his hands and smiled. For him, one show was as good as another.

And Ky Roman gave him one.

Slamming the flat wooden seat of the stool into the face of one of the grimy men who held the woman, he grabbed the other by the ear with his free hand and yanked hard. The ear ripped half away from the screaming man's skull and propelled him back to Blake, who finished him off with a rap on the head with the butt of his pistol. The ne'er-do-well Ky had smacked with the stool lay in a heap on the floor—either unconscious or sensible enough to stay down and out of the path of the seething fury that was Hezikiah Roman.

The dark-eyed bartender stared in disbelief as Roman dragged the sobbing, half-naked woman off the table and passed her back to Blake before bringing the stool crashing down on the wooden bar between them. The bulk of the stool broke away and left two feet of splintered pine the size of a short bat. Without pausing, the marshal kicked the bar over with a mighty shove of his boot, trapping the bartender between it at the short wall. Before the dazed man could form a plan, Roman was on top of him, smashing the wooden baton across the arm that held the strop.

The wounded man squealed out in pain. A gush of tears quenched the fire in his eyes and he dropped the leather. "She is only a whore, *patrone.*"

Ky growled again from low in his chest. He clubbed the blubbering barkeep across the shoulders, and sent him sprawling against the overturned bar. The stick shattered at the blow, and Ky dropped what was left to the ground as if he'd expected it to happen that way. The lawman took up the strop without pausing and he looked up at the woman in Blake's arms.

"Some things you don't even do to a whore," Roman spit through clenched teeth, and laid the wide leather across the man's back and buttocks. When he tried to rise, the marshal pushed him down with the sole of his boot and struck him again and again. Ky whipped until his hat fell off and sweat dripped from the end of his nose. When it was apparent the bartender was unconscious, Roman toed him over with a boot toe. He was still alive, but long past feeling the effects of the beating. When he came to, he would feel them for quite a while.

Roman regained his hat and tipped it to the woman. She'd found her composure despite the fact that most of her pink bottom still poked out the back of her shredded dress.

"They call me Cora," she said through a sniffle. Extending a hand toward the marshal, she smiled through a tear-streaked face. "If I had to guess, I'd say you were Clay's friends."

Blake's head snapped around. "You know Clay Madsen."

Cora smiled and patted Blake's elbow. "Why, yes, honey boy, we're old friends as of twenty minutes ago." She brushed a wilted lock of red hair out of her eyes. "Really, he's the first man to treat me nice in a long time." Her eyes shone in the lamplight. "You two are the second and third."

"Did Clay say where he was going?" Blake felt Madsen and his father must have been onto something since they were already gone from the saloon.

"Sure did." Cora let her head loll dreamily and sighed. "He paid for a whole night with me. Hell, more than that—what he paid could have had me for a month—and that's if I decided to charge a handsome gentleman like him. Then he told Franco to keep off me for the night. Said he'd be back to look in on me, but Franco didn't believe him." She sniffled and wiped a tear from her eye with the heel of her hand. "After Clay left, the bastard took my money and whipped me for bein' nice. As if that ain't what he pays me to do anyhow."

It suddenly occurred to Cora that Franco still had her money. She trotted over and rolled him over to get at his pockets. The bartender's body arched back across the demolished bar rubble like he was trying to do a back-flip. She squatted beside him, the tattered cloth of her dress falling between her fleshy pale thighs like a flimsy green loincloth. She searched around under his whiskey-stained apron until she came up with a wad of cash the size of her fist. Money in hand, she rose and stared down at the man who moments before had beaten her without mercy. Rearing back on one leg, she gave him three solid kicks with her bare foot to his unprotected groin. Cora was built low to the ground and had powerful legs. Franco's eyes fluttered but stayed closed, and his lips parted in a mournful moan as he drew himself into a tight ball like a dead spider. Even through the veil of his unconscious stupor, Franco could feel some pain.

Blake winced within himself. He hoped he never passed out in front of a woman who hated him that much.

Ky leaned over and whispered, "He's lucky. Your mama would have used a knife."

Cora looked up at the two lawmen. "Please tell Clay thank you for me. I need to get gone before Franco comes to his senses and shoots me—or worse."

"I'd be happy to tell Mr. Madsen whatever you want me to, ma'am, if you'd be so kind as to point us in the right direction." Roman still breathed heavily. He kept his head tilted back to keep from looking at the stout pink hips that peeked between the rags of Cora's dress.

Her hand shot to her mouth and she giggled. "I'm so sorry. I never did tell you, did I? Him and his friend was looking for Lucius Feak, so I sent 'em over to Moira Gumm's place. Feak used to take a fancy to me." Cora held up her nubby fingers and sneered. "Til he decided I wasn't his style. Moira ain't got the sense God gave a gopher. She's hoein' the same row, so she's in for the same treatment sooner or later."

Cora gave the men directions, and started to shuffle off toward her small room sectioned off in the back of the tent. Franco's cruel beating was still evident on her bottom and in her gait.

Ky started to leave, then turned. "Ma'am," he said, clearing his throat. Now that the excitement was over, he had a hard time even looking her in the eye. He took some bills out of his wallet and offered them to her. "Do you have anywhere to go?"

She took the money and gave him a coy wink. "I'm still young, sir. A gal like me will have places to go for a few more years anyway. With all the boys in the fire camps around these parts, I'm sure I can be of some service out there somewheres."

Roman's shoulders drooped. "But you could take this money along with what Clay gave you and make a new start for yourself—away from men like that." He pointed to the heap that was Franco.

"Doin' what?" Cora smiled, but a tear rolled down her pudgy cheek. "Listen, mister, I don't know how to sew and I don't aim to learn now. I can't cook worth a damn and even if I could, the way I been livin' no good man like you or Clay would ever take up with me. You see, I already got it figured that I ain't never gonna see no heaven on earth. I'm just hopin' to sock enough away while I got somethin' to offer that I don't have to live in Hell all the time—till after I'm dead."

She sniffed and rubbed her eyes with both fists. "You best go find your friends. If it's Lucius Feak you're huntin', they'll need the help."

CHAPTER 12

Billy Scudder was mad enough to choke a cat to death with his bare hands. Who did that son of a bitch Feak think he was anyhow, ordering him around like that in front of the A-patch and all? Billy had a good mind to stand up to him next time and show him Mama Scudder hadn't raised no sucky baby. No, sir! Not by a long shot she hadn't. Billy was tough as any man around and he knew it.

The whiskey he'd shared with the Indians earlier that evening had clouded his thinking, and he couldn't seem to come up with as many curse words as usual. He compensated by using the same ones over and over as he urged his gaunt pony into the deserted back alleys of

Taft and cussed the mortal soul of Lucius Feak.

Killing the boy would be no problem—if it weren't for the witch. Mama Scudder had taught Billy much more than how to kill a person. She'd also taught him to have enough good sense to be scared of witches. Once, when he left the curtain open after dark with the lantern lit in the front room of their house, she'd nearly caved in his head with a stick of stove wood. "Them Mexican *brujas* are out there watchin' for fools liken you," she'd said. "Fools who leave their curtains open in the night so they can slip in on their spirits and give you the *mal ojo*—the evil eye—or suck the life's breath right out of you so's they can raise their dead sweethearts or some such thing."

Mama'd seen it done, she said. Mama knew about things like that.

Billy wished the sheriff back in Santa Fe wouldn't have hung Mama. She could have given him some good advice about this particular witch. She would surely know what to do.

The jail was near now, only half a block away. Scudder got off his horse and tied it to a short vine maple growing along the alley. In the distance, a hound sent up a mournful howl. The shiver going up Billy's spine met a trickle of sweat rolling down it. He belched up a particularly harsh whiskey burp that burned his throat and brought tears to his eyes.

He coughed and spit to clear his mouth. Billy seemed to remember Mama saying witches liked to steer clear of crosses. Not having such a thing handy, he bent to the dusty street and stirred his spitball into a muddy cake. He smeared the greasy mixture between his fingers and held it up close to his face so he could get a good look at it in the darkness. Satisfied it would mark him sufficiently, he smeared the sticky goo in the shape of a jagged cross on his forehead. If Mama was right, he would be safe from any witch trying to suck out his life's breath to raise her dead sweetheart—or any such thing.

He checked the rounds in his Colt, then slid it back into the holster that rode high on his hip. The deputy would be no problem; few men were as quick or as eager to kill as Billy Scudder. He tapped the wood handle of the large bowie knife on the other side of his belt. He'd use the blade to kill them all if the Indian witch didn't get in the way. A knife would be quieter—bloody, but not so much fuss as a pistol barkin' in the night.

Scudder touched the rough mark on his forehead where the muddy spot was beginning to dry. He started into the darkness, down the alley toward the jail. The dog howled again, and Scudder felt his bowels go loose like something broke inside him. That was the last thing he needed. He needed to concentrate on protecting himself from the witch and her *mal ojo,* not worrying that he might crap his pants. He paused to relieve himself under a clothesline full of long underwear behind a quiet shack along the alley.

"Mama," he whispered into the black night air while he plucked a cotton sock off the line to clean himself. "I sure hope you told me right about witches." Even as he questioned his dead mother, he ducked slightly, anticipating the piece of stove wood that inevitably landed somewhere on his head or shoulders when he'd shown any sign of doubt in her word. When nothing happened, Billy Scudder pulled up his britches, screwed up his courage, and walked toward the back of the jail. The bowie knife gleamed in the moonlight, and the sparkle of a plan that would take care of the deputy, the boy, and the witch began to form in his mind.

Shad hadn't let go of Maggie's skirt since he woke from his sleep at Dr. Bruner's office. The poor boy had seen enough misery to last him a lifetime, and though he was beginning to come out of his stupor, his eyes still held a wistful, faraway look. He held onto her as if she were the only anchor that kept him from drifting away. Though Shad refused to leave Maggie's side, he had been taken with Madsen. The big, swaggering Texan made faces and clowned with the boy enough to coax out a smile or two. Clay had always had an endearing way with women and small children. Women wanted to mother him and children considered him a playmate.

John Loudermilk puttered around with his coffee grinder in the front office, whistling some song Maggie had never heard before but that seemed to be his favorite. The deputy had wanted to lock Shad and Maggie in a cell for their own protection, but she wouldn't hear of it. In the end, he'd put her in a storeroom behind the office alongside the two ten-by-ten cells. The small room, no more than a third cell without the bars, had two cots, a pile of wool blankets, and a barrel of drinking water.

All the prisoners had been released on their own recognizance to help fight the forest fires. Apart from Maggie, Shad, and Deputy Loudermilk, the jail was empty.

"I'm hot, Miss Maggie," Shad said, lying on a cot with his head in her lap.

"Me too." She tousled the little boy's blond hair. "My husband says I'm always hot unless it's snowing." Her thoughts drifted to Trap while she patted Shad's cheek. "I'll show you something my mother taught me when I was a little girl."

Shad sat up and rubbed his eyes. It was late, but he'd slept away much of the day and was wide awake now. Maggie had taken off the absurd little jacket and knee socks he'd been wearing, and cut the knickers into a much cooler pair of shorts. A heavy woolen blanket covered the open barred window high above the cot. The covering kept anyone from looking in, but held off any breeze as well.

"You come sit over here for a minute and watch me." The window was over six feet off the ground, but Maggie didn't want Shad anywhere near it when she took down the blanket. He would be an easy target for someone outside with a ladder.

Using a wooden bucket, she dipped enough water from the barrel to completely submerge the woolen window covering. She carried the bucket to the window, and then used the cot as a stepladder to replace the dripping blanket on its nails in front of the iron bars. Water streamed from the bottom. Another blanket, rolled into a long tube and placed along the floor, caught the drizzling runoff.

"Sit here." She pointed to the cot beneath the window and stepped to the door.

Loudermilk still shuffled in the other room with his grinder.

"Now," Maggie said, her hand on the knob. "Watch what happens when I open the door and give the air a place to go." She cracked the door a few inches, and watched the blanket over the window billow out as a breath of wind blew against it from outside.

"That's nice," Shad said, leaning his head back to feel the cool air cascade down from the wet blanket over his head. His feet stuck straight out in front of him on the wide cot. "Mama was always hot too. She would have . . ."

Maggie cocked her head to one side and trained her ears toward the cracked door. The boy kept talking, but she didn't hear what he said. For as long as she could remember, Maggie had felt a peculiar tickle when things weren't quite right—as if her heart had walked through a spiderweb. Her mother said it was a gift from the spirits. Trap's father said it was a spiritual gift.

"What would you say to some Indian tea to help you sleep?" Maggie took the medicine bag from her neck and held it up in front of her. She smiled to keep from frightening him. "It's one of the special things I keep in my bag here."

"All right. Will it taste funny?"

Maggie strained to hear Loudermilk's movements. Nothing. "You'll like it. It's sweet—like licorice. I need to get some hot water from the front. Be right back."

Shad scooted to the edge of the cot and hopped to the floor. "I'll come with you."

Maggie raised her hand. "No, you stay here. I'll only be a minute." Her voice was sharper than she intended, and his eyes went wide. Pointing to the cot, she put a finger to her lips and motioned him back there. The boy obeyed, but his breathing grew shallow and his eyes lost their focus. He was slipping back into his stupor. It couldn't be helped. Maggie couldn't afford to have him clinging to her if her fears were realized. He was safer back here.

The door yawned open a crack, and Maggie peeked into the hall. The front office was quiet. Light from the lamp spilled down past the cells and cast a spiked shadow from the key ring on the wall.

Shad sat back under the window, tight-chinned, like he might break down at any moment. It broke her heart to leave him.

"Be right back." She grabbed her rifle, hoping Shad didn't notice, and pulled the door shut behind her. The door leading to the back alley lay off to her left. It was still closed and barred from the inside. In front of her lay a small corridor with the two cells. It ended at a second door to the deputy's office. To her right, a funnel of light at the end of a short hall led into the same room.

In the front office, John Loudermilk's coffee grinder lay in pieces on the wooden floor. One of the double-barrel shotguns was missing from the rack behind a cluttered desk, but the deputy was nowhere to be found. Maggie stepped to the front door. The bolt was locked, but there were scuff marks on the floor in front of it and the thick timber bar that should have been in brackets leaned against the wall.

The tickling feeling grew stronger in her chest, and Maggie fought the urge to run blindly back to Shad. With the rifle in both hands, she peeked around the open door that connected to the small alcove in front of the two cells. It was dark and hot. The smell of human sweat and boredom from the recent prisoners' confinement hung in the stale air. A tawny rat moved across the far wall of the closest cell, its claws clicking against the wooden floor. Maggie shuddered, but rats were the least of her fears.

"John," she whispered, holding the rifle out in front of her.

Nothing. Nothing, but the prickling web pulling across her heart.

Heavy footfalls echoed off the walkway outside the front door. The bolt rattled while someone gave it a shake. Maggie considered replacing the thick cross-beam, but decided against it when she realized she'd have to put down her rifle to lift the heavy timber. Only then, as she stepped away from the doorway, did she notice the boot heel jutting from behind the cluttered office desk. It was John Loudermilk. His shotgun lay beside him along with a half-dozen errant wanted posters in a growing pool of blood. Maggie knew enough of death to see there was nothing she could do for the poor deputy.

A pitiful scream from the storeroom rent the night.

Shad.

Straining to hear another sound from the back room, she began to move toward the boy. She rounded the corner and ran headlong into a shadowed figure in the darkness. As she crashed into him, the rifle slipped from her hands and clattered to the floor. Face-to-face, close enough to feel his sour breath against her forehead, Maggie could smell blood on his clothes. She shoved as hard as she could with both hands. At the same instant the intruder lashed out with a knife.

Shad opened the door behind them, bathing the hallway in light. The man with the knife froze like a cockroach caught in the flare of a newly lit lamp. His eyes wide as silver dollars, he looked Maggie in the face and screamed.

He wheeled, stumbling on his own feet, and ran out the back door, slamming it behind him.

Breathing heavily, Maggie scooped up her rifle and peeked cautiously inside the storage room door, scanning for danger. She'd seen Shad out of the corner of her eye when he opened the door, but the piercing screech from her would-be killer had sent him back into the little room. Maggie scanned for other intruders.

Trap had taught her an old saying he used many times to save his own life when it came to attackers—*see one, think two*. Luckily, it seemed this killer was alone.

The boy stood in front of the cot, tears streaming down his face.

"I heard a noise," Shad sobbed. "Sorry I hollered, but I couldn't hide again while they killed you too Miss Maggie."

The blanket above him still billowed in the breeze. Maggie bolted the door solidly behind her, then took Shad in her arms and held him.

"It's all right now. He's gone."

When she backed away, Maggie saw the front of Shad's shirt was covered in blood. She frantically searched for wounds on his chest. He sniffed and pointed to her.

"It's not me, Miss Maggie. It's you."

She looked down. The front of her dress, across her breast, had been slashed by the man's razor-sharp blade. She'd been able to push away fast enough that the cut was only superficial, but blood oozed from the long gash that ran almost from armpit to armpit. Shad looked at her in growing horror.

"Are you going to die?"

"I'm fine," she assured him. "It's only a scra . . ."

The sound was faint at first, just a creaking of wood barely audible above Maggie's breath. The creak grew louder directly outside the door. Maggie trained her rifle on the threshold. She chided herself for not barring the front entry when she'd had the chance. A toss of her head told Shad to get back behind her on the cot.

Seconds ticked by, and she realized her forehead was dripping with sweat. She sat motionless as a loud rapping bowed the storeroom door. Expecting someone to burst through it at any moment, she let her finger tighten on the trigger.

The knocking stopped.

Maggie risked a glance over her shoulder at Shad, who still sat unmoving on the cot. A coarse chuckle came in under the door, along with a peculiar crackling sound she couldn't quite place.

Then she smelled it. Smoke. The jail was on fire.

Maggie put her shoulder to the door and shoved. It didn't budge. Someone had boarded it shut from the outside. Whoever killed John Loudermilk planned to burn them all alive. She would have to move quickly if they were to survive.

Looking back at Shad, she prayed for guidance. Instinctively, she reached for the leather bag around her neck. Moist blood covered her chest.

The medicine bag was gone.

Taft's volunteer bucket brigade turned out with amazing speed at the first sign of flames from the jail. No one cared so much about who might be inside, especially the lawman. They were more interested in getting the blaze put out before it could jump to the nearby Berryman Tavern and its large supply of whiskey. The mere mention of a spark could reduce any of the nearby buildings to ashes.

Billy Scudder sat panting in the shadows at the end of the train platform, a block away. The Indian witch's medicine bag rested in the palm of his hand. He must have cut it off when he lashed out at her in the dark. He felt foolish for screaming, but that wasn't the worst of it. When the door had opened and light spilled out into the hallway, the woman before him had borne an uncanny resemblance to his mama. The same mama the sheriff in New Mexico had hung by her neck until she was good and dead. The same mama that had a fair aim with a stick of stove wood when she got riled. The sight of her rattled Billy's bones and scared him so bad he'd wet his britches.

After he ran outside, Billy realized the witch had beguiled him. She'd turned herself into his mama to save her skin. The fact that he'd lost control of his bladder infuriated the trembling outlaw. There was fresh blood on his knife along with the darker stain from the dead lawman. He knew he'd cut her, but he didn't know how bad. Feak would be furious if the witch showed up alive, so he had to make sure.

The boy still needed killing. Billy had started to go back in and finish the job, but made it only as far as the front office. The chance he might run headlong into his mama again hit him like a shovel in the face. That's when he came up with the idea to burn the whole building down. No one would ever suspect arson. There were fires all over the mountains; a stray spark could have blown in from anywhere. He'd been able to scrounge up some nails and a hammer from the deputy's desk. The rest was easy.

From his hiding place by the train station, Scudder watched the flames lick away at the heavy, stacked timbers of the wooden jail and nodded to himself. That would teach the damn witch to take on Mama's visage.

A long line of people, some still in their nightclothes, formed a bucket line from a water trough to the building, but they weren't doing much good. Most of their efforts went toward the Berryman Tavern.

Scudder rubbed his sparse mustache and drew a ragged breath, trying to rid himself of some of the tension he had from meeting the witch face-to-face. By now, he hoped his mama was giving her a good welcoming to Hell.

Billy clambered to his feet and caught a whiff of himself. It wouldn't do to go back to Feak and the A-patch smelling like he'd pissed himself. He remembered the clothesline he'd passed on his way to the jail, and headed in that direction. The same looseness he'd felt in his bowels came back to haunt him again, and he picked up his pace.

Even from over a block away, Scudder could feel the fire against his back. The witch and the boy were both dead by now; they had to be.

CHAPTER 13

"Couldn't get a good look, but I think there's only one man in there with her. He's kind of a grump." Trap used his .45-70 to point at the shack. Moonlight glinted lazily off the octagonal barrel in the hazy blue darkness. "She called him Sam."

"A customer?" Clay rubbed a thumb and forefinger down his drooping mustache.

"That's what I'm thinkin'. I'd like to have a look around for tracks out back. There's a privy beyond that stump row there from the door. Should be a whole load of tracks going back and forth. As far as I can tell, it's the only way in or out."

"A whore's door nearly always leads to the back," Clay whispered. The rough catch still lingered in his voice. He had a way of taking on strays. Given time, Cora would become his project for redemption whether she was willing or not.

Clay looked intently at the shack for a moment, then waved his pistol toward it. "Shall we go interrupt poor Sam's riotous evening?" His voice smoothed out at the prospect of adventure. All but a hint of the melancholy that had filled him fled by the time they reached the door. The shine of tears that moistened his eyes only moments before was replaced by the glint of mischief as he rapped on the wood with the edge of a closed fist.

"Later." A tired voice barely made it through the thin

walls. If a voice could have a hue, this one was drab.

"Can't wait." Clay stood to the right of the door while he knocked again. Harder this time; a persistent knock that bowed the door in on its hinges and left no doubt that the one knocking was there to stay. Trap took up a position oblique to Clay's, a few feet back with his rifle trained on the threshold—just in case they were wrong and it was Feak who was inside.

"Be gone, damn you." This time it was a man's voice, thin and brittle as cheap glass. More whining plea than threat, it was hard to take as an order. "Can't you see she's got the book in the window?"

Clay looked back at Trap, who bobbed his head at an ornately bound book with a red cloth spine, resting inside the cloudy window on the edge of the sill. A small circle of dust and grime was rubbed away to make the book visible through the otherwise opaque glass.

"Must be her sign that she's otherwise occupied." Clay said, loud enough for everyone within a block to hear. A few shanties down, a dog began to bark at the disturbance.

"You're damn right that's what it is," the voice whined from inside.

"Open the door, Sammy." Clay's mouth was a wide grin. He was enjoying this far too much.

"Now, you look, mister. I was here first. Off with you." Sam's voice took on an edge now. It was louder, and close to the door.

Trap withdrew another step into the shadows as the

door creaked open an inch. A metal belt buckle jingled inside, and the black barrel of a pistol nosed its way out at chest level.

"I said get outta here. You're a slow learner whoever . . ." The intense heat of his preoccupation with Moira had imbued Sam with a little too much counterfeit bravery.

Clay grabbed the pistol easily and shouldered his way in through the door.

"Wh . . . wha . . . what do you think you're doin'?" Sam was even thinner than his voice, with a long craning neck that seemed too narrow to hold his lolling head upright. He wore no shirt, and hadn't had the time to get his suspenders up over bony shoulders. A bony hand held up the bunched front of his sagging britches.

As soon as Clay breeched the door, Trap moved up and peeked in. A sallow woman, with lifeless hair the color of sun-bleached wood, slumped in a rumpled pile of sheets on a sagging bed along the sidewall. Beads of sweat covered her forehead. Knobby bare legs hung like sticks, akimbo from under the frayed hem of a dingy sheet. Jutting collarbones peeked out from above. It seemed absurd that such a woman would pretend any sort of modesty under the circumstances. Even Trap found it hard to believe anyone could pick a woman like this over the robust and smiling Cora.

Inside the shack, the tight air had the dank, sour odor of an illness. If not for the welcome scent of wood smoke that came through the open door, Trap felt he might get sick to his stomach.

Clay shook his head at the gangly man in front of him. "You know, friend, women are worse than whiskey for giving a man a swelled-up view of his own abilities." He emptied the offending revolver, shell by shell.

Sam's eyes twitched as if he'd been shot each time one of the heavy bullets clattered to the wooden floor. He hitched up his pants, looked back over a bony shoulder at Moira, and attempted to hitch up his courage.

"Now see here." The raw whine caught in his throat, but he plowed ahead in a stutter. "I d . . . done p . . . paid."

Clay took a deep breath, swelling his already puffed chest, and advanced on the quaking man. "Mister, I got the only two reasons I need to put a boot in your ass. I'm mad and you're handy. Now, you best git while I'm in the mood to let you."

Sam's head sunk on the end of his long neck and settled in the hollow of his chest, which looked like it was made for it. Deflated, he picked up his shirt and slinked to the door.

"I'll come back later," he said to Moira. "You still owe me."

She shrugged and ignored him, apparently more concerned now with the new men in her life. Trap stepped in as Sam disappeared through the doorway. A muffled yelp came through the door behind him, and Ky stepped in following Trap.

"I believe you let one get away," Roman observed.

Blake came in next and winked at his father. The two new men finally got a reaction from the sullen woman when she realized she wasn't dealing with customers.

"Now, what could you all want with me?" Moira groaned, raising her arms above her head to slither into a threadbare yellow dress. She squinted through rheumy eyes, as if she were looking into the sun, though the lamp globe was so covered with lampblack it hardly gave off any light.

Clay pulled up a wobbly wooden chair and flipped it around so he could sit and lean forward across the backrest while he spoke. He sat only a few feet from the bed.

"We're lookin' for a man you're familiar with."

"I'm familiar with a whole passel of men." There was a sense of gloom about her as heavy and squalid as the room. Without warning, she launched into a coughing fit that added some color to her face for a moment. It made the vein on the side of her neck bulge with effort. Spittle pooled in frothy bits at the corners of her mouth. When she regained her composure and her face had returned to its normal pallid hue, Clay began again.

"This one likes to cut the fingers off of young girls."

"Did Cora send you? That little whore, I'll tear her heart out for this." Moira's words came hard and vehement from an impassive face, like fire from the cold steel barrel of a gun.

Trap thought it funny how a woman like this could call another woman a whore and consider it an insult. He let his eyes play around the small room, as much to give them something to look at besides Moira as anything. "Blake, take a look at those quilts." He pointed his rifle at a pile of blankets against the far wall.

Clay rested his chin on his hands along the back of the chair and closed his eyes. "Listen, hon, you got a dark future ahead of you. As things stand now, the only thing that'll save you from the gallows is if the vigilantes get to you first and hang you from a tree."

Moira sat forward and cocked her head to one side. Only the slightest bit of animation perked the corners of her otherwise lifeless eyes. Her voice was as gray and lifeless as the faded pillows behind her. A peculiar rattle gurgled in her lungs when she spoke. "I don't know what you're talkin' about. I ain't done nothin' worth anybody hangin' me over."

Clay nodded. "Consortin' with murderous men . . ."

She snorted, coughed again, and spit something thick and putrid into a rusty can by the bed. "If consortin' was enough, my neck woulda been stretched long ago. Hell, you'd have to hang all the sports in this little burg."

"And going along with a kidnapping." Blake squatted on the rough floor beside a pile of soiled quilts. "The Kenworth girl was here. Looks like they made her sleep on the floor." The young lawman used the barrel of his pistol to poke through the dirty blankets. A louse scurried down the front sight and he shook it off in disgust. "There're some bloody rags here. Looks like they came off a bandaged finger."

Clay turned his attention back to Moira, opening both palms in front of him. "There's nothin' we can do for you if the Kenworth girl dies."

Ky moved up beside him. "If that girl dies, young lady, I'll come back and hang you myself." Roman stared hard across his hooked nose. He was not a man to make idle threats. If Roman said you were about to hang, you'd best start in with your praying.

Moira threw up her hands. "Look, fellas. She was alive when she left here. What did you want me to do? Slip off and report this to the old fart of a railroad agent? He's got the croup so fierce, Lucius woulda killed him before he got halfway up the street. I'm only one woman. What was I supposed to do?"

Clay looked at her and nodded slowly. The other three men were content to let him do the talking. "I see what you mean. But chew on this for a second, kiddo. What you do from now on can make a big difference in your future." He paused for a moment, staring at the hardened face. "Did Feak say where he planned to take the girl?"

Moira's head twitched slightly. "I know they were taking her to meet somebody else. This wasn't all Lucius's idea, you know."

"Who?" Ky couldn't help but chime in. "Who are they supposed to meet?"

"Didn't say." Moira shrugged. "I'd tell you if I knew. When he mentioned it, Lucius just called him the boss."

"Did Lucius say which way they were goin'?" Clay looked at Ky while he spoke.

"Nope. But I'm pretty sure they were headed deeper into the mountains. Whoever they're meetin' was a private sort of fella. Didn't want to be seen around here."

“When is this meeting supposed to take place?” Ky asked as Blake joined the men beside the bed.

“Look, gents.” Moira lay back on the sagging bed and covered her face with a forearm. “I told you what I know and I know that ain’t much. Lucius keeps important matters between hisself and the Apaches. He don’t even tell that stupid kid, Scudder.”

Clay glanced back at Trap and Blake. “The Indians with Feak are Apaches then?”

Moira nodded behind her arm.

“How many?”

“Two. A youngster, about the age of that young buck here with you.” She peered over her forearm at Blake. “And an older one with a scarred-up face. He wears an eye patch, but he’s got enough meanness in him that one lonesome eye will melt you for sure.”

Trap looked over at Ky, who met his gaze with a nod.

“Did Lucius ever call these Apaches by their names? Ky touched his pistol absentmindedly as he spoke.

“Not so as I would remember. I called ’em Ugly and Uglier. Most of the time they was off somewhere and Lucius had me . . . otherwise occupied, if you know what I mean.”

“What about this Scudder kid?” Clay reached out with his boot toe and kicked at the bed to keep Moira focused. “Tell us about him.”

“Billy Scudder. He’s a mean one, he is. Gets his jollies by threatenin’ me, but he’s too scared of Lucius to take it any further than that.”

“When did they go?” Clay stood and hitched his belt

like he was ready to leave. Leaving seemed like a good idea to Trap. The closeness of the room and the sour sell of the woman worked hard against his churning stomach. Even with the cracks in the walls, there didn't seem to be enough air in the tiny room for everyone.

"Just after sundown—about a half hour before old Sam came by." Moira suddenly swung her legs over the edge of the bed and sat upright. "Listen, boys, are you about to take me to jail or what? The night is still young and I got appointments to keep if you ain't."

"I reckon that's up to you," Clay said. He took a half step backward and almost bumped into Ky. Even he was surprised by the woman's sudden boldness.

Her face suddenly took on the hardened edge of a flint knife. "Well, don't you think you're scaring' me with all your talk of hangin' and vigilante boogermen. I know Lucius Feak. I been a witness to what he's capable of. He's just as likely to come back and kill me if I talk to you or if I don't—it don't make no difference. My life ain't worth a pinch anyhow and I know it. I don't reckon I'll make it past this coming winter no matter what happens." She coughed again, as if to illustrate her point, and wiped her mouth with the back of a filthy sleeve.

"So go ahead and hang me if you're of a mind to. The way I see it, you can stay on here and pester me or you can go on and catch Lucius and his bunch."

Clay shook his head and followed the others out the door without another word.

• • •

Outside in the alley, Clay leaned back against a table-sized stump and spit at the dirt. "I've never felt like I needed a bath as bad as I do now—and I mean a good scrubbin' too, not just a soak-and-ponder bath."

"I know what you mean," Ky said before he turned to Trap. "Any one of you ever heard of this Lucius Feak character?"

All the men shook their heads.

"What about the Apache with the eye patch?" Blake said to his father. "I caught the way you three looked at each other when she mentioned him."

"Maybe somebody from a long time ago, son." Trap shot a quick glance at Roman.

"A very long time ago. And if it's who I think it is, he doesn't think too much of me," Ky said.

"Come on, boys," Clay groaned. "Explain it all to the youngster after we've gone to roost. My old bones are sore and it's too dark to track for a few hours yet. I've got a hankerin' for a thick beefsteak. I'll lay odds our pretty Miss Cora can rustle us up some before she shows me a soft bed while you make your hard, miserable camp." Without waiting for a reply, Clay began to pick his way around the stumps and downed trees toward the back of the Snake Pit.

Ky gave a tentative cough. "Madsen, there's been a bit of a change in developments since you last visited Miss Cora. . . ."

CHAPTER 14

Angela's horse was a poor, puddin'-footed thing with feet as big as frying pans and thick ribs that jutted from black slab sides like slats on a hay bin. It was old to boot and prone to stumbling even on the flat. The broken mountain ground was murder, and the horse spent more time down on both knees than it did on its four large feet. Both hands tied together in front of her, Angela had to claw at the saddle horn to keep from falling off into the darkness over the side of the steep trail. The jagged nub of her little finger pained her past the point of hysteria, and even the cruel rawhide gag the older Apache had tied around her mouth did little to take her mind off the stomach-churning ache in her hand.

Angela knew how to ride. There were two fine stables not far from her house in Boston. But now, tied, weakened, and injured, she found it impossible to keep her seat. Each plodding misstep of the lumbering horse jammed or jostled the shard of bone. Her teeth slammed against the stiff gag. Tears poured from her eyes and ran in muddy lines down her filthy cheeks.

Feak led the way on his big sorrel horse, almost out of sight in the darkness. The younger Apache followed him, just ahead of Angela. Juan Caesar brought up the rear. She knew he was back there, but didn't dare turn around to see. It seemed to infuriate him when she looked at him, as if her mere glance was an insult to his scarred face. If she slowed or moved her head to look back, he jabbed at her cruelly with a long cedar branch he'd carved to a rough point and carried for the sole purpose of punishing her.

They'd left Moira's shortly after sunset, keeping to rough mountain trails well away from the railroad. The wilted prostitute had shown a tiny shred of decency when she'd offered to take Angela to the privy before they left. Feak agreed, but threatened to cut off both their noses if Angela made a run for it. He sent the young Apache to stand guard.

Breathing open-mouthed around the gag parched and dried Angela's throat, but she was afraid to drink any more for fear she'd have to go to the bathroom again. It didn't really matter because no one offered her any water anyway.

Apart from the groan of clambering horses, the creak of saddle leather, and the occasional scuff of a horseshoe against sharp rocks, the group moved in a silent parade. The air grew noticeably cooler as they gained elevation. Smoke still permeated the surroundings, and once in a while she could even see the far-off orange glow of a smoldering fire. But now and then, the telltale hint of cedar or spiced scent of Grande fir kicked up on a gentle breeze. The crisp air soothed Angela like a sip of springwater and for the first time in two days, she felt like she could breath.

The trail, such as it was, snaked back and forth in a zigzag pattern, working its way up the black mountains before them. Angela's stomach flew into her mouth as her clumsy horse tripped over a root or river rock when they crossed one of the numerous little creeks and gullies that wrinkled the hillside. She gripped the saddle horn like a madwoman for fear of falling off and receiving a severe beating from the stick-wielding Juan Caesar, and somehow managed to keep her seat on the ungainly horse as it clambered up the other side. The effort brought more tears to her eyes and shot spasms of light through her head as bright as a fireworks show over Boston Harbor.

In the darkness, she heard her mother's nasal voice chiding her about wearing pants around such men. Her brain was fevered, and she shook her head to clear it. Deep voices drifted across a small switchback on the trail above her. She'd been hearing mutterings of one kind or another for the past several hours, and she tried to ignore them. But lights danced in the darkness along with the new voices. Lantern lights—and singing men.

Angela shut her eyes and held her breath. She dared not hold out hope for a rescue. When she opened them again, Javi, who'd been in front of her, was gone. She risked a glance behind her, and saw Juan Caesar had dissolved into the inky darkness as well.

"Pete, is that you?" a jovial voice holloed from a junction in the trail above them. Small rocks skittered down the mountain as men milled about in one spot in the darkness. The glow from three lanterns cast huge shadows among the trees.

"Who's askin'?" Feak yelled tentatively.

"Pete? It's George White. The old man sent me to look after you. Fires looked like they might pen you down." The voice from the blackness was more cautious now. "Am I talkin' to Pete Seaver?"

Lucius Feak cursed under his breath and drew his pistol.

Firemen.

Angela's breath quickened. From the lanterns it looked like there were at least three of them, maybe more. They might stand a chance against her captors if she could warn them. She looked behind her again to make certain Juan Caesar wasn't about to smack her with a stick. She craned her neck in an effort to stretch the leather gag and give her more room. It cut at the corners of her chapped mouth and she tasted blood on her cracked lips. She wouldn't be able to make herself understood, but she could definitely scream.

And scream she did. A loud, wailing cry that summed up all the trials and torments of her last two days as it curdled the cool night air. She tried to lunge her horse up the mountain past Feak, to the firefighters who meant her safety and freedom. The outlaw turned and glared at her.

She'd misjudged how narrow the trail was as well as her stupid horse's desire to expend no more energy than necessary to make it up the hill. Feak wheeled his mount in one smooth motion and clouted her smartly in the temple with the fist that held his pistol. Angela kept screaming when he hit her, but reeled as blue and yellow lights exploded behind her eyes. Miraculously, she kept her seat in the saddle. When the pain dulled enough for her vision to clear, she saw Feak pointing the gun at her belly.

"You best be keepin' quite," he hissed though the blackness. "I'll kill you slow after I let the A-patch have a go at you if you don't shut your gob."

"Who's out there?" All three lantern lights flickered out at once. The voice above them was less than fifty feet away. "What's going on here? Identify yourselves."

Feak held the gun barrel to his lips to remind Angela to keep quiet. "We're just out here for the fires same as you," he yelled up the mountain.

"Who screamed?" George White demanded through the darkness, his voice firm as wrought iron. He spoke more quietly to his men, but it was clearly audible filtering through the trees. "McGowan! Baker! Spread out and stay quiet!" Again, he spoke with authority. "Listen, whoever you are. Identify yourselves. I am a duly appointed agent with the federal government and until I am satisfied as to what's going on around here, you should consider yourselves under arrest."

Feak scoffed at such talk. "Come on down here and we'll talk."

"Come up and show your . . ."

Gunfire split the darkness on a bald knob above them. An odd moan, like the air hissing out of a India-rubber balloon, caused Angela to cringe in pity. There was a clatter in the rocks above them and something heavy slid down the mountain. A chilling scream followed off to the right, and she knew another man had died.

“McGowan? Baker?” The demanding tone bled from White’s voice with every syllable. “Are you all right? Who’s out there?”

Feak chuckled in the darkness. “I reckon they just be busy arrestin’ a couple of my men.”

“Now see here. We’re firefighters in the employ of the U.S. Forest Ser . . .” White’s voice trailed off into silence.

A short moment later, a low loon-whistle wafted down through the trees. Feak reholstered his sidearm and twisted in his saddle to face Angela. Little moonlight filtered down through the smoke and thick canopy of branches, but Feak’s yellow sneer was plainly visible in the darkness.

“It’s all over now, little britches. Go ahead and scream if you feel a mind to, but you best follow me up the trail. Them A-patch wouldn’t want me to be losin’ their little treasure just yet.”

Juan Caesar was busy pulling the scalp off a dead man with silver-white hair when they arrived at the site of the massacre. He used his foot to brace himself against the dead man’s shoulder while he pulled. The popping sound the small circle of flesh made when it tore away from the bone caused Angela’s stomach to lurch and she vomited around her leather gag.

Slumping in the saddle, she turned away only to see Javi walking out of the underbrush holding a lit lantern in one hand and two bloody scalps in the other. He smiled and offered the tangled masses of hair to Angela.

When she shook her head, he shrugged and grabbed one of the scalps in his teeth as if he were about to bite off a piece.

"Suit yourself," he said around the morsel of flesh, "but it's good grub."

Angela heaved again, tasting the bitterness already in her mouth. She never been in a spot where things were so desperate, where there seemed no escape—no relief, no comfort. With each passing moment, the realization formed more clearly in her fevered mind. Sooner or later, she would end up like one of these poor dead souls—murdered and mutilated only to have her defiled body become an object of entertainment and derision for these savage men. Three more men were dead now, for no reason but that they got in the way. Bitter tears of complete despair caught in Angela's throat at the thought that she might have prevented their deaths—had she only been braver and ignored Feak's threat. Her screaming might have given them a chance.

Feak walked up beside her and put a rough hand on her thigh. He spoke quietly as he stroked her above the knee, his voice a scornful hiss in her ear.

"Quit your blubberin', little britches. This is the last pee break you'll be gettin' for a while, so you best take advantage of it. The A-patch will be busy for a minute or two butcherin' up the bodies so as to make things look real Injun-like. If I was you, I'd be droppin' my drawers while they was otherwise occupied. I got my orders to deliver you unsullied, but that Juan Caesar, he hates whites. I seen what he can do to a pale woman like you, and it ain't at all a pretty picture. If he was to get an opportunity . . ." Feak licked his lips. "I don't know as I could even slow him down, let alone stop him."

Even in the darkness, Angela could see a glistening sheen of whiskey-dull lust in his black eyes. It didn't matter anymore. If he wanted to rape her he would. If he decided to hack off another piece of her, just for entertainment, he would. There was absolutely nothing she could do about it except fight and prolong the inevitable. She knew she would fight when the moment came—but for now, she needed to go to the bathroom.

A few feet away, in a ghostly pool of yellow lantern light, the two Apaches stooped over the lifeless corpse of George White. Engrossed in their own brutal actions, they paid no attention to Angela.

She looked down at Feak and nodded weakly, straining her jaw against the filthy leather gag. Her lips and mouth were cracked and raw from the constant rubbing of the wide strap. She'd been able to chew the corners down somewhat, but it still kept her from closing her mouth completely. Drool and dried blood matted the tangled strands of her once-beautiful auburn hair to her cheeks.

Feak helped her down from the horse and chuckled to himself when she said "Thank you" out of habit. "You really don't belong out here. Do you, little britches?" He gave her a rough shove in the behind and hissed at her again, all humor draining from his ice-cold voice,

"Don't you be thankin' me just yet. Hurry and get your squattin' done. If you try to run, I'll cut your nose off and feed it to Javi. He's right partial to woman nose. Eats 'em like candy."

Angela bit down hard on the gag to keep from screaming again. She felt insane for thanking the man who only hours before had brutally hacked off her finger. He would likely be the one to kill her—or at the very least order her death—in the not-too-distant future.

Stepping behind a nearby cedar tree, she fumbled with the buttons on her britches, careful to keep from bumping the inflamed shard of bone where her little finger used to be. She knew Feak was watching her from the darkness, and found she didn't care. For some unexplainable reason, she began to laugh softly to herself. She thought of how Mother would be able to say, "I told you so." Boston seemed so far away. For as long as Angela could remember now, her world had been nothing but rough men and savage Indians.

When Angela was finished and buttoned up her pants, she couldn't help but chuckle, even though the action hurt her mouth. She wondered how Mother would handle such men—or how such men would handle Mother.

If Lucius Feak had known the big sorrel possessed such a tendency to hold air, he never would have stolen it in the first place. The outlaw heard the noise in the thick brush behind him while he was busy tightening his cinch. A crackling rustle of branches rubbing together.

The forest at night held so many sounds, he ignored the noise at first, but it came again, more tentative than before. Most animals didn't creep around at night; they either walked along like they didn't have a care in the world or ran off, crashing wildly through the underbrush. A cougar might creep, or even a bear if it was hunting—but men, they most always went sneaking around when they were in the woods.

Another dry branch snapped in the shadows. Feak heard someone catch their breath. He looked up at the Apaches, who were still busy dragging the bodies of their victims out onto the trail so they would be easily discovered.

This whole plan set Feak's nerves on end. He'd never gone out and done so many bad things and then left so much sign on purpose. It went against his instincts to leave so many things undone. Killing was one thing, but leaving the bodies in the open where any lawman with half a brain could find them, that was just plum crazy.

Another rattle of a branch jostled the darkness behind him, followed by the swish of a limb against clothing. Feak let the loose end of the latigo drop, and slowly reached for the near rein with his left hand while his right slid down to his pistol. The stupid girl sat moaning in her saddle on the other side of him. Feak eased his horse around, putting himself on the ground between both animals, the girl to his back. If things turned sour,

Feak could easily jump on his horse and slip off into the darkness.

Training his revolver across the seat of his saddle, the outlaw yelled into the darkness—as much to warn Juan Caesar and Javier of approaching danger as to evoke an answer.

"Get out here so we can see you!" Lucius's voice was a fierce growl, and his horse threw its head and snorted with a start. Steel bits jingled in the still night, and the girl caught her breath behind him. Both Apaches vanished into the blackness.

"Hey, hey, hey!" came a tentative voice from the dark line of mottled shadows at the edge of the trail. "Don't shoot. It's only us."

Lucius relaxed when he heard the voice. The Indians heard it too, and reappeared from the shadows to resume their grizzly fun.

Holstering his gun, Feak finished tightening his cinch. When the two men moved in closer, he spoke to them without looking up.

"You two are liable to get your throats cut—sneakin' up like a couple of Papago Injuns. Get your horses and let's get movin'. We got a little ways to go yet before we meet the big boss."

Billy Scudder held up a leather bag. The white elk ivories adorning the outside caught the nearby lantern light and seemed to glow in his hand.

"She be dead then?" Feak trained his eyes on the young outlaw.

Scudder grunted. "Cut her guts out with my own

knife. Boy's too. They won't cause you no more trouble."

Javier walked in from the darkness, chewing on something. He looked at the decorated bag dangling in Scudder's hand. "There are those among my people that believe the owner's ghost inhabits their medicine bag after they die. They say if you hang onto one that belongs to someone else, pieces of you start to rot off. Bad medicine." The young Apache stared into Scudder's eyes. "I always bury or burn them after I'm through with my business."

Billy looked down at his hand, his eyes wide in horror as if the rotting process might have already begun. He held it out to his companion, who spun the leather drawstring back and forth around a thick forefinger. "Billy, you're a slobberin' idiot," the new man said, shaking his head. "That Apache buck is just tryin' to make a fool of you, and I'd say he's doin' a good job of it."

Javier shrugged, fishing something from his back teeth with the tip of his tongue. He turned to walk back to where he'd tied his horse in the trees. "Suit yourself," he said over his shoulder. "When pieces of you begin to stink and turn black, there will be nothing you can do."

"You don't scare me, you thievin' red bastard."

Juan Caesar perked up at the insult, and moved like quicksilver from his place in the shadows to beside the other Apache.

Feak began to panic. "Hold on here, boys. Everybody be simmerin' down now. The boss wouldn't take kindly to us killin' each other before the job's done. Let's us all just play nice for a little longer. We got some money now, but we got a chance at a hell of a lot more if we just see this through."

The two Indians eyed the other men for a long minute. Feak didn't know about Scudder and the newcomer, but the Apaches scared him, and he didn't mind saying so. Controlling them was like trying to eat a soup sandwich. They did as they pleased when it pleased them. He wasn't sure the money meant much to them, and suspected they only came along with hot revenge burning a hole in their brains.

Everyone jerked, including Feak's horse, when Juan Caesar wheeled and walked away into the darkness. Feak let out the half lung of air he'd been holding.

"I wish you could be keepin' your fool mouth shut till all this is over," Lucius said. "I think it would be wise for you to remember what them A-patch done to that old boy back at Goblin Creek." Lucius climbed into the saddle and spit, his nervous grimace a blue-gray gash across his face. "After you're mounted, you be ridin' up here by me. I got a little plan. Think we might need to do a little changin' out on our horses."

The newcomer dangled the medicine bag in front of Scudder's face. He curled his own ring finger down so it looked like it had already fallen off. "You want this back, Billy?"

Scudder tried to put on a brave face, but he wouldn't get near the bag. "Naw, you go ahead and hang onto it. Maybe it'll bring you some luck."

CHAPTER 15

Maggie rolled a wet blanket lengthwise and stuffed it under the door to keep out as much of the smoke as she could. It was difficult to move with Shad dogging her every move, but she didn't have the heart to tell him to sit down. She could hear the crackling of burning timbers outside mingled with the shouts of men working to put out the fire. Already, smoke poured in through cracks in the storeroom walls like fingers on a ghostly apparition, and threatened to suffocate them before the fire actually got to them. Maggie had a fleeting thought that it would likely be better to pass out from smoke than be burned alive. But it wasn't in her nature to give up. She was no quitter.

The temperature in the stuffy room was already rising. Maggie put her hand on the door. It was hot enough to the touch that she couldn't keep her hand on it for more than a second or two. Shad put his hand next to hers, and immediately jerked it away.

He yelped and looked at her. "I don't want to hide anymore. I'd rather just die out here with you. Are we going to die, Miss Maggie?"

"I don't know," she said with an honest shrug that appeared more relaxed than she really was. "I'm not ready to die quite yet. I'd like to see some grandchildren and watch you grow up." Her mind raced while she spoke.

The crackling outside the door grew louder, and the blanket she'd stuffed under the door began to smolder. Sticky black pitch boiled out of seams in the thick wooden door.

Maggie cast her eyes back and forth around the room, struggled to figure out what to do. Jumping up on the cot, she yanked at the iron bars that blocked the window above her head. She'd hoped one might be loose enough to get Shad out, even if she was doomed.

More men's voices buzzed past the window and she cried out.

"Help us! There's a child in here with me!" The roar of flames and snapping of timbers combined with the general hubbub of the bucket crew and covered any pleas for help.

One of the five bars in the window did wiggle in her hand a bit. If she could just get one out, Shad might be able to get though.

"Shad, honey." She glanced over he shoulder at the boy while she continued to work at the bar. "I need you to do me a favor."

"No, please, Miss Maggie. I can't. I can't hide and let you get killed." He was racked with a series of violent sobbing coughs.

"I'm not asking you to hide, child. I need you to get my rifle. I may be able to shoot this bar loose so you . . . we can climb out through here."

He slowed his crying and handed her the gun, plugging his ears with the palms of both hands after she took it.

Maggie figured it would be better to shoot at the wood that held the thick iron than the bars themselves. She set the muzzle where she thought it would do the most good, then turned her head before she pulled the trigger to keep from getting flying splinters in her eyes. It was becoming more and more difficult to breath. The entire door smoked as if it were ready to burst into flames.

"Shad!" she barked after she shot, and levered another shell into her rifle. "Can you throw that bucket of water against the door?"

The boy jumped off the cot and did as he was told. The water hit the superheated wood with a great hiss of steam, turning the room into a sauna.

"Good job," Maggie said between pulling the trigger. "Keep doing that and we may be able to get out of here."

Someone outside screamed for everyone to get away from the burning building, warning that the ammunition inside was cooking off in the fire.

Six deafening shots later, she leaned the gun against the wall. Wrapping both hands around the loose iron bar, she bore down against it with a mighty heave. It didn't move. If anything, the stubborn bar seemed more solid than before.

She still had four rounds left, but was loath to shoot the gun dry. Even if she did succeed in getting the boy out, someone out there still wanted to kill him. Trap had always told her to leave an extra round or two. She'd learned better than to empty her weapon back with her own people when she was only thirteen, during the Battle of Big Hole, but she chose to let Trap believe he was the one to teach her.

"There's not much water left, Miss Maggie." Shad said, splashing another bucket against the steaming door.

The situation looked hopeless. For her entire life, Maggie Sundown O'Shannon had been a great believer in hope. Now, there seemed to be no avenue of escape, no Trap O'Shannon there to help her save herself from the evil things of the world. He was busy on the trail as he'd been so many times before, depending on her to take care of herself.

He would not—could not come. No one would.

Maggie slumped down on the cot and motioned Shad to her with a flick of her hand. The smoke and steam were thick now, and she could hardly see him. It would only be a matter of seconds before the door ignited and flames rushed into the room. She tried to say something to comfort the boy, but found a hard knot in her throat so she couldn't speak. She tried to sing the song she'd used to comfort him at Dr. Bruner's office, but sobs gripped her chest and she began to cry.

Shad leaned against her, coughing. "It's all right, Miss Maggie. I only said I wouldn't hide. Why don't you hide this time?"

Maggie rubbed her eyes and looked at the boy through the thickening smoke. "Why all this talk of hiding?"

"It was awful dark in that box, and I could hear Mama

screaming . . . I don't want to go in there again."

"That was on the coach, child," Maggie said, pulling the poor boys head closer to her breast. "You won't have to go in there anymore, I promise."

Shad wriggled away from her grip. "I know that. I'm talking about the one under the bed."

"What?"

"There's another hole under the bed. I was going to hide in it when you went out and the man cut you, but it was too dark. I'm scared, but you . . ."

Maggie lifted the boy up and slid the bed to one side. Along the floor was a trapdoor. With no time to lose, she yanked on the metal ring and found it opened easily. It was indeed dark down the square hole, but the air was remarkably cool and free from smoke.

"Come with me, Shad." Maggie coughed, grabbing her rifle off the cot and hiking up her dress so she could step down on the wooden ladder she could just make out in the blackness.

"No, it's too dark," said Shad.

She took his hand. "I need you to protect me."

The door burst into flames.

"Hurry, Shad, we need to go now. We'll protect each other."

The boy looked at the flaming door, then down at the black cavern below him. He took a step toward her, and Maggie pulled him in before he could change his mind.

Once they were inside the narrow crawl space, it was relatively easy to work their way to the latticework vent at the side of the building. Shadows and light from the fire reflecting off the hotel cast eerie orange shadows along the dirt floor. Spiders and rat droppings littered the ground, but Maggie was happy to be away from the fire and didn't care. Shad hung onto the hem of her dress while she crawled on her hands and knees to the louvered wooden vent.

People milled about outside. They'd suspended their bucket work, now only watching for stray sparks that threatened the nearby hotel.

Maggie used the butt of her rifle to break the brittle wood away from the vent. It was almost too hot to breathe around the opening, but it was the only way out and she was overjoyed to have it.

A man in striped bib overalls and no shirt stared in shock and dropped his empty bucket as she pushed a wriggling Shad through the small opening and squirmed out with her rifle directly on his heels.

A group of volunteers, including the man in overalls, ran forward to brave the flames and grabbed the two scorched survivors and dragged them to safety. Doc Bruner was in the crowd. He herded them away quickly before any of the local townsfolk could recover from the shock of seeing them escape from the belly of such a fiery beast.

When they were a half block away, the doctor looked at them and whistled under his breath at the wound across Maggie's chest.

"I should put some ointment on that. You've been through it, young lady. Looks like you may need stitches."

Maggie chuckled in spite of her appearance at the thought of anyone calling her young. "May we stay for a while at your place? It might put you in danger."

The doctor shook his head in amazement. "Of course, of course. I wouldn't have it any other way. I wish my wife would have had your pluck."

Pluck. Maggie knew she had many qualities, but she'd never been told she had pluck. She'd have to tell Trap about that one.

Turning to get a last look at the fire that had almost beaten her, Maggie froze in her tracks.

Well away from the blaze, at the fringe of the bucket brigade, stood a man from the past—a man she was certain had been dead for over twenty years.

CHAPTER 16

August 20, Early Morning

Trap O'Shannon woke before the fires with the dream of Maggie's breath like a warm breeze in his ear. His back and shoulders ached from the packed earthen bed. Clay stirred when he heard Trap roll out, and threw his arms back in a long, yawning stretch. It was just after four in the morning, and dawn was only beginning to gather up her orange skirts behind the eastern mountains.

"Blast this cold, hard ground for a mattress," Madsen said through his yawn. "If you boys wouldn't have trounced that bartender, Franco so soundly, I might have been able to spend the night with Cora on a real bed in that little room of hers."

Blake sat up in his bedroll and rubbed a hand through his mussed black hair. Ky was already standing and making water a few yards away. His shirttail hung loose with leather suspenders around his britches. He looked over his shoulder at Clay.

"Sure you would. I only gave the man a severe thrashing. I do believe you would have killed him had you come back and found your rotund Miss Cora in the same position we found her."

Madsen stumbled to one knee and pushed himself up, still cussing the ground. "Indeed I would have, sir. That is a plain fact, but I might point out that if Franco was dead, I would still have had a bed to sleep in. As it stands now, with the job half done, Cora's sought a place to roost her bones elsewhere and I am forced to spend my repose against the cold, unfeeling bosom of Mother Earth." He glanced over at Blake.

"You don't know Roman. He don't get angry, he gets indignant. Believe me, that's much worse. When you're full of righteous indignation like he gets, he believes the Good Lord is on his side. That's when he gets hard to stop. Spit in his face, he'll wipe it off and walk away. Mistreat an innocent—even an innocent whore—and you best watch yourself 'cause you're about to receive one of Captain Roman's famous layin' on of hands."

Once on his feet, Clay put both hands on his knees and pushed himself to a semi-upright position. Still hunched forward like a man twice his age, he hobbled to the edge of the woods to relieve himself. Trap watched him walk back and stoop slowly to retrieve his blankets.

"What are you looking at, O'Shannon?" Madsen smiled at his friend. "I don't see you up and boundin' about like a prairie dog either. I reckon my bladder wakes up a mite quicker than my old back does—too many rank horses and fistfights in my time."

Trap nodded. He was every bit as sore and bent as Clay, and it took him as long to get up in the morning; he just did it without all the moans and groans. Trap had never possessed his friend's flair for the dramatic.

After wolfing down a quick breakfast of coffee—except for Ky, who stuck with water—and cold lamb and tortillas compliments of Maggie, the four lawmen took to their saddles. Trap settled into the lead. He had a general idea of the kidnappers' direction of travel after they'd left Moira Gumm's place. First light was always his preference for tracking. In a few minutes the sun would be low and bright on the horizon, its long shadow casting over the parched ground to make all kinds of sign virtually jump out at the eye.

The outlaws had traveled in single file. Someone had ridden a clumsy, big-footed horse that stumbled back and forth along the trail without any guidance from its rider—likely the Kenworth girl. All four sets of tracks led along the rough road toward the mountains to the west—into the High and Lonesome. A glow of pink and orange already tinged the hazy fog that clung to the highest peaks. Smoke from a dozen spot fires billowed straight up from the dark green forests in giant plumes, shooting skyward, then flattening out as it cooled on the chilly pillow of morning air.

The kidnappers' trail led directly into the fires.

Clay jabbered quietly while they rode, intent on imparting some of his wisdom to Blake whether he wanted to hear it or not.

"You know why the Nez Percé rode Appaloosas into battle?" Clay gave Blake's spotted horse the once-over from under the brim of his hat.

Blake shook his head.

"On accounta they wanted to be good and mad when they got there." Clay slapped his leg and guffawed at his own joke. "Your mama used to threaten to skin me alive the way I picked on her favorite ponies so much."

Trap rolled his eyes and winked at his son. "Don't let him get started, boy. Take it from me. He'll wear you out if you let him."

"You just pay attention to the trail, O'Shannon." Clay waved off his old friend. "This here conversation doesn't concern you. How old are you now, Blake?"

"Twenty-four."

"You know, my daddy once told me a man couldn't call hisself a man till he was past thirty. Well, sir, I hit thirty-one and paid the old man a visit. He looked me over and up and down and says to me, 'Son, it takes some men a mite longer than others.' "

Trap slid out of his saddle and squatted beside the jumble of tracks in the dust. He studied them for a while, touching the ground with his ungloved hand. Hashkee stood by stoically, ears pinned back and grumpy, but otherwise obedient. At length, Trap stood, took off his hat, and scanned their back trail. He had a habit of chewing on the inside of his cheek when something troubled him.

"Blake, come check my eyes, son, and tell me how many tracks you count," he said, rescuing the boy from Clay's tutelage.

The younger O'Shannon spurred his Appaloosa up next to his father and dismounted. He looked at the ground, studying it for a moment, and then scanned the valley behind them.

"Four?"

"That's the way I figured it."

Ky and Clay rode up to take a look.

Though none of them would ever admit it, deep down they all gave at least a pinch of credence to the notion that tracking expertise was a gift at which Indians—especially those with Apache blood—excelled. Expert trackers in their own right, either Roman or Madsen could follow bandits across bare stone if pressed. But if Trap was around, they always yielded to that extra sense of his that no one ever even tried to explain.

"So we're short by one?" Ky rubbed his chin, ruminating on the new information.

"That we are, Captain," Trap said. "There were five sets of tracks leaving the site of the massacre: the four bandits and the girl's. Looks to me like they put the girl on this plow horse." He poked the leather tip of

Hashkee's reins at the huge tracks that meandered along the narrow road.

"She wouldn't be able to outrun anyone on that beast," Clay said, perusing the large impressions. "I think I dated a gal with feet that big once—she had a pretty face, though, and a butt like a barmaid. Come to think of it, she never did go lame on me."

Roman rolled his eyes. "So one of them's split off. Blake, you make it your job to watch our back trail for a piece while your pa concentrates on the tracking. Clay and I will keep our eyes peeled to the sides."

It was the way they'd traveled in the old days. Trap on and off his horse, studying the ground, setting the pace, while the others in the squad watched for ambush. Once in a while, if the trail became forthright and relatively simple to follow, Trap might ask for a break to ease the strain on his eyes, but more often than not, the break turned into a teaching session with Trap as the headmaster, pointing out this subtle nuance or that about whatever tracks they followed. There were so many things a footprint could tell a person, if he just listened.

Trap was fairly certain by the overlay of the tracks that he knew which horse Feak was riding. It had a loose front shoe on the left side and it stayed pretty much to the trail. It was obviously the lead horse, and many of its tracks were partially obscured by those left by the puddin'-foot. When it stopped, the horse always pranced on its front feet; an action likely caused by someone heavy-handed on the bits. Considering what he'd been up to, Trap didn't figure Feak to be a man with a light touch when it came to horses—or anything else for that matter. The other two sets of tracks were more precise, moving in straight lines, one in front of the puddin'-foot and one behind it, sometimes fanning out in opposite directions but always returning to their spots in line. These he picked for the two Apache mounts.

As time passed, Trap began to learn even more about them. The rear horse was most likely ridden by the older Indian because the lead fanned out on slightly more scouting trips while the rear horse stayed in place. A younger Apache would usually defer to his elder and generally do more of the work in the little group. Trap studied each set of tracks for the slight differences in hoof angle, drag, shoe and nail type, and gait so he could tell them apart as individuals in case another member of the group split off for any length of time. He used his pencil stub to scratch out some notes in his little book. Time was he'd kept all such information in his head—but those times were gone.

The kidnappers stayed to the trail and tracking them was no more of a job than following—a fact that gnawed at the men's craws considerably. In the old days, it hadn't been uncommon to follow the trail of a person who wanted to be followed, but when they did, it always meant an ambush.

By eight in the morning, the sun was full up and blazing down through the thick brown haze that was so full of sap it stung the nose and eyes and left a sticky film on clothes and skin. Even the horses began to be bothered by it, and became more agitated with every mile. Hashkee in particular had a kink in his tail. No matter how hard he coaxed, Trap couldn't soothe him. Though the animal never hesitated, every step was a growling, pin-eared reminder of how unhappy he was with the situation. Clay had observed once that Hashkee was the type of mule who'd walk off a cliff with you if you pointed him that way, then cuss you all the way to the bottom and kick you in the afterlife.

Blake, with his younger eyes, was the first to notice the crows and magpies flitting and fighting through smoke and yellow pine up the mountain switchback a scant hundred yards ahead of them.

"Think something might be dead up there?" He stood in his saddle to get a better look.

The older O'Shannon shook his head and put out an overturned hand. "Don't stand up like that, son. Men standing tall sometimes get shot off their mounts."

Blake dropped back to his seat immediately with a sheepish look.

"Don't look so glum, boy," Clay said, trotting up next to him. "Me and your pa learned that lesson the hard way. Lucky for us, the guy who taught us was a poor marksman and only winged me." Clay rolled his shoulder to illustrate the wound.

"I think Blake's right." Ky squinted against the cool layer of smoke that flowed downhill like a pungent river. "Something's not right up there. Could be an animal, but we'd best not take that chance. Trap, that mule of yours still climb?"

O'Shannon nodded and touched a knuckle to his forehead in a sloppy salute.

"Good. You and Blake spread out to either side and go poke around up ahead. Clay and I will take up positions back here with rifles and watch for any movement at your approach." The Arizona marshal turned to look at Madsen. "That is, if you're not feeling too old and stove up from all your life's escapades."

Clay scoffed. "Scoot on up yon hill, O'Shannon boys." He slipped his rifle, boot and all, off the saddle and threw a leg over the horn to hop nimbly off his horse. "I still got some sass left in me." He held his rifle in one hand, and took off his hat to squint up at the direction of the screeching birds. "Can't see too well that far off, but we'll do our best not to hit either of you."

The Texan grinned at Blake and gave him a conspiratorial wink. "Now, don't you worry, sonny. Time was I could shoot the *cojones* off a horsefly at a hundred yards. As old as I am now, I just have to aim for the whole bug."

Trap sighed and then motioned up the trail with his chin. "You go to the north, son. Don't be afraid to sing out if you see anything. If it's an ambush, they already know we're here."

Ten minutes later found Trap on a panting Hashkee overlooking the birds from a shadowed copse of tamarack on a little knoll above them. He called out to Blake and the men below, then let out the little extra bit of air he always kept back in his lungs when he was ghosting around on half breaths in what Madsen called his panther mode.

"More dead," Trap sighed to himself. He stole a moment to let himself worry about Maggie. She was a capable woman who'd proven herself in pitched battle more than once. But the missing track nagged at him. One of these raw killers was unaccounted for, and that fact alone was enough to leave his mind in a constant whirl of worry.

Blake and his Appaloosa appeared out of some floppy-topped hemlock trees along the trail to the north of the bodies. He waved up at his father, who had already pointed his mule down the hillside and was half-sliding, half-riding toward him.

"I got a track here I've not seen before," Blake said. "It's got a hooked shoe on the back right."

Trapped smiled inside himself at how well his boy was doing. It didn't surprise him—Maggie was his mother after all—but he couldn't help but be pleased.

"Looks like these three unfortunate souls bumped into our killers during the night," Ky said, his hat in hand when he and Clay made it up the switchback.

All three of the dead were positioned across the narrow trail. Each had an exposed circle of white skull where they'd been scalped. They had been killed with a knife, all from behind. A white-haired man, young but obviously the oldest of the three, had defensive wounds on his hands where it looked like he'd been able to put up a fight at least. All were stripped of their clothes and mutilated in the same manner as the blond man at the stage massacre site.

Clay spit vehemently into the dust. "I'm sure looking forward to the time I meet up with these folks."

"Blake found a new track over here, Captain," Trap said from up the trail. "Looks like two new riders have joined up."

"Sure they're not from the firefighters' horses?"

Blake motioned back to the woods with his rifle. "I think the dead men were on foot. I came across a mess of tracks back there where one of them was killed. Didn't see any hoofprints."

Trap stood and walked up the path. "One of these belongs to our missing rider from yesterday; more than likely it's Billy Scudder. The other track looks familiar, but I can't place where I've seen it." He perused the ground as he walked. "Yep, the two newcomers came out of the brush here, leading their horses."

He poked around in the trees for a few moments, then whistled softly under his breath. "The girl was still alive last night. She made water here behind this tree. All the tracks join up again up the trail."

Clay rode in alongside Ky. "Moira said Feak was supposed to meet someone he called the boss."

Ky nodded and tapped his saddle horn. He bowed his head in one of the little prayers he was wont to say from time to time. Everyone stood silently until he was finished.

"We best get some rocks over these poor souls to

keep the magpies off them till we can notify someone to come get the bodies." Returning his hat to his head, Roman dismounted and looked around at the clouds of smoke coming up from behind the mountains. "I imagine there are fire crews all over up here. Somebody's bound to be wondering about them."

CHAPTER 17

Horace Zelinski slung a faded canvas rucksack over his back and tapped the canteen at his belt to make sure it had water in it. He constantly warned the men to drink. It reminded Daniel Rainwater of his own mother, the way the man took care of everyone over whom he had stewardship. When Zelinski was nearby, Big Ox and Taggart kept to themselves, unwilling to do anything in front of him. Now that he was preparing to leave, both men glared at the two Indian boys with open hostility.

The fire boss gathered the crew around him in a little green glade of hemlock and cedars to explain his plan. "You men can obviously tell there's a big fire brewing over that mountain to the southwest. It's uncommonly dark for this early in the day, and the wind has an edge to it that puts some fear in me, I don't mind saying."

Daniel and Joseph looked at each other, then up at the huge cloud of smoke that billowed up behind the black mountain five miles away. It rose into the hazy blue, its top knocked queerly to one side like the pompadour on a Nez Percé warrior. The Flathead elders had warned them about the late summer winds before they left to volunteer.

Dry wind and fire always spelled disaster.

Zelinski continued his speech. "I'm going to do some scouting and see just how big the fire is. I'm leaving McGill in charge. He knows exactly where we are and I'm sure the two Indian boys do as well. I should be back before nightfall, but if you get into something you can't handle, follow them to safety." He stooped to rub the shaggy head of the wolfhound at his side. "In the meantime, work on a firebreak along this creek. If the fire makes it over that mountain, we can stop it here." He stomped a foot and pointed to the ground before him. "Right here, lads. This is where we stop it."

Even with the air of bravado in his voice, Daniel knew the fire boss was more than concerned about what lay in wait for him on the other side of the mountain.

Before Zelinski was out of sight, McGill tightened the blue bandanna over his balding head and hoisted his ax. Without saying a word to the rest of the men, he walked toward the small creek and began to work on the firebreak. He was a good man and a hard worker, but possessed none of the charismatic leadership qualities of Zelinski or George White. Rather than giving orders, McGill seemed to hope he would inspire the men to work because he did—a tactic that might be successful with some of the group—but not Monroe and Taggart.

Daniel Rainwater shouldered his ax and threw a grubbing hoe to Joseph. Zelinski was still visible making his way up the mountain trail on the far side of the trees. It wouldn't be long before he'd be out of the sound range of a gunshot.

Big Ox swaggered up to the two boys with Roan Taggart at his heels. "He's about gone, young 'uns." Monroe shook his head and sniffed, wiping his nose on the back of his forearm. "I reckon it's only a matter of time before you niggers get what's comin' to you."

The big man was close enough that Daniel could smell the acid odor of canned tomatoes on his foul breath. "Just get to work, Ox," said one of the men, an older fellow everyone called Swede, slapping Monroe heartily on the back. "Don't you go scaring the children."

"You ready for our wrestlin' match?" Bandy Rollins had a way of materializing out of nowhere. It was an odd skill for a man who took up so much space wherever he stood.

Big Ox coughed. "You heard Zelinski. Why don't you get to work and mind your own business?"

"Oh, he wouldn't mind. He told me I was welcome to fight whenever I pleased."

"Go ahead and fight yourself then. I'm goin' to work." Monroe turned his back just as a tall black trooper in a sweat-soaked uniform ran up and whispered urgently in the corporal's ear.

Rollins suddenly became animated, gesturing up and down with his huge hands before dismissing the other trooper with a curt nod. When he turned to face Rainwater and Joseph, his face was set and tense.

"You boys gotta look after your own selves for a while. Company G's bein' recalled back to Avery. Seems like they got 'em a bad fire and they evacuatin' the whole town by train." The trooper suddenly brightened and slapped his leg. "Why don't you boys come and go with me. I can get you out on the trains. It sure enough ain't safe for you here."

"Mr. Zelinski told us to stay here in case the fire comes this way," Daniel said with more commitment than he actually felt.

Rollins nodded his great head slowly, his eyes shut for a moment while he came to a decision. "All right then. I'll likely hang, but I reckon I should go on over there right now then and shoot Mr. Ox between the eyes before I go." The corporal hitched up his pants and started for the tree line.

Joseph broke his customary silence. "Don't worry about us, Bandy. We can take care of Monroe and his stinking partner."

Rollins turned back with a shrug. "Suit yourself then. I'll be back as quick as I can." He leaned in to the two Indian boys and took on a solemn tone. "You listen good to ol' Bandy now. If either one of those two comes near you, kill 'em quick. Don't pussyfoot around or they'll get you for sure. You can't trust none of these yayhoos 'cept maybe McGill, so slip away right off."

The corporal winked. "When I come back I'll wrestle the son of a bitch and save the world a bullet."

CHAPTER 18

"You remember ol' Go Go Gomez?" Clay let his boots hang out of the stirrups while he rode to rest his knees. "What was his first name?"

"Enrique," Roman said. He'd always made it a point to know the given names of every trooper under his command.

Clay nodded. "That's right, Enrique Gomez. Damn, that boy could run. I wonder whatever happened to ol' Go Go."

"Died," Roman offered, his eyes on the horizon.

"In Cuba with you and the Rough Riders?"

"Nope, just died. Late last year. Stomach something or other, I heard."

Clay stared at his saddle horn and shook his head. "Damn. He was younger than me." He looked up at Trap. "You ever think about gettin' old?"

The trail was clear enough that Trap could read it from atop Hashkee. He kept his head down, but glanced up from under his hat brim at Clay's question. "I reckon I do now and again. But I don't feel all that old."

Clay slowed his bay and pointed hard at Trap to emphasize his words. "Well, I read that in these United States the average man don't live to see fifty. In fact they don't even live to see forty-nine."

Trap scratched his chin and studied the tracks. He was glad Blake had faded back to be a rear guard and was spared such depressing talk. "I don't plan on dyin' anytime in the next year."

Clay slapped his thigh with a leather glove. "Well, I don't neither, but that's the point. You just never know."

"I hope you boys aren't thinking you're too doggone ancient," Ky said from his mount, a few yards through the buck brush to Trap's right. "Since I'm considerably older than either one of you."

"Yeah." Clay shook his head back and forth with an undisguised smirk. "But you look old. Hell, you and Trap both look like you could be grandpas. You two make me afeard to get too near a mirror on account of what I might find lookin' back at me."

"It might surprise you at that. I noticed you wear your hat a lot more than you used to," Ky mused. "Is that because that great mop of yours is thinning a bit?"

"I don't believe it is," Madsen said, snugging his hat down tighter on his head. "But even if it was, the ladies would just want to rub it all the more."

Trap leaned back slightly in the saddle and lifted his reins. Saying nothing, he stared down at the trail for a full minute, shaking his head slowly from side to side. He waved Blake up and groaned.

"What is it, Trap?" Ky urged his lanky horse over next to the trail. "Looks like the trail splits here."

"Indeed it does, Captain." Trap pointed up the dust-blown path that was wide enough for three riders abreast. "Four went that way and two—our hook-shoed newcomer and the puddin'-footed nag—went west up this old wagon track that runs along an old Nez Percé trail—dead into the High Lonesome."

"What lies down that trail?" Ky nodded south after the four sets of tracks.

Trap looked at Blake. "I don't rightly know," Trap said.

The young O'Shannon took off his hat and rubbed the sweat out of his eyes with a blue bandanna. "I'm not certain. I never been this far out, but I've heard tell of an old placer outfit that used to work off Old Man Creek. I'm thinking there would apt to be some buildings and such there, but the gold played out long ago. I reckon they're mostly abandoned."

Roman crossed his arms across the pommel of his saddle and looked up into the old Nez Percé Corridor. His gray eyes squinted as if he was trying to penetrate the smoke haze that permeated the dense undergrowth of the jack pine forest.

"You say the puddin'-foot went deeper into the High Lonesome?"

"It did," Trap said," but I can't be certain the girl's still sittin' the same horse."

Clay nodded in agreement. "It's a pretty moldy old trick to switch horses to throw us off the trail."

"I don't see anywhere they changed, but they could have done it without getting off the horses." Blake rode down the back trail a ways and searched the dust for clues. "They did a lot of milling around back here."

Ky gazed up the mountain slope again, his brow creased in thought. "And that way leads directly into the midst of all the fires."

The three other trackers sat quietly in their saddles and studied the ground, looking up every few seconds and scanning their surroundings, but always returning to the ground with their eyes so as to give Marshal Roman plenty of time to make a decision regarding their plan of action.

"Denihii," Ky said at length, using O'Shannon's Apache moniker. He drew a slow steady breath through his hawkish nose—a sure sign he'd come to a conclusion. "Can you tell me how long ago the riders passed this way?"

Trap nodded. "Half a day—if that. We're close."

"Let me tell you how I see it then, boys," Roman said. "And remember, this isn't the Army so feel free to question me. With all these fires, we're apt to be cut off from either trail at any time. I'm not familiar enough with this country to know what kind of a game these people are up to, but I'm not prepared to leave here without the Kenworth girl. I am loath to split our forces, but I propose taking Blake with me for a reconnoiter of the mine area by Old Man Creek while you two slip up this old wagon track toward the fires as quick as you safely can and see what sign you can cut. If you find anything that leads you to believe they've taken the girl in that direction, or you find the group has reunited somehow by means of a side trail, one of you watch while the other scoots back to get us. We'll follow the same counsel if we see anything of the girl in our direction."

"If we have the chance, we'll just take her back when we come on 'em." Clay wasn't much for a lot of waiting when his quarry was in sight and everyone knew it.

"*If* you can do it safely." Roman narrowed an eye and stared hard enough at his old subordinate to make most men look away. "I trust your judgment."

Clay grinned. "No, you don't, Captain. You can't help but like me, but you never did learn to trust me to be anything but a hothead. Trap'll be along to lord it over me and you trust *his* judgment, so I guess that'll have to do." He took off his hat and made a wide, sweeping gesture toward the High and Lonesome. "After you, partner. Let's go give the captain something to fret over."

CHAPTER 19

The side trip to the ghost town was not part of the plan and never had been. Lucius Feak had thought that up all by himself. The more he pondered on his decision to deviate from the original arrangements, the more frightened he got—and Feak was not an easy man to scare. Even now, it wasn't the kind of skin-crawling, trembling, piss-your-pants kind of fear he saw in other people's eyes.

This was deeper. Much deeper. It was as if he knew he was finished, like the final seconds of realization a condemned man must feel in the moment before the rope tightens around his throat and snaps his neck—a kind of broken-bone ache that seeped through his entire body like the smoke in the air round him.

Maybe the boss would agree with him about the place. Anything was possible, although from what he'd seen of the boss, he wasn't a man who liked anyone changing his plans.

The abandoned house where Feak chose to hole up was still in decent shape considering it hadn't been lived in for over five years. Dust and cobwebs covered the inside of the small single room. There was porcupine damage to some of the wood, and the lone window on the west wall had been pried out, presumably by the place's frugal former inhabitants who thought they could put the glass panes to good use elsewhere. Apart from the window, the previous owners had not taken much. There was still a small wood stove in the corner, complete with a dust-covered pile of split kindling. A rusted coffeepot sat on top of the old stove, and two sets of matching plates lay abandoned on the table. The more Lucius chewed on it, the more he thought the cabin probably never had a window in the first place and the oilpaper covering had likely just rotted away. It didn't matter, and Lucius Feak wasn't the type of man to spend too much time pondering over one subject.

The sight of the plates and stove reminded him he was hungry.

He struck a match on the sole of his worn leather boot and held the fire to the half-burned stub of a cigar. He puffed for a minute to get it going, reasoning that with all the smoke in the air, he might as well not put off any more of his guilty pleasures than he needed to. Though the cigar tasted good, it didn't do much for his parched throat and grumbling stomach.

"What I really want is a hot beefsteak, a bottle of whiskey, and a soft woman."

Juan Caesar looked up from where he squatted with his partner, playing cards on a piece of red cloth. "We got a woman and Javi's deer haunch."

They'd seen numerous animals fleeing the fires throughout the day, and the younger Apache had shot a fleeing doe with his bow. Leaving most of the animal to rot, he'd cut out the tender back-straps and one of the hams and slung them over his saddle.

"Well, we ain't got no whiskey, and that's what I really need." Feak rubbed his cracked lips and puffed on the cigar. "There's so much smoke, I don't reckon it would hurt to get a little fire goin' in that stove and rustle us up some of that deer meat."

Javier looked up from his cards long enough to sneer. "I'm not cooking when there's a woman here to do it. You won't let us use her for anything else—she should have to cook."

The young Apache chuckled and threw his hand down on the red cloth next to a small pile of money. Juan Caesar swore an unintelligible oath and threw down his own cards. Rising, he glared at Feak and then down at the girl, who lay feverish and pale in the back corner away from the window hole on a pallet of filthy saddle blankets. His already scarred face was twisted in anger at losing to his younger companion, and he looked ready to take it out on someone. Feak was his paymaster, so Angela was the obvious choice.

Prodding her in the thigh with his toe, he glowered over her. “You cook us some grub.” His voice was sharp and cruel as a bloody knife.

Angela drew her knees to her chest and turned away from him, moaning quietly.

The one-eyed Apache let fly a vehement string of Spanish oaths since his own language was scarce on such terms. Squatting next to the pitiful girl, he grabbed her knee and rolled her roughly back to face him. She cowered there, sobbing around the leather gag that was still in her mouth, her injured hand drawn up to her chest to protect it.

The Apache’s good eye flashed like black obsidian and he licked his lips. His hand still rested on the girl’s knee.

Feak could see where this was going, and it only added to the sickening fear that piled up inside him. He was a mean hombre and he knew it, but in a fight against these two Apache, it would be touch and go who would emerge the victor. It put him in a real quandary.

The boss had given strict orders about what not to do with the girl. But the Apache were friends of the boss, and the only way to stop them if they got their blood up was to kill them—something the boss wouldn’t take too kindly to either.

Lucius was in a pure fix. He leaned the rickety wooden chair back against the wall and blew a smoke ring into the already close air. When backed against a wall with an impossible decision, it was customary for him to do the thing that required the least effort—and that usually meant making no decision at all.

Angela decided early into her abduction she would fight, no matter the odds, the moment any of the men tried to rape her. It was not part of her internal makeup to lay back and take such things, even if it might keep her alive for a few more hours. Her face hurt from the harsh rawhide gag and her hand had swollen up to the elbow. Even through her fever, she had enough of a grasp on reality to know she would likely lose her hand, if not her whole arm—if she made it out of this at all.

The one-eyed Apache pushed at her knees, and she pulled them up as if to shield her chest, grateful, at least for the moment, that she had defied her mother and worn britches. From the corner of her eye, she could see the Javier towering above her, waiting his turn. She understood the futility of fighting, had even played it over and over in her mind while she rode the night before. But fight she would, hopefully angering the men enough they would strike out in haste and kill her quickly.

Perhaps Feak would end it with a bullet or one of the Apache would finish her with a knife. She didn't care. As long as she could make them do it quickly, death would be a welcome respite from her constant pain.

Thinking her half-unconscious, Juan Caesar leaned in closer, ripping at the brass buttons in front of her britches. She knew she should wait, but the way she was curled put his forearm next to her face and almost out of instinctive reaction, Angela sank her teeth into the sinewy bronze flesh.

The Indian jerked away and covered the gushing wound with his other hand. Instead of killing her instantly as she had hoped, he only glared at her harder. After a moment, he turned to his grinning young partner and said something in quick Apache. Angela couldn't understand the words, but she caught the meaning.

You go first.

Javier nodded smugly and slowly drew his knife. Feak, who'd been Angela's protector of sorts, did nothing but sit and watch.

"I'm going to cut off your clothes," the young Apache said. "The more you fight, the better—and the more of your skin comes off with your drawers. It will make a fine snack."

Angela started to scream, but the rickety slat door flew open and slammed against the wall. The scream caught in her throat.

Feak and both Apaches looked toward the noise, and Angela pulled herself up so her back was to the wall and hugged her knees.

Though the outside light was sparse, it was still brighter than the dismal interior of the cabin and the figure at the door stood backlit in the doorway, filling the space with his enormous dark silhouette. The stranger wore a flat-brimmed hat tipped low over a shadowed face and carried some kind of sack in his left hand. A long-barreled dragoon pistol occupied the right.

His voice carried in on the smoke like a hoarse whisper, though it was easy enough to hear. All three men jumped when they heard it.

"What in Hell's blazes is happening here?"

"Be careful!" Angela screamed, fearing the newcomer would be killed like the firefighters as soon as the Apaches regained their senses. "These men are killers—scoundrels holding me prisoner." It felt good to say it out loud.

The figure turned to study her for a moment, then looked back at Feak, ignoring her altogether. The gun still hung, poised like the head of a rattler, in his right hand.

"I asked you a question." The voice was cold and rasped enough to take off skin. Angela realized a man with such a voice was not likely to be any salvation.

Feak squirmed and dropped his cigar on the ground. He stomped it out nervously. "The bitch took a hunk outta Juan's arm. Javi was just about to teach her some manners and tie her up so she couldn't hurt no one."

The dark figure stood there motionless for a full minute, his shoulders moving up and down slowly as he breathed. When he spoke again, Feak yelped softly as if he'd been shot.

"If anyone needs a lesson in manners, I'll be the one to do the teaching." The man heaved the cloth sack he'd carried into the center of the room. It hit the packed earth with a dull thud, and the severed head of

Billy Scudder rolled out to face Angela.

Three days before, such a horrific sight might have caused Angela to faint, but now she could hardly work up a shudder. Though she'd wished him dead for the cruelty he'd meted out to Betty, she bowed her head to her knees to escape the hollow dead eyes and hideous gash of a mouth that seemed not to have changed much since between life and death.

"Young William and I already had our lesson for the day," the man said matter-of-factly as he stepped through the doorway. He holstered the pistol, but the tensions of the other men remained taut enough that anyone could snap. "Seems he went back and tried to kill that boy along with O'Shannon's wife."

"He mighta been able to identify us," Feak said weakly, unable to tear his eyes away from Billy Scudder's head.

"So?" The newcomer took off his hat and ran a freckled hand through thinning, sandy-colored hair. Every move he made evoked a twitch or jerk from Feak. "We want them to catch us or the plan doesn't work. If O'Shannon learns of a plan to kill Maggie, he'll quit the trail immediately. I know him, you imbecile. That's why I make the plans. The man loves his wife above all else." The man drew a deep breath and let it out again through a bulbous nose, webbed with tiny red veins from too much hard liquor. "If Trap O'Shannon turns back now and misses our rendezvous, Mr. Feak, I'm holding you personally accountable. Young William there is just a lesson." He smiled. "I told you I'd be the teacher."

Lucius nodded weakly.

"All right then. Get the girl ready to move. As I said before—nothing should happen to her yet." He glared at the Apaches with narrow, slate-gray eyes. "I want her untouched for the time being. Do you understand?"

Both men grunted, and Javier finally put away his knife.

The newcomer offered a friendly smile and opened his hands in peace. "I don't care about the reward money. You men can keep all of it. My business is with O'Shannon and his friends. Bring the girl where we planned." He pulled his hat on again and turned before stepping out the door.

"And don't cross me again."

CHAPTER 20

There were five men in all. Running like a wronged woman was after them with a meat cleaver.

Zelinski stopped at the crest of a bald knob, blew off some steam, and took off his hat while the gaggle of men scrambled up the loose scree on hands and knees. Mopping the sweat from his forehead, he let his gaze shift to the blossoming cloud of gray and white smoke coming from the low mountains behind them. When the men got closer, he recognized the leader as Joe Voss, a forest supervisor from Missoula.

The fire boss took a swig from his canteen and

handed it to Voss as the men took the ridgetop beside him.

"Horace," Voss said, taking a long pull of water. "You're going the wrong way." He was a tall man with watery, noncommitting eyes, befitting the vaporous politics that had helped him rise to his lofty position within the Forest Service. Certain Voss wouldn't know which end of the ax to hit the tree with, Zelinski was surprised to find him leading a group through the Clearwater.

"Fancy that." Zelinski nodded. "Looks like I'm goin' the right direction if you boys are running from a fire. That's what you pay me for, isn't it?"

"Not this fire, Horace. Get your men and get out of here. I understand there are evacuation trains headed for Avery. The colored boys from the Army have been called in from the field to help with the move."

"What?" Zelinski felt the dry, superheated wind whip across his face. The news hit him hard.

A stub of a man with round spectacles that kept sliding off the end of his chopped-off little nose reached out for the canteen from Voss. "Milton Brandice, Bureau of Entomology." He pushed up his glasses again and raised the canteen toward Zelinski. "Do you mind?"

"Go ahead. Bureau of . . . what did you say?"

When Brandice had drunk his fill, he pushed the canteen toward Zelinski, who motioned to the other men. "If you go easy, you might each get enough to wash the ash out of your gullets."

"Bureau of Entomology," Brandice replied, using his forefinger to push the glasses back into his squint. Zelinski couldn't help but think if the man would just relax his face, they might stay put. "I'm a beetle specialist. Three of us are. The Secretary sent us out here to study beetle-killed trees and their causal relationship to forest fires."

Brandice was what the field folks in the Service called a patent-leather man. Someone who stayed at his desk back East, read books, and wore fancy shoes. Zelinski shook his head. "I can't believe it, Voss. I beg for more men to fight fires and you folks send people with bug specialties."

"Shut up, Horace. Look back there." The forest superintendent took off his hat and used it to gesture toward a greasy yellow haze that all but blotted out the sun. A huge black and gray cloud boiled up five miles distant. Zelinski knew the mountains in front of the smoke rose at least 2500 feet from the valleys behind them. The smoke towered over three times as high as the mountains—more than a mile—before being sheered off at the top by a high-altitude wind. "It won't matter how many men you have once that rolls over you."

"We used to have horses," a forlorn-looking bug specialist Zelinski hadn't noticed before said, shaking his ruddy face sadly. "Fire took them all, so now we run, walk, and crawl. It doesn't matter, it'll catch us no matter what we do. I'm sure of it."

Brandice handed the man the canteen. "Calm down,

Prescott. It's not as bad as all that. Avery's mostly downhill from here." He looked at Zelinski. "Right?"

"Sort of. Down, then up again a time or two, but you're not far off the mark. What's this you say about your horses, Voss?"

The superintendent continued to stare at the smoke. "That's what I'm trying to tell you. It's an inferno back there. We'd tied our pack stock and riding horses up next to a small stream that runs through Ruby Canyon. Brandice wanted to climb up and check on a bunch of beetle kill along the ridgeline above us. The going was rocky and I'm not much of a horseman, so I thought we'd give the animals a rest. If we'd been down in that canyon . . ." Voss trailed off and shook his head. His moist eyes narrow and rimmed in red, he turned to look Zelinski full in the face. "There was a wind, H. A wind like I've never seen in the mountains. When we got to the top of the ridgeline, I could see a small fire smoldering about half a mile from the horses on the other side of the creek. One instant it was a small fire, barely putting off a piddle of smoke; the next there was a horrible belch of wind and fire and the whole valley was a wall of flames, rushing below us. It all happened so fast the horses just disappeared in a river of fire. I don't think they even looked up from their grazing.

"The fire raced down the valley. I thought it would stop when it got to Boulder Canyon, but it just jumped half a mile of rock and kept going. The only thing that saved us was we were beside it and not in its path."

"What the deuce is that?" Brandice shaded his

squinting eyes and looking up at the hazy sky.

All around them, tiny glowing embers the size of stickpins whirled on the wind. The air seemed alive with millions of orange lights.

"Pine needles," Zelinski whispered, more to himself than to the bug specialist. "Another ten minutes and it will be brands as big as your arm." He nodded to Voss. "You were right, Joe. I was going the wrong way."

The fire boss shouldered his rucksack and started down the backside of the hill at a lope, knowing the others would follow. His boys were a good enough lot, but they would never be able to make it out of this. George White had not returned, and if the 25th had been recalled to Avery, then they were all on their own.

The time for scouting was over. It was time to retreat.

CHAPTER 21

A furious wind shook the dry spruce along the ridgeline the way a dog might shake a snake. A heavy pall of resinous smoke rode the wind through the whipping trees and stung the trackers' eyes and noses. Blake had his bandanna pulled up over his face to help filter out some of the smoke, but it did little good. Ky had the lead and ducked his head against the wind, the brim of his hat folding down over his eyes from the force of it.

Dropping off the lee side of the ridgeline, he followed the trail down and away from the brunt of the wind before reining his sorrel to a halt beside a charred twist of lightning-killed ponderosa. The mountain fell away abruptly, and the trail began to wind through a park of white pine. A ground fire had already swept through the area and cleaned out all the debris and snags beneath the huge trees without doing anything to them but blacken their skirts. The thin trickle of a mountain waterfall beside the debris and tailings of an old mine was barely visible through the haze on the rocky cliffs a half mile distant. The fan of green grass and shrubs that followed the only water in the area gave the bleak gray dress of the rocks a green apron.

"There's the mine you were talking about." Roman spoke above the wind that folded the brim of his hat down over his forehead.

Blake nodded. "There are some old shacks down in the bottom. If we move up a little, we should be able to have a good view of them from up here without getting too close."

Ky nodded, holding his hat down with a gloved hand against a sudden gust. Unbuckling his pommel bag, he produced a small brass telescope. "Bring your rifle and let's go see what we're up against."

Blake slid his .45-70, a twin of his father's Marlin, out of the saddle boot and followed the marshal up the trail. He could see why his father and Clay had had no trouble following such a man. Roman listened to what the situation dictated and acted. Always moving forward, Ky Roman seemed an icon of action in a profession where politicians were the rule and preferred to send others to implement their plans. He himself was a doer, and led from the front rather than a desk.

Once inside the dim forest, they made their way to a small outcropping that overlooked the narrow valley some two hundred feet below. A towering ponderosa pine sat squarely in the middle of the outcropping. Its girth was too big for Ky and Blake to both get their arms around, and made a perfect spot for them to hide behind and study the three tumbledown buildings that made up the old placer mine.

A sun-bleached outhouse had been blown over by the wind—recently from the look of it—and the lonely wooden seat stood out in the open, a few yards from what had been the main house. A chicken coop with a tar-paper roof sat abandoned and caving in on the far side next to a small stream that led from the waterfall.

"Not too wise to put the chickens that close to the water supply," Ky mused, taking off his hat and lying down next to the pine tree.

Blake took up a position with his rifle next to him, scanning the scene. At first, he saw nothing. Then, a flash of movement caught his eye through the broken window of the shack. He pointed it out to Roman.

"I see. Someone's in there all right," the marshal said, letting his spyglass swing slowly in a wide arc across the valley. "The horse tracks lead over to that thick stand of fir to the left there. I can just make out the outline of a horse in the shadows." Roman lowered the glass and rubbed his eyes with a bandanna. "If it weren't for the smoke, I'd be able to make out how many there are."

He gave the telescope to Blake. “See if you can tell.”

Blake looked, then shook his head. “I can’t make out the horses.” He moved the glass back to the broken window and jumped when he saw more movement. An Indian walked past the window, holding something in his hand. Blake fiddled with the telescope, drawing it in and out to focus on the dark recesses of the shack’s interior.

“I can’t be sure,” he said, squinting with his other eye. “But I think I see the Kenworth girl. She’s leaning up against the other wall.” He coughed and dabbed at his eyes again, blinked to clear them from smoke, then adjusted the telescope some more. “Yep, it’s her.” Blake felt a wave of exhilaration wash over him.

“We got ’em.” Roman took the glass back and studied the area for another full minute before he said anything. Even as he spoke, he kept his eyes on the dilapidated shack.

“Remember, we’re chasing four horses. That means three in there with her—and that’s if the others didn’t swing around and join up. They must have known we would follow them, and yet they chose a place out in the middle of the valley where we were sure to find them. It makes for a rough approach, but it also leaves them little room for an escape. If not for the girl, I’d say you and I just sit here and wait them out. I’m not happy about her chances if we rush them with just two of us. We’d take them, but the girl might perish in the endeavor. Bad odds all around.” Roman shook his head while he spoke around the telescope. Blake had to roll right up next to him to hear him over the rising wind.

"I'll stay here and keep watch." Ky lowered the glass. "Looks like they got a little fire going, so I expect they'll stay here for a while. You rush back up the trail and tell your pa and Clay to come runnin'. With all of us in on this, we'll have the girl back home by nightfall."

Almost immediately after Blake disappeared into the swirling smoke, Juan Caesar stepped out of the shack. Roman watched him walk out of the wind beside the chicken coop and make water. Seeing the Apache after so many years made Ky's mind swim. He had assumed the old outlaw was long dead, his thieving, murdering ways having overtaken him somewhere along the way. He watched the prowling way his old enemy moved when he walked, the slow way he swung his head back and forth to compensate for the lack of vision in his bad eye.

Ky Roman was not a man prone to bad dreams, but memories of Juan Caesar had been responsible for many a sleepless night over the past twenty-five years. The fact that the Apache had once been a trusted soldier made matters even worse. Roman had handpicked him as a scout. When Juan Caesar went renegade and began to wreak havoc outside the reservation, the young lieutenant had taken it as a personal insult.

Watching the man he'd once trusted took Ky back to Arizona. For a moment, he felt the desert heat and sandstone beneath him instead of Rocky Mountain granite.

He could hear the screams of the women on the wind. The memory of the carnage he'd witnessed made him wish he'd not been so hasty to send Blake back. If Juan Caesar had his way, the Kenworth girl was in a very poor state indeed. The man had almost cost Roman his life. In return he'd taken the Apache's eye. . . .

Ky drifted back to the fight that had almost killed him. The way Irene had been proud that he'd been strong and brave, but deeply troubled that he, Hezekiah Roman, the man she knew as a gentle, God-fearing father, could be so brutal as to beat another human so badly it would cost him his sight in one eye . . .

The smoke-filled wind whirred against Ky's ears. He was focused on Juan Caesar, and failed to hear the crunching of twigs behind him. When he did notice a small rock roll across the ground beside his elbow, he assumed it was Blake returning with some news. After all, his quarry was before him, in the valley.

"Run into a fire?" he said without looking up.

"It's good to see you, Hezekiah."

The voice, almost lost on the wind, made Ky's blood run cold. After hearing of the Apaches with Feak, he'd been able to prepare himself for an eventual meeting with Juan Caesar.

Nothing had prepared him for this.

He lowered the telescope and stood, turning slowly with his back against the huge orange pine tree. Before him stood a ghost from his past.

"How have you been, Captain?" The man was smaller than Ky remembered. Age could do that. But every bit as dangerous. The same wan smile across a ruddy face, the same nose that signified the unhealthy love for hard drink he'd developed toward the end. The fire of pure hate still burned in the darkness behind the man's green eyes.

"Did you make out ol' Caesar down there?"

Ky nodded, still unable to believe his own eyes. "I'm surprised to see either one of you."

"Thought I was dead, didn't you, Hezekiah? Everybody did." The man smiled. "You'd be surprised at the things a dead man can get away with. I even checked in on Irene while you were up in Spokane."

The air rushed out of Ky's lungs. "You what?"

The apparition raised a gloved hand. "She's all right. She didn't even know I was around. I just wanted to have a look at her for old times sake. I wanted to see all of you." His green eyes narrowed and flared in intensity. "Especially our little half-breed friend. How is he these days?"

"He's well, considering." Ky chided himself for his position. The ghost had moved to less than an arm's length away. Ky had nowhere to retreat with the tree at his back. He felt for his pistol.

"Don't do that, Captain. The one I want is O'Shannon. My quarrel is with him alone. The rest of you are dross. Whatever happens in all this, I had no part in hurting Maggie. That was never part of the plan."

"What do you mean? Now look here, Jo . . ."

The long steel blade went completely through Ky,

pinning him to the pine. The voice was quiet but sharp, as the ghost pushed the knife home and held it in place against Ky's struggles.

"No! You look here, you arrogant wretch." The voice strained as the man held Roman in place with a forearm across his chest, just above the blade. "I am sick to here with you people thinking you know so much more than everyone else. O'Shannon thought he could play God with my life. Now it's my turn to play God with him. I've done a pretty fair job, don't you think?"

Ky shuddered and tried to get a breath. He tasted the salt of blood and felt the strength leave his legs. The man withdrew the knife and slipped Roman's pistol out of the holster and tossed it to one side. The strength bled from Ky's legs and he slid to a crouch at the base of the tree.

The cruel ghost squatted beside him and smiled. He was close enough, Ky could make out the sour smell of whiskey and meat. "I didn't harm Irene. Not yet anyway. Who knows, I may go back and let her convert me to that church of hers like she did you. That seemed to work her into a lather, didn't it? A few words from the Good Book is all it takes to get her going, if I remember correctly."

Ky could only gasp. He heard a gurgling noise and realized it was his puny effort at trying to talk. "Jo . . . Maggie?"

The man shook his head and snorted. "That's just like you, Roman. You're done for and you know it, but still you check on that miserable half-breed's woman." He wiped Ky's blood off the knife on his pants leg. "She's fine for now. Not that they didn't try, the fools. I'll have to look in on her myself after I'm done with our little Trapper."

The redheaded man patted Ky on the shoulder—softly, as if to reassure him. "I've got to go now. You shouldn't linger too long. Look at this as a blessing. You'll know soon if all the philosophy you've studied over these years has any truth to it."

Alone with the wind and smoke, Ky pressed both hands against his abdomen, trying to staunch the flow of blood that poured from his belly and covered his shirt and trousers.

He'd lost all track of time, but knew Blake would be back with the others soon. He had to hold on until then. His killer had been right—he was done for. But he had to warn the others of the danger.

He had to stay alive long enough to tell them who he'd seen.

CHAPTER 22

Blake slid off his horse and led him in so as to stay undetected by the outlaws in the valley below. Behind him, Trap smelled blood on the wind and knew something was wrong before he saw Ky leaning against the pine tree. All three men ran to his side. Blake kept a wary eye toward the mine. Ky saw him and shook his head feebly.

"Gone," he groaned. "After you left . . . took the girl . . . could . . . only watch . . ." A solitary tear rolled down from the corner of one eye.

Trap stooped down beside his friend and tried to check the wound. Thick blood oozed, dark as oil, between Roman's clenched fingers. His teeth were clenched and his breathing labored. When Trap tried to look under his bloody hands, Ky shook his head again and smiled up at him.

"Leave it . . . no use."

Clay's face teetered between sorrow and murderous rage. "Who did this to you, Ky?"

The wounded man tried to speak. Leaning his head back against the tree and staring up at the sky, he seemed to be gathering all his strength. He opened his mouth, and then swallowed against a spasm of pain.

"Johannes," he groaned.

Trap looked over at Clay, who came up next to the two men and knelt beside them.

"Hold on there, Ky." Clay touched his friend's shoulder. "Stay with us. You'll be seeing Johannes soon enough."

Roman smiled weakly and struggled through three quick, shallow breaths. "Johannes . . . alive . . . Trap!" He let go of his stomach and grabbed O'Shannon by the sleeve with a bloody hand. Blood began to flow from the wound in earnest, and Ky's already ashen face took on a blue-green hue. His voice was a tight whisper, and the others had to lean in close to hear him over the howling wind.

"Maggie's . . . safe . . . now . . . but watch out . . . Johannes is alive . . ." His eyes fluttered and closed for a moment while he labored though another series of breaths. His body seemed to relax and the twisted grimace of pain lines fled his face.

"Adios, boys," he said, almost in his old voice, only weaker. "Look after Irene for me. Tell her . . . I'll be waitin'." He looked up at Clay and grinned. "I thought you . . . might like to know, Madsen, . . . this . . . doesn't hurt like we thought it would."

Roman's face went slack. Trap put an open hand gently over his eyes, closing them and feeling the last bit of warmth before his friend's body grew cold.

"Son of a bitch!" Clay screamed ferociously over the roar of the wind, his hat a crumpled wad of felt in his clenched fist.

Trap stood and put a hand out to hush him. "They'll hear you."

Clay jerked away. He turned toward the valley and spread his brawny arms out to the sides. "Bring 'em on!" he shouted. "Let them come and try to kill us and see where it lands 'em. Juan Caesar, you one-eyed bastard, come on up and see what I got for your other eye!"

Blake looked nervously toward his father at Madsen's outburst. Trap shook his head slowly and held up a palm to keep Blake back. He knew Clay well enough to know the more vocal portion of the anger would blow over like a hailstorm, while the quieter, more dangerous part would seethe and smolder inside of him until it exploded out on whoever was responsible for Ky's death—or anyone else who got in between him and revenge.

"What do you think he meant by talkin' about Johannes?" Clay said while he knelt and used his small hand shovel to scrape out a makeshift grave until they could get back and move Ky to a proper gravesite back in Arizona, nearer his wife. The ground was baked hard, and he did little except scratch at the pine needles and forest litter a few inches deep. "Ky said Johannes was still alive."

Trap chewed on the inside of his cheek and shrugged. "Do you think he could be?"

Clay paused in his digging and looked up at Trap. "We never did find no body, but there's no way he could have lived through that explosion. It would have torn him to pieces."

"Or buried him alive," Trap said, staring into space, thinking about the past.

"Who's Johannes?" Blake stood by, alternately checking the trail behind them and the valley floor below.

Clay threw the shovel down in disgust and pushed himself to his feet. Tears dripped off the end of his nose. "This is bullshit. I can't dig in this rock." His voice was gravelly from his screaming fit into the wind. "We'll have to take the captain down and leave him in that shack and hope the birds leave him be till we get back."

Clay put a hand on Blake's shoulder and sniffed.

"Johannes Webber served in the same unit as your pa and me under the command of our good captain here. He died when you were a baby—at least we thought he did."

"Why would he want to kill Marshal Roman?"

"That's a good question, son," Trap said. "He had a pretty good reason to hate me, but the captain and him were always on good terms. It's a story that takes too long to tell for now. We should settle the captain and get on the trail. That's where the answers are."

Clay took off his hat again and folded his hands in front of him. "I wonder if we should say any special words seein' as how he was a Mormon and all."

Trap removed his hat, as did Blake.

"I don't really know," Trap said. He wished Maggie was there, or his father. Either would know infinitely more on the matters of religion than he did. "I suppose we should just make our own peace with it, in our own way—that's what we always done when he was alive and we were buryin' someone else."

Clay nodded, his head moving up and down slowly while his eyes blazed.

"Peace!" he finally spit. "I can't make no peace. But I will say this. If Johannes Webber is still alive, Ky Roman won't be seein' him in Heaven anytime soon 'cause I aim to send him to Hell the next time I run across him."

Both Trap and Blake looked at each other, then replaced their hats.

"Amen," they said at the same time.

After they wrapped Ky in his own bedroll, they loaded him across the back of his lanky sorrel and started wearily down the steep trail for the abandoned mine shack. Trap took the lead and Blake and Clay followed, leading Roman's horse.

"Can I ask you something, Mr. Madsen?" Blake knew his father was well out of earshot because of the blowing wind.

"What is it, lad?" Clay looked straight ahead, but urged his mount forward to match stride with Blake's Appaloosa.

"What did my pa mean when he said Johannes Webber had reason to hate him?"

Clay reined up and let his hands rest across the pommel of his saddle. He looked straight at Blake, and sighed. "It's a story best left to your father to tell. But suffice it to say, Webber is insane. Always has been, if you ask me. I never did have much use for him—thought he had a bad smell about him—but your pa and the captain, they took him in like the stray dog he was. He is a smart one, though . . . and he firmly believes your pa had a hand in killin' his woman."

CHAPTER 23

Big Ox Monroe grabbed Joseph from behind, pinning his arms to his side and lifting his feet off the ground while he squeezed the life out of him. Daniel Rainwater looked up from felling a tangled hemlock snag just in time to see it happen. He raised the ax in protest, but before he could move, he felt a sickening blow on the back of his head.

Reeling in pain and nausea, the boy slumped to his knees, and then fainted.

Rainwater came to his senses a few moments later with Roan Taggart sitting heavy on his back and pulling his hands together with rough cord that the food rations came wrapped in. It cut deeply into his wrists, and Daniel bit his lip to steel himself against the pain. When Taggart rolled him over, he saw Joseph, also tied with his hands behind his back, sitting, slumped against the downed hemlock snag a few feet away.

A man Daniel had never seen before sat on a muscular dun horse at the edge of the little glade. He was a big man, with a barrel chest and a head of thick gray hair combed straight back like a wood duck. His face was red, as if he were exerting himself at some heavy task instead of merely sitting in the saddle, and he breathed through his nose in loud puffs and snorts like a train getting ready to pull away from the platform.

". . . do it the way I tell you and you can be rid of the thievin' nits and stay out of trouble to boot. Get the rest of the crew over here and put the question to them. Ask 'em what should be done with redskins who would steal from their own fellow workmen," the man on the horse said to Big Ox, who nodded like a schoolboy getting instructions.

"Right, none of them will take to a cardsharp," Monroe replied.

The red-faced man shook his head. His huffing grew even more intense. "Not cheatin' at cards, you moron, stealing from your kit. Put some of the money and things from your outfit in their pockets. When the others see that, most of 'em will side with you right off. I'll step in as a disinterested third party and back up your story. That should even convince any nigger-lovers you got in the group."

When he'd pulled the knots tight behind Daniel's back, Roan Taggart stood up and kicked him between the shoulder blades, sending him headlong onto his face. The Indian boy rolled onto his side, curling into a ball to protect himself from another blow. Instead of kicking him again, Taggart chuckled and looked up at Monroe.

"He ain't so cocky once his wings is clipped." He raised one leg and let out a ripping fart.

"Leave him be, you imbecile." The man on the dun shook his head in disgust, his nostrils flaring like an angry horse. "I don't care what you do with 'em once the others decide to hang 'em. The fires are movin' this way. Once they're hung, we can leave 'em to burn."

Ox Monroe had the remaining fire crew rounded up beside the hemlock snag in less than ten minutes. Each small group of men came in cautiously from their respective duties, eyeing the prisoners as they gathered around. Monroe had already primed the pump with stories of their treachery.

Zelinski had left Cyrus McGill holding the reins of the small outfit of firefighters in his absence. McGill was a young man, not yet in his thirties, with a tendency toward premature baldness and hands that looked slightly too large for his sinewy arms. Though he was a strong and capable woodsman, McGill didn't have much of a hold on the men, and Daniel didn't expect he would do much to intercede where Big Ox was involved.

Taggart worked on getting the ropes ready to hang the boys while Monroe produced the evidence of their misconduct: a wad of folded bills and a silver watch that he said belonged to his departed uncle.

Joseph sat silently across from Daniel at the base of the hemlock, his dark eyes locked on the crowd. Daniel thought it funny that Joseph could look so unrepentant for something he didn't do. It actually made him look guilty.

"What have they got to say for themselves?" McGill did show a little backbone at least.

The newcomer on the dun horse stepped down at this and strode forward, huffing and puffing like he might run down anyone who got in his way.

"My name's Tom Ledbetter," he said. "I don't know how many of you folks know about this because of your service up here with the fires, but there's been a bad killin' back down in the Bitterroot. A pretty young gal's gone missin' and another was butchered up somethin' awful. Two men massacred as well." Ledbetter stopped to let his words seep in to the smoky crowd. "It was Injuns just like these that did it. I'm on their trail now."

McGill rubbed his thinning, mouse-colored hair. "Well, I hate to hear about that, but these here Indians been with us for over a week. I doubt they had anything to do with it."

Ledbetter sneered. "I'm not sayin' they had anything to do with it. I'm just sayin it's natural for an Injun to be up to no good. Your own boys here got the evidence that they been up to just that." He turned to the rest of the murmuring group, ignoring McGill as if he were no more than a flyspeck. "I ask you men, what kind of people would steal from their own troop? Are you to trust a sneak thief with your life? It's dangerous enough out here with all these fires. I heard two men already died up at Moon Pass. It could just as easily have been two of you, especially if you can't even trust those who work alongside you."

The murmur swept through the crowd again. An old Swedish fellow in the back suggested they banish the boys to their own fate among the fires.

Ledbetter threw back his head as if in horrible pain.

"I ain't talkin' about sending these redskins off so they can hurt someone else. Didn't Ox tell you that sullen one there tried to stab him when he caught 'em stealin'?"

Monroe's head snapped up at that information, but the crowd was so focused on the two boys now, Daniel doubted anyone noticed. Stealing was one thing; trying to kill someone was a different thing altogether. None of the men would be able to work if they thought they might get a knife in the back as soon as it was turned.

The old Swede bowed his head at the revelation. "Well, we have to do somethin' about that then." His voice was low, just loud enough for Daniel to hear.

"That's what I'm tellin' you. These two are a threat to the whole group. You should get rid of 'em like you would a rabid dog before more people get hurt."

The muttering of the fire crew swelled as they whispered among themselves. McGill had his back to Daniel, and it was impossible to hear the conversation. From the hard looks on the soot-covered faces, it was easy to tell things weren't looking good.

At length, the men began to nod. Some, including the old Swede, took off their hats and stared with long, solemn faces at the two boys.

McGill shook his head violently while the two ropes Taggart had prepared were thrown over a slanting tamarack that had fallen into the crook of another, above and slightly behind the hemlock snag. Neither boy struggled when they were dragged to their feet and placed on the scarred black stump of the snag. Taggart placed rough pack-rope nooses around their necks and stepped back, grinning openly.

McGill waved his hands back and forth, and stepped in front of the boys so they could lean their knees against his shoulders.

"This is all wrong. We should wait till the boss gets back. We got no right to do this."

"You got no right to stop it now that everyone's

decided," Ledbetter said with a matter-of-fact nod. "It was a jury of their peers."

"I ain't letting you do this, mister." McGill drew his sheath knife to cut the boys' hands free.

"Step aside, damn you." Ledbetter put a hand on his pistol. "Can't you get it through your thick skull . . ."

"Hello the camp!" A roaring voice that rivaled Horace Zelinski's rattled the trees and caused Ledbetter to slump. Daniel turned with the rest of the fire crew and watched three men ride in through the smoky trees. The men weren't smiling.

Ledbetter's twisted face tightened when he looked up, the muscles in his red cheeks clenching above his jaw. He was only a few feet from Daniel, his hand still resting on his gun. Big Ox and Roan Taggart stood to his right. All three men looked as if they'd been caught rustling cattle.

"You know these folks?" Monroe fidgeted with his knife handle and clicked his gold teeth.

Ledbetter nodded. "I do. They're the lawmen lookin' for the Injuns who done the massacre I told you about. Two of 'em are Injuns themselves." His clenched voice was low and breathy. "They picked a hell of a poor time to show up."

Daniel Rainwater leaned his knees against McGill's shoulders and watched the lawmen ride in slowly, like panthers sniffing the air. A large white man with a great curling mustache took the lead atop a muscular bay horse. A young Indian who looked to Daniel like a Nez Percé followed with an older man who could have been

Indian. Each man had hard, unflinching eyes that appeared to drink in all around them at one long look. They had stern, hard-put faces that looked as if they'd seen much sadness lately. There was an air of decisiveness about them that frightened Daniel. He hoped these men didn't want to see them hang, for if they did, he knew he surely would.

"What do you reckon they want?" Big Ox's brown eyes widened and darted back and forth between the new arrivals and Mr. Ledbetter.

Ledbetter stood planted for a long moment, then shrugged and turned away. "How am I supposed to know? Don't let 'em stop you from your hangin', though. You've come too far to turn back now. Push the nits off and let 'em swing before anyone stops you."

"What do you mean *my* hangin'? You was the one to think of all this." Big Ox's huge head kept swinging back and forth between Ledbetter and the newcomers.

Taggart, unnerved at his compatriot's hesitation, raised a singed, roan-colored eyebrow and loosed a squeaky fart.

CHAPTER 24

"Looks like you boys are havin' yourselves a little party," Clay Madsen said. He reined up a few feet from the two Flathead boys, who teetered precariously on top of the hemlock snag. Though it was just after noon, the heavy forest and thick smoke made it seem like dusk.

Clay had to lean forward to give the crowd a glimpse of the marshal's badge Ky had given him. The balding man who propped up the two guests of honor gave him a smile of relief a mile wide. He looked as if he might cry with pure, unabashed gratitude when he saw the badge.

"These Injuns stoled from my kit and were plannin' to kill me," a filthy, soot-covered giant said, stepping forward. Tom Ledbetter stood back and looked on but said nothing.

"What's your name, sir?" Clay stared down at the man with gold teeth. On top of his horse, it didn't matter how tall the giant was. Clay was taller and had the psychological advantage.

"Ox Monroe. Folks call me Big Ox."

"Well, Mr. Monroe, it looks like we got us a ticklish situation here," Clay said, leaning back and stretching his neck to one side. Trap and Blake both had their rifles handy across their laps. "I do believe it would be better if these boys stepped down from there for a minute while we sort this all out."

Blake stepped down from his Appaloosa and moved to the makeshift gallows to help the bald man. Trap let his finger slide across the trigger of his Marlin.

"Look here now." Monroe raised a hand, his eyes flashing. "You men got no cause to stop this hangin'. We're out here fightin' these fires for the federal government and we got no time to lollygag with any more of a trial. We need swift justice so's we can get on with our work."

Blake pulled the knife from the scabbard on his belt and cut the ropes binding the two Indian boys' hands. He didn't even look at Monroe. "You make a move to stop me, sir, and swift justice is exactly what you're gonna get."

Trap smiled inside at the grit he saw in his son. He was indeed Maggie's boy. The only two men worth worrying over were Big Ox and Ledbetter. Everyone else looked to be followers, blown like dandelion fuzz by whichever wind was strongest. And all appeared to be smart enough to see the prevailing wind was against the blustering giant. Clay and Blake could easily handle a blowhard like Monroe. Ledbetter never did anything but stand on the sidelines and egg others into doing the dirty work.

The fact that they were there to stop the hanging at all was just pure luck for the boys. It was a track that led them to the fire camp—the track with the hooked back right shoe. It had split off from the others a quarter mile back at the edge of a wide firebreak. Trap had heard voices through the trees, and after a short vote they decided any man who'd been riding with the kidnappers was worth talking to, especially if he'd had anything to do with Ky's death.

The little fire brigade possessed only a motley-looking trio of worn-out pack mules who stood forlorn and singed in a small rope corral at the edge of the glade beside a muddy wallow of hoofprints that had once been a poor excuse for a stream that angled off of Granite Creek. As far as Trap could see, there was only one saddle horse—Ledbetter's big dun. Unless he missed his guess, it had a hooked shoe on its right hind foot. Ledbetter had tethered the animal at the far edge of camp, and it was difficult to see through the drifting smoke and dusky shadows.

Trap slid his rifle back into its scabbard. Throwing a leg over the saddle, he hopped to the ground, leaving Hashkee ground tied and grumpy. Considering Ledbetter's past behavior, Trap was looking forward to a little face-to-face discussion about why he happened to be riding with known killers.

The crowd of dirty, tired men milled about in a loose group and watched Clay explain the facts of life to Monroe. Unwilling to lose face in front of all his peers, the big oaf stood defiantly in front of the Texan's horse, touching the hilt of the long knife that hung from his belt.

"These niggers was found guilty by all the men here—even the cue ball." He nodded his big head toward McGill. "He don't have the guts to see it through, but he was in on the decision. You got no right to stop us."

Clay groaned and slid off his gelding so he could look Monroe in the eyes. He was a half a hat shorter, but that didn't matter. Standing brim to brim, Clay tapped the silver badge on his chest. "I don't even need this to stop an illegal hangin', but I got it just the same and you can count your blessings I do, 'cause if I didn't I'd plant you here and now."

Ox stared hard with coal-black eyes, but he took a

half a step back as if to steady himself. "You can go to hell, mister. We ain't scared of no law."

Clay closed the distance between them and sneered.

"I don't know what you mean by *we,* big'un. Your partner there's shakin' like a puppy passin' a peach pit. It's just me and you."

Monroe waved Clay off. "Go on then. Take your red nigger friends and get out of here then if you love 'em so much."

"No, sir," Clay said smugly. "Don't believe I will. You'll be the one doin' the leavin'. Real easy now, drop your knife and that rusty old hog-leg on the ground." Madsen turned his attention to Taggart, who stood with both hands raised high in the air. "You too, stinky. Weapons in the dirt."

Taggart complied, but Monroe blustered.

"What makes you think you can just blow in here like this and start givin' orders like you own the place? You so cocksure I won't best you?"

Clay rubbed his goatee with his left hand. His twinkling eyes never left his opponent. "Oh, I reckon there's always that possibility." He chuckled. "I suppose there's a chance I could have a heart seizure because you're puttin' so much fear in me—but it ain't likely." Madsen's face clouded over. "I'm sick of messin' with you, Ox. Throw down your gun or pull it; makes no never-mind to me."

Monroe let out a deep breath, deflating so he looked like he shrunk a good six inches. He studied his own boots while he slowly lowered his pistol and bowie knife to the ground.

Trap truly enjoyed seeing his old friend work. He normally would have stood by and watched, but Ledbetter had eased back through the smoky shadows to climb back on his horse.

"Hold on there, Mr. Ledbetter." Trap stepped in front of the dun as Ledbetter tried to slip out past the crowd.

The right rear track of the horse hooked noticeably.

"You step aside, runt," said Ledbetter. "I stopped for you once. I'll be damned if I'm gonna do it again. If you and your friends are more interested in savin' Injuns than catchin' the ones responsible for the massacre, then I'll have to go do it myself." The muscles in Ledbetter's beet-colored jaws bunched and clenched after he spoke. His mouth pulled back into a tight grimace as the skin on his thick neck tightened in hatred. Ledbetter jerked back on the dun's reins. The horse pranced sideways, fighting the bit.

O'Shannon's eyes widened as the big animal came to a halt broadside to him. Hanging from the saddle horn of Ledbetter's dun was a finely crafted leather bag with elk ivory and porcupine quillwork. Trap felt as if he'd been kicked in the stomach, and he had to steady himself to keep from dropping to his knees.

It was Maggie's medicine bag.

Trap looked at it in horror and imagined all the terrible things a man like Ledbetter would do with an Indian woman if given the chance. He should never have left her—not the way things were. Not with folks feeling so worked up.

Trap felt a sickening ache fill the void that occurred when he first saw the small leather pouch—as if all the joy had gushed from him like water from a broken pitcher. She would never have lost the bag. It held the things that were important to her, locks of her children's hair, spiritual things she was never far from—it would have to be taken from her by force . . .

Ledbetter mistook Trap's unsteadiness for fear and lowered his reins to goad him a bit. "What do you think of my new saddle ornament?" He'd obviously figured out Trap was an Indian, and couldn't seem to resist the opportunity to gloat over the fact he'd gotten the better of another redskin, even it happened to be a woman. It was a deadly error on his part.

"It looks right nice on my saddle. Don't you think? I heard tell the squaw it belonged to was a witch." Ledbetter smirked and patted the bag. "There's all sorts of goodies in here. Maybe they'll bring me some luck. That damn old coyote bitch don't need it anymore."

Trap struck like a rattlesnake, stepping on Ledbetter's boot toe to vault into the saddle facing him, just back of the horn. His left hand grasped the loose muslin of the bigger man's shirt while his right drew the bone-handled knife from his belt as he moved.

Ledbetter had time to give a startled grunt as he was joined in the saddle by 160 pounds of furious Apache. "What the . . . ?" He was able to get his revolver out of the holster, but Trap's arm snaked around his elbow, locking the arm out straight in front of them. There was the glint of a knife blade between the two men. Ledbetter growled in surprise and pain. He struggled to turn the gun toward Trap, but the little tracker yanked up hard on the man's elbow with a mighty heave.

Ledbetter cried out in pain and his finger convulsed on the trigger. A horrific boom rocked the smoky glade and the poor dun horse collapsed under the two grappling men, a forty-five slug through the back of its head.

Trap used his forehead to butt Ledbetter in the nose as they rolled off the dead horse, but kept his grip on the arm to keep from getting shot himself.

Ledbetter was no weakling, and once the initial shock of Trap's surprise attack passed, he wasted no time in returning Trap's head butt with one of his own. Pulling in tight, face to sweating face, Ledbetter slowly began to wrench his gun arm free from Trap's grip.

"That was my horse, you stupid son of a bitch," he grunted through clenched teeth.

Trap could feel Ledbetter's arm bending—slipping free. The pistol began to move across his back. The tracker drove his knee hard into the big man's groin and sank his teeth into a bulbous nose. Before Ledbetter could recover, Trap's knife found its way between his ribs. He worked it back and forth with two quick flicks, severing Ledbetter's heart. He felt the man go weak beside him, heard the gun clatter to the earth.

Trap spit out the bloody mess that had been Ledbetter's nose and staggered slowly to his feet. Kicking the gun away, he gently lifted the medicine bag off the saddle horn atop the dead horse.

O'Shannon stared down at the dying man and tried to catch his breath as he smelled the soft leather pouch.

"That was my wife."

CHAPTER 25

Everyone in the glade, including Ox Monroe, stood in silent wonderment at the outcome of the fight. Tom Ledbetter had been a force to be reckoned with and though Trap O'Shannon was obviously no slouch, without knowing about the medicine bag, few would have guessed he could prove to be so deadly.

"I've never seen him like that," Blake whispered. The speed with which his father had dispatched Ledbetter gave pause to everyone in the group. For a moment, even the wind seemed to lull. "It was like an execution."

Clay leaned in next to the boy and slowly shook his head.

"There's a mighty big difference in the way you and your pa view things." The Texan chewed on the corner of his mustache in thought. "Your pa ever tell you our unit's motto?"

Blake nodded, unable to take his eyes off his father. "*Sanguis Frigitus*. He told me it means *calm in the face of danger*."

"That it does . . . in a way. But it more literally describes your pa. It means *Cold Blood.* You look at this little escapade as a law-enforcement matter where a civilized legal system can make everything right and proper. If you have to arrest someone or even kill them in the line of duty, then it's well and good—but it's always a last resort. Your pa, well, he sees this as war, a kill-or-be-killed kind of thing where the battle lines are clear as a slap in the yap."

"How do *you* see it?" Blake still watched his father as he spoke.

"Like your pa, I reckon. Though it wasn't always that way. Trap O'Shannon was born a warrior. I was sort of formed into one in his image."

Across the clearing, Trap grabbed the saddle horn with both hands and swung up on Hashkee. His chest still heaved from the battle and his eyes glowed with an intensity Blake had never seen. He dug his heels into the mule's flanks and bolted the short yards between him and the others.

"I'm going to check on your mother." Trap reined up next to his son and held up the medicine bag. "You keep the trail with Clay. He'll look out for you."

Madsen stepped in close to Trap and grabbed a handful of saddle string. He patted his friend on the knee in an effort to calm him.

"I know what you're thinkin', Trapper, and it just ain't so. She's fine. I know Maggie, and it would take more than some blowhard to bring her down."

"That's what I always thought about the captain." Trap stared into the wind.

"I hear you, but even the captain said Maggie was all right. Johannes told him so."

O'Shannon shook his head. "Let go of my saddle, Clay. I've got to go. You know it and so does my son."

Blake gave a somber nod. He felt the same anxiety his father did, the same hollow dread at the thought of his mother in the hands of a person who blamed every problem they had on Indians. He wanted to go check on her himself, but at the same time he'd always believed he shared a deep spiritual connection with her and his father both.

"Pa," Blake said, his voice halting. "I . . . I'm as scared as you are. But don't you think we'd know—feel it if anything happened to her? When I was a little boy, she used to tell me you two were connected that way."

Trap didn't speak, but looked down at Clay, who held his saddle strings. His eyes still blazed with barely controlled fury.

Clay stepped back, holding his hat down against the rising wind. "I'll back your play, partner, you know that—whatever you decide to do."

With a brisk nod, Trap wheeled his mule and trotted off to the east without another word.

"This don't bode well," Clay said to no one in particular.

"Guess we should get on the trail then," Blake said. He felt a little dizzy after his father's quick departure, and it took him a minute to get his feet back under him.

Clay chewed on the curl of his mustache and gave him a wink. "A couple of sharp-eyed hunters like you and me, we'll bring the girl back all right." He surveyed the rest of the fire crew, who stood staring in shocked disbelief. The two Indian boys still had the rough nooses around their necks where Blake had cut them down from the snag.

"You boys might as well take those neckties off," Clay said. "I think enough folks have died for the time bein'. These men seem to have lost their appetite for a hangin'. Ain't that a fact, Mr. Big Ox Monroe?"

Monroe nodded, his eyes still glued to Ledbetter's body and his dead horse. "Sure thing."

"Good enough," Clay groaned when he climbed aboard his bay. "Y'all behave yourselves 'cause I aim to come back and check.

"Now, Blake, I've worked with your daddy on the finer points of philosophy for lo, these many years and he ain't learned a blessed thing. Let's see if I can do a little better with . . ."

"You men get what food and water you can carry and follow me!" Horace Zelinski's voice roared over the howling wind. The fire crew all looked as if the cavalry had arrived when they caught sight of their boss. They huddled around him as he strode into camp, enveloping the gaggle of wide-eyed men who accompanied him. To Blake's surprise, his father rode slowly behind the procession, veering off to join him and Clay.

"We've got about a half an hour," the fire boss yelled over the whirling melee of dust and wind. "Maybe a little longer before this whole area is smack in the middle of a firestorm."

Taggart, who stood a few feet from Blake, gave the

fire boss a naively mournful look. "What does he mean firestorm?"

"The wind," the Indian boy with the smiling eyes said solemnly. "It's the wind blowing the fires together like a blacksmith's forge."

As if Zelinski had struck a match and set them on fire himself, the entire camp became a rush of furious activity as everyone gathered canteens, blankets, and what tins of canned ham and tomatoes they could cram in their pockets and pokes. Zelinski supervised, issuing orders and keeping things running as smoothly as they could for men who were running for their very lives.

The intensity of the wind grew with each passing minute and by the time the men were ready, the flurry of glowing needles had reached them.

"Any minute now," Zelinski screamed over the wind, holding his hat down with the flat of his hand. "Any minute now, we'll see spot fires spring up from all this falling debris that's being driven before the fire. Don't stop to put them out, it won't matter. Our only chance is to make it to an old mine adit I know about two miles from here."

Trap reined up beside Clay.

"Fire's got the whole landscape to the east and south cut off. I got to go around and up over the mountains to circle back down to Taft."

Clay smoothed his mustache and nodded. "What's keeping you then?"

"That fire boss said he saw some settlers headed up the mountains to the northwest between here and

Avery—over Porcupine Pass. Two Indians, two white men, and a girl."

"You aim to tell me and Blake so we can go after them?" Clay stood in his stirrups and rocked back and forth with anticipation.

"I'm going too," Trap grunted. "It's on the way."

CHAPTER 26

A steady drizzle of sweat poured down Lucius Feak's spine despite the driving wind that whipped at his loose cotton shirt. Without any hair to help keep it on, his hat had blown off miles before, and gone rolling on its side through the buck brush and dry bear grass like it wanted to flee as badly as Lucius did. Horrible luck to have hat come off in the wind.

Webber had made him cut the gag off the girl, but she still rode along in silence with her mouth half open, looking at him with a kind of catatonic out-of-her-head stare that made his flesh crawl like it was festering. If it were up to him, he'd have killed her long ago, but he didn't care to end up like the witless Billy Scudder.

Even the Apaches had the jitters, and old Juan Caesar kept checking his back trail as if the devil himself was behind them. Lucius smiled at such a thought—Apaches believing in the devil, that would be something. That was like the devil believing in his own self. Feak found himself wondering if the devil might be just a little bit scared of Apaches—until Johannes Webber's voice, flat and crisp above the wind, yanked him out of his thoughts.

"You must leave O'Shannon alive. Kill the others. Make him watch those he cares about vanish from him. But be watchful. The Scout Trackers are nothing to be trifled with. They are excellent marksmen, and Trap is as brutal as Juan Caesar in his own way. Split them up, pick them off one by one, but leave Trap O'Shannon to me."

Johannes glared at Caesar, who kept looking over his shoulder.

"This is not like you, my friend, to be so afraid of another man," Johannes said.

The one-eyed Apache turned to face the group and scoffed, a murderous scowl across his scarred face.

"It is no man I fear." He gestured over his shoulder with his chin. "It is the fire. We cannot fight against that. It's grown too large even to outrun, I think."

"Focus on the task at hand," Webber said, his face not quite concealing the utter contempt he had for anyone who might stand in the way of his planned destiny.

"Once you have killed O'Shannon's only son, then take from him his dearest friend." Webber grabbed the reins of the Angela's horse and gigged his own gelding cruelly in the ribs, leading her away from the other men. "Leave Trap to me, and don't worry, the fires will be the least of your problems."

Angela couldn't tell if it was the fever or merely the hot wind that made her feel as if her face was on fire. Her lips were badly cracked and bleeding, but any moisture in her mouth had long since dried up from breathing around the rawhide gag. Her tongue felt foreign to her own mouth, as if she'd bitten off a piece of meat too big to swallow. Her jaw ached as bad as her injured finger, and she found it difficult to keep her eyes open. If only she could have a sip of water, that might ease the swelling in her tongue and ease the pain in her face.

Webber slowed his horse and urged her stumbling mount up next to him with the reins. Smiling at her softly as if he were a favorite uncle, he shook his head and clucked.

"Feak and his ilk are heathen scum, Miss Kenworth. I apologize for their rough treatment of you." He drew a long sheath knife from his belt and used it to cut the bands that held her wrists. She saw blood on the blade, and found herself wondering if it was the same knife he'd used to cut off Billy Scudder's head. Once her hands were free, he offered her his canteen.

Angela drank greedily, the cool water running down both sides of her blood-encrusted lips and spilling onto the saddle horn. It cooled her throat and gave her the energy to cry.

"Don't fret yourself, my dear," Webber said. He took the canteen back and hung it across his saddle horn. "They won't harm you again. My old friends will make short work of them. I'm certain of that."

Angela wondered if she were hearing things.

"I thought you wanted them to kill your old friends." Her voice was hoarse and raw and her mouth didn't work quite right from the long hours in the gag. But Webber understood.

"If things go as I have planned, they will, but I'm sure some, if not all of them, will die as well."

"What about me?" Angela sniffed, rubbing her eyes with the heel of her good hand.

"What about you?" Webber's lips pulled back in a flat grin—almost a grimace. "You are the bait that brings O'Shannon to me. You will be fine, my dear. Just fine."

Angela slumped in the saddle. Although she was no longer tied, she was still being led just the same to a certain death, if not by the cruel men who'd had her before, then by the madman who had her now. She sniffed the air and watched a flurry of glowing sparks dance on the wind before they landed on the dry grass.

Maybe it wouldn't be the men who killed her at all.

CHAPTER 27

"Have to say, I don't like it one bit," Madsen said amid a cloud of whirling ash and cinders. "I feel like a goose in the middle of a cookstove."

The others rode along in silence, Trap watching the ground while Blake scanned the trees around them.

"And another thing." Clay used the tip of his reins to point at Trap. "I don't like the way that Zelinski character said we should head toward some 'distant valley.' That sounds too much like the afterlife if you ask me."

The wind howled through a thick stand of paper birch

that had miraculously escaped a previous fire. The white-barked trees stood out in stark contrast to the surrounding black landscape.

"I ain't never seen anything like this in all my life." Clay whistled above the moan of wind that surged through the gray haze of the birch forest.

A black bear sow with two white-collared cubs the size of feeder pigs hustled past him in the trees. Scarcely half a minute behind the bruins, a small herd of whitetail deer trotted through, only a few feet away from the horses. A fresh young doe, her sides heaving from panic and exertion, froze in mid-step when she noticed the men. Snorting, she stomped a slender foreleg and blinked huge brown eyes—as if in wondering awe that anything would be so foolish as to amble before the approaching flames. She was close enough that the men could see the wind ruffle her soft brown undercoat of hair.

Clay tipped his hat, and the doe seemed to vaporize into a flash of snow-white tail and a blur of tawny brown. When she had vanished along with her friends, Clay shook his head and stared after them.

"It's like the deer are chasin' after the bear. Just don't seem proper."

"They're likely the only ones with any sense," Trap said, chewing on the inside of his cheek. The specter of what might have happened to Maggie hung over him heavier than the thick billows of smoke and ash that swirled by with the wind. His gut told him she was all right, but he'd never rest until he was certain. If he had really believed she was dead, he would have turned around and let the fire overtake him, for without Maggie, life would be totally void of worth or flavor. He cursed himself for leaving her in the first place, with all the danger that was in the air.

He knew better. That's why he'd stayed alive for so many years living the kind of life he'd lived.

The three trackers rode as quickly as they could and still keep a reasonable trail. They traveled over a fresh ground burn, and step-by-step tracking, though possible, was painfully slow. Instead, they followed the natural lines of drift. With a general direction of travel from the last known set of tracks and the description of the area where Zelinski had seen the group, Trap decided to follow the flow of the land. Unless they were pushed, people as well as animals tended to follow natural contours and drainages. In the forests there were only so many routes a horse could take with all the blowdown and tangled snags.

The drainage they searched now was a maze of scorched, moss-covered logs and shallow creek beds that resembled a great green quilt bunched together in a fan of wrinkles. Head-sized chunks of granite littered the low washes and wreaked havoc on the horses' footing.

The wind blasted every bit of debris out from among the trees and ditches. Hundreds of animals, including elk and moose, had already followed the same natural routes of escape, so finding a decent identifiable track without inching along was next to impossible.

His eyes to the ground, deafened by the whir of wind in his ears, Trap traveled on for several minutes before he glanced up and realized he couldn't see Blake. Clay, quiet for an unnaturally long spell, was off to his left, flanking him and keeping a sharp eye ahead. With the fire, there wasn't much chance of anyone sneaking up behind them.

Trap turned in his saddle and scanned every direction. Blake was nowhere to be found. The way the land rippled, he could have been below the lip of a wash twenty feet away and still been out of sight, and so Trap didn't worry at first. Instead, he gave a shrill whistle like the call of a hawk. He received no answer, so he tried again, cupping his hands in front of his face to focus the sound to his right and then his left.

Nothing.

Alarmed now, he waved at Clay, who was already picking his way around a knee-high blow down to ride up next to him.

"Where's Blake?" Clay leaned in close and yelled above the wind.

"That's what I was going to ask you." Trap began to get the feeling he knew he would feel if anything happened to Maggie or Blake—a sickness down to his center that spread like palsy over his entire body—a deep, broken-bone sort of ache that made it hard to catch a breath.

Something was terribly wrong.

Blake O'Shannon was off his horse when he realized

someone was watching him. He couldn't see anyone, and the wind moaned so mournfully that the idea of hearing anything above it was unthinkable. A shudder up his spine and a prickling along the short hairs on the back of his neck told him eyes were on him. He chanced a look to his left, where his father and Clay should have been. He saw nothing but a tangle of wilted hemlock trees, devil's club, and smoke.

The young deputy chided himself for straying too far away from his companions. He knew better than to venture out on his own, and had been happy to follow such knowledgeable men as his father, Ky Roman, and Clay Madsen. Maybe Madsen had been right about not being a real man until you were thirty. Blake was not the type to panic, but he was smart enough to realize the chances of survival on his own in the midst of hostile forces and a rapidly approaching fire were less than poor.

He got the prickly feeling on his neck again, even reached up to touch it, hoping he was wrong, hoping it was just the wind hitting him above the collar.

The rattlesnakelike thrum of wilted huckleberry shrubs gave him the warning. Alerted by the familiar noise off to the right, Blake's Appaloosa gelding expected a snake and jerked against the reins. Blake fell backward and stumbled on the uneven terrain of the mossy wash where he stood.

The arrow whistled by him and lodged in the red bark of an alder, now naked of all its leaves before the driving wind. It missed the startled lawman by scant inches.

The wind had saved his life.

Blake fell to the ground so quickly, an onlooker would have thought the arrow hit him. He pressed himself flat against the forest floor and tried to make himself as small a target as possible. It was a little less smoky in the small hollow, and he could smell a hint of the huckleberries above him, fragrant even amid the fires. The line of bushes that had warned him of danger formed a thick barrier along a three-foot hummock of moss and deadfall to his immediate right. This flimsy bulwark was all that stood between him and whoever shot the arrow.

He thought of calling out for his father or Clay, but didn't want to get them shot because of his stupidity.

He couldn't just lay there forever, though, and he knew his father. It wouldn't be long before he'd come to check on him, especially being so worried about his mother.

A sudden tingle ran up Blake's spine, and he steeled himself when he heard a change in the wind above him. Danger was near now. He rolled onto his back.

The one-eyed Apache stood above him, a long knife in his hand, coming up to check and see if he was dead. He didn't have a bow, and was likely covered by someone who did from a safer vantage point. The attackers obviously didn't want to risk alerting Trap or Clay by using a gun.

Juan Caesar sprang as soon as Blake turned. The Apache was surprisingly agile for a man of his age. He landed on Blake with his knees, hard enough to take the wind from the boy's lungs and crack at least two ribs. Blake was just able to catch the arm that held the knife. He pushed it off to the side so the knife landed in the duff only inches from his neck.

Clawing at the one-eyed Apache's back, Blake kneed him in the groin, trying to push him off before he could regain control of the knife. Caesar's grip loosened enough for Blake to get a foot up and deliver a terrific blow to the Indian's exposed belly with the flat of his boot. Caesar flew backward, staggering from the impact, and coughing as he tried to catch his breath in the thick smoke.

The knife disappeared into the thick huckleberry shrubs. When the renegade chanced a look for it, Blake sprang on him. Juan Caesar was strong, but without a blade in his hands he was no match for Blake's youth and stamina. Trap and his friends had wrestled with the boy since he was no more than a sprout. Man or not, Blake knew about hand-to-hand combat.

Feinting with his left hand, Blake drove a crushing right hook into his opponent's temple, capitalizing on his lack of vision. The Apache reeled, staggered by the blow. Blake's right fist shot out again, catching Juan Caesar low in the jaw and spinning him around in the loose duff and pine needles. Worried about the second Apache, Blake grabbed the disoriented renegade in a choke hold from behind and drew him close. He continued his struggles and Blake tightened his forearm, stopping the circulation in the man's neck.

Blake looked right, then left, dragging Juan Caesar

with him. The Apache was still conscious, but just barely. It was impossible to see more than a few feet in the thick smoke, and the gathering wind made hearing anyone approach impossible. He strained his ears and thought he heard his father's whistle, but couldn't be sure. It could just as easily have been the other renegade or Feak.

Blake coughed from his exertions. The sticky smoke stung the back of his throat. Sweat ran into his eyes. He closed them and pressed his face against the back of Juan Caesar's greasy hair to gain some relief. It smelled of grease and spoiled meat.

Blake's mind raced while he tried to think of a way out of his situation. If he let the renegade go, he'd revive in a few minutes and the fight would start all over again. Blake drew his revolver with his free hand, holding the Apache close with his left arm. He knew what his father would do in this situation. This was war. There was no time to take a prisoner who would not hesitate to put a bullet in him the next time they met.

The shrill whistle came again, high and piercing over the wind. It was impossible to tell from which direction in the wind and whipping, moaning trees, but it was close. A crash in the brush made him spin to the right, his revolver at the ready. Two cow elk blew by on the wind, nothing but tan-rumped blurs. The noise of their passing was drowned out almost immediately by the forest that seemed to be alive with wind.

Bits of limbs, needles, and leaves began to separate from the trees and be driven before the wind. Grit and sand, picked up in the rush, flew into Blake's eyes, and he rubbed them with the back of his gun hand in an effort to keep them clear. His arm began to cramp from the constant effort of holding it around Juan Caesar's neck.

He felt the familiar tingling in his neck that his mother had taught him to recognize as a sign of danger. He dragged the unconscious Apache with him to get his back against the thick trunk of a ponderosa pine a few yards away. He heard movement, saw a shadow ghost through the frenzied green and yellow shadows of smoke and wind-whipped trees.

Someone was out there, circling him.

The brush was too thick to stay on horseback. Trap had to lead Hashkee over or around the numerous deadfall and blowdown snags that cluttered the thick forest. The mule was a better jumper than Madsen's bay gelding, and Trap made good time while he studied the ground looking for any sign that might tell him he'd intersected his son's trail. He looked mainly for horse tracks, knowing Blake's big-footed Appy would leave infinitely more sign than moccasin or even boot prints.

He knew Clay followed only yards behind, keeping a sharp eye through the smoke for anything "with teeth" as he would say. They were moving in a general direction away from the fire, a fact that made it easier to get both animals' cooperation.

The whine of a pistol shot above the wind brought Trap up short. He froze, straining to hear any other sign of danger. Hearing nothing but the wind, he dropped Hashkee's reins and slid his Marlin out of the saddle boot before bounding off in the direction of the shot in a half crouch.

Clay caught up to him at Blake's Appaloosa, whose reins had tangled around the snaking branches of a vine maple. He carried his pistol, and led Trap's mule and his own gelding with his left hand. The bay nickered at the sight of the other horse, and Hashkee gave a tedious groan, showing a white eye at having to work so hard jumping all the deadfall. Apart from being agitated over the wind and his natural aversion to the scent of fire, the Appy was in good shape—no blood or injury that Trap could find.

Trap surveyed the ground at the horse's feet. Few tracks remained on the windswept surface beyond the prancing circle the horse had dug around the vine maple. Another shot echoed through the trees.

Trap looked at his friend.

"Sounded like the boyo's Remington to me, bud. That's a good sign."

Trap nodded, his jaw set in grim determination, his eyes narrow.

"Watch yourself," he said above the wind.

"Lead on." Clay pointed in the direction of the shot with his pistol. "I'm right behind you."

Clay tied the two animals so they'd be around if they were needed, but would still be able to break free if they pulled hard enough and escape the fire if things took a turn for the worse.

• • •

Blake felt Javier's presence before he heard him, and spun Juan Caesar around a fraction of a second before the shot.

The older Apache stiffened. For a moment, Blake thought he was waking up, and attempted to apply more pressure with the V of his bicep and forearm. Suddenly weak on his feet, Blake stumbled, letting Juan Caesar slide to the ground in front of him in a dead heap.

A young Apache stood before him only a few yards away, his stringy black hair whipping across his cruel face in the wind. A blue steel revolver still pointed directly at Blake.

Blake tried to raise his own pistol, but found himself curiously weak, as if he were mired in the middle of a nightmare where someone was shooting at him and he could only move in slow motion.

The young lawman willed his gun hand up to face the threat, but no matter how hard he tried, he couldn't make it move. The Apache gave a crooked grin when the pistol fired harmlessly into the ground, then fell harmlessly out of Blake's hand.

Blake swayed on his feet, squinting to make out the form of the man who was about to kill him. The salty, copper taste of blood rose in his throat. The mere act of standing against the furious battering of wind suddenly seemed more of a chore than he could manage. He stumbled backward, grabbing for a handful of flimsy huckleberry brush as he fell.

Javier walked slowly toward him, seemingly unperturbed that he'd killed his own confederate only moments before. It was enough to him that the same bullet had passed through and through to hit the lawman.

"Caesar told me your white blood would make you weak," the Apache sneered.

Blake started to speak, but decided against it. Talking to a maniac like the one before him was pointless. His own pistol had landed less than two feet from where he sat heaving, his back against a rotting log. Blake tried not to look at it, knowing he would be dead in the short time it took him to get to it the way the other man covered him.

The young Apache squinted against the wind and looked down in disdain. He slid his long-barreled Colt back into the flap holster on his belt and drew a long skinning knife. It was obvious he no longer considered Blake a threat worthy of a bullet.

Blake pressed a hand against the jagged hole in his thigh. It didn't seem to be bleeding as badly as he thought it would be considering his sudden weakness. Javier took a slow step toward him. Blake eyed the revolver again and steeled himself for the attack he knew was about to come. He couldn't just sit still and let himself be carved up. His mind raced back to the men he'd seen butchered already by this man and his friends. No, he'd die fighting, no matter how weak he was. Even the thought of it made him stronger.

The fire was closer now, the pungent smell of wood smoke heavier on the wind. Even the young Apache looked up to take note. Blake had shifted his weight to make a rolling move for his pistol when he heard another shot, this time from behind him, beyond the rattling huckleberry brush.

Javier's face twisted in angry surprise. He dropped to one knee and put a hand to his side. Up again in an instant, the young renegade bolted for a nearby line of fir trees and disappeared into the shadows.

Blake clenched his eyes shut in relief and leaned his head back against the snag, expecting to see his father or Mr. Madsen at any moment. Instead he heard a bawling voice he'd never heard before carry through the whirling.

"Everthing all right over there?"

Blake froze, fearing it was Feak. Shooting their own didn't seem to bother anyone in the murderous group of kidnapers.

"This here's Corporal Bandy Rollins, United States Army," the voice yelled above the wind. It was tentative but friendly. "I'd be obliged to find out whose life it is I just saved."

Blake knew there was an Army presence in woods because of the fires. He raised his left hand from behind the snag and waved so Rollins could see where he was.

A beefy colored man in filthy military khakis knelt over Blake when Trap came into the clearing. A rifle leaned against a nearby tree, out of the black man's reach, but Trap leveled his Marlin to be on the safe side.

Blake raised his hand in a feeble gesture. There was

enough grin on his face to let Trap relax a measure.

"This mountain saved my life, Pa,"

Bandy Rollins looked up grimly from where he attempted to dress the wound in Blake's thigh. The soldier introduced himself without getting up.

"I don't know for certain if I saved his life yet or not."

Trap handed his rifle to Clay and knelt beside his son and the corporal. Blake's britches were cut away to reveal a thumb-size hole in the front of his thigh. Bandy rolled him slightly so they could have a look at the back side of his leg. Bits of flesh hung in tatters, crusted with pine needles and dirt. Blood poured into a growing pool on the dirt.

"I'm thinkin' they nicked an artery, maybe even clipped the bone." Rollins pressed his broad hand over the wound. He looked back in the direction of the wind. "We got to move him soon, though. He'd sure enough die if we stay here. We all will."

"I don't think I can outrun this, Pa. I can't even stand up."

"Nonsense." Trap put a hand on his son's forehead. "Your mama wouldn't be very pleased with me if we let that handsome Nez Percé hair of yours get all singed."

Blake chuckled weakly, and then winced. "So you're willing to admit she's still alive."

Trap nodded. "I'm too scared of her not to. Now let's get you on your horse and around this mountain to go with the fire crew. That ranger seems to know his business."

"You mean Mr. Zelinski?" Rollins's face brightened.

"You know him?" Clay toed Juan Caesar. Gave him a swift boot to the temple to make sure he wasn't playing possum.

"Yessir, I know him. My company was workin' right alongside him till they got called back to Avery. There was two Indian boys with him. I'm worried somethin' awful about 'em. I just know that Monroe character is up to no good. That's why I'm here. I got permission to come back and tell them about the relief trains. I wanted to check up on my two friends."

"Mercy, Rollins." Clay grinned. "You talk as much as I do." He filled the corporal in quickly on the attempted lynching.

"He's takin' the boys to a mine?"

Trap put the finishing touches on a tight bandage around Blake's thigh. "A place called the Ruby Creek Adit. Said they'd be safe there."

"I know the place," Rollins said. "Let's get this boy there. He needs to get somewhere fast so the bleedin' will stop. The people are like ants, just running outta these hills for their lives. Seen a man and young woman as foolish as me, ridin' back in towards the fire. Most likely they forgot somethin' or another they consider more important than their own mortal lives."

Blake winced and looked up, blinking. "What did the man and woman look like?"

"What are you talkin' about, son?" Rollins patted Blake's shoulder. "Hush now. Let's get you up on a horse."

Blake reeled when he got to his feet. His face was set

in a tense mask as he tried to disguise his agony. "With this leg, I don't think I can fork a horse."

"Where did you see this man and woman riding back towards the fire?" Clay asked.

"They were ridin' along just below a hogback ridge-line 'bout two drainages over. Why?"

Clay explained their pursuit.

"Poor girl." Rollins's already sad expression took on a wilted look. "That fella she's with must have taken leave of all his senses. I seen a huge plume of smoke risin' up over that biggest batch of mountains to the south. What with the wind a-whippin' so, it'll be right on top of 'em in no time. If he don't bring her out, she's good as dead."

Trap took a deep breath. It went against his grain to leave the care of someone he loved to anyone else, but he didn't know the way to the adit. Corporal Rollins, as sharp as he was, would be no match for Johannes Webber's cruel intellect.

"Corporal, could you take my boy to the adit and see that he's safe?"

Bandy raised an eyebrow, but gave a nodding shrug. "I'll carry him. It would be easier on him than riding, but not much."

"Clay, could you go with them?" Trap looked at his friend.

Madsen let his head loll back and forth. "I could, but I won't. This mountainous corporal here will have no trouble seein' to Blake's safety. I don't think it would be a good idea for him and me to be together very long. I'd have to compete too much for talkin' time. Besides, I got as much of a score to settle with Webber as you do. Ky Roman was a good friend of mine if you'll recall." He winked at Blake. "Not to mention the fact that Maggie would never forgive me if I didn't look after your sorry little hide."

Corporal Rollins took a sniff of the wind and shook his head in disbelief that anyone would willingly go back into the fire.

"I say you all done flipped your wigs." His hangdog eyes squinted into the smoke. "But I reckon it don't really matter much. We all apt to get cooked anyhow."

CHAPTER 28

"I hope you got some idea of where you're takin' us, Trapper," Clay groaned a few yards behind as they forded an ash-choked stream. It was littered with the white bellies of dead trout, killed by rising lye levels in the water. His voice was loud, but Trap could only just hear it above the howling wind. Both men had long since given up wearing their hats and lashed them down firmly behind their saddles.

In point of fact, Trap was only guessing at the route, following natural lines of drift from the ridgeline where Rollins had seen the man and woman. He was haunted by the recurring notion that they were following a couple of settlers gone back to get a milk cow, and not Johannes Webber and Angela Kenworth at all. Tracking over the wind-driven ground was slow and tedious, but he was heartened when he stumbled over a fresh set of horse tracks in a section of bear grass burned over from an earlier fire.

The area had been logged, and dozens of smoking stumps dotted the gently sloping hillside like short quills on a black porcupine. Above the hill was an apron of loose gray talus fanning out from a large mountain to the north. Turned earth in a line to the west of the talus rock, along with the depressions of tents and a split-rail eating table, showed the remains of a fire camp. The fire had swept through only hours before, burning itself out against the rocky bulwark of the mountain. It had been a small blaze compared to the one behind them.

Trap twisted in the saddle to look southwest, and shuddered in spite of himself. An enormous gray-black cloud billowed thousands of feet above the tumble of mountains north of the St. Joe River. Ghostly orange gasses churned inside the cloud, casting menacing shadows as the whole mass rolled toward them at an incredible pace.

"Oh, my Lord!" Trap heard Clay over his shoulder, and turned back to see him dismount and stoop next to a smoldering stump.

O'Shannon urged Hashkee forward to see what had Clay so distraught. When he drew closer, he realized it was no stump but a badly burned body.

Blackened beyond recognition by the searing heat of the previous ground fire, it resembled the stumps around it more than a human being.

“The poor thing’s feet are completely gone,” Clay moaned. “I ain’t certain, but I think it’s a woman.”

Trap slid off his mule and took a deep breath before he got too near the corpse. The body was facedown, its hands drawn up underneath in a sort of fetal position. The head was turned back, as if to watch the fire that killed it.

“Think it could be Angela Kenworth?” Clay let out a deep breath and looked up at his friend, his eyes already glassy with tears.

“Let’s turn her over and see if she’s missing a finger.” Trap scanned the surrounding trees and rocks. He expected to see Johannes looking down at them with a rifle. This would be just like him.

“Oh, no. No, no, no not her . . .” Clay said as they rolled the body over as gently as they could. “Poor sweet, pitiful thing.”

The body was missing not one, but two fingers. Though her face was badly deformed and twisted into a grimace by the fire, the turtle-shell comb Clay had given her earlier and the swatch of green taffeta dress revealed too plainly it was Cora, Clay’s new friend from the Snake Pit bar.

“Why did she have to come up here, Trap? Why couldn’t she . . .” Clay caught himself, breathing heavily. He stood to untie the leather strings that held his bedroll. “Ground’s too hard to bury her. You mind helpin’ me get her rolled into a blanket and leaned up against one of these stumps?”

Trap put a hand on his friend's shoulder. "That fire's gonna drive through here again, Clay. It'll turn what's left of this place to dust."

Madsen shrugged. "I know it, Trap. But supposing it doesn't. We can't just leave her layin' here for the coyotes and crows."

Clay spread the blanket out beside Cora's body, his back to the wind so it didn't fight him. He muttered to himself as he worked, sniffing and shaking his head. Trap couldn't make out everything he said, but he knew the gist of it.

"Poor thing just couldn't get a break, could you? I hope you had you some happy times in your life, darlin'." Madsen suddenly looked up at Trap. "You think she ever had any good happen to her at all?"

"She met you. That appeared to make her smile."

"You reckon life is just that, sadness with a tiny sprinkle of good only once in a great while?"

"What do you mean?" Trap was sorry as soon as he spoke. Asking such a question was like pulling the cork out of Clay Madsen, and only *he* knew when his ramblings would stop pouring out. Luckily, he kept working as he spoke.

"If you think back on it, can you ever think of a time when everything fit just right—as if the Good Lord might have intended you to be happy once in a while and not just livin in one degree of misery or another?"

"I reckon I been happy enough," Trap said, helping hold the rolled blanket at Cora's feet so Clay could tie it with a length of leather cord from his saddle kit.

"I ain't talking about just not bein' sad." Clay snorted and gave an exasperated shrug. "I mean truly, sublimely happy. That moment of perfection when there's no wind and the sights and the sounds and the company all bundle up together like . . . I don't know. . . ."

Trap knew better than to get in front of Clay when he was heading off on a philosophical gallop.

"I never thought on it that way, but I guess I been happy like that with my Maggie."

"Yeah, but what you and Maggie have ain't even normal. I think that's what galls Johannes so awful. He always thought he should be the one of us who found that sublime sort of partnership with a woman."

Trap scratched his head at all the talk of awe-inspiring relationships. His marriage to Maggie was what it was and that was it. Talking about it made him feel uncomfortable, almost naked.

"I know you've been happy, Clay." Trap focused the talk back on Madsen. "I've seen you laugh your head off on more than one occasion, if I recall correctly."

"Laughing don't necessarily mean you're happy." Clay stroked the crown of Cora's charred head with the tip of his finger. "She laughed. I seen her. But I'd bet you the ranch she wasn't very happy."

"Yeah, but you've been happy."

"A few times, I reckon. I could likely count them without too much effort, though." Clay sniffed. "Two come to mind. One was when I was married to Inez and we took that little trip out to Sedona. There was this evenin' thunderstorm followed by the prettiest sunset you ever saw, all bright and yellow orange across the desert—but my Inez, she was even brighter." Clay wiped his nose with the back of a gloved hand. "I know a man shouldn't pick a favorite. Inez wasn't the handsomest woman I married, but she had a way about her that made me feel like I was drownin' when I wasn't around her. She was salve to my soul—like Maggie is to you." Clay rubbed his eyes and blinked to clear them. "Your wife is still alive, you know."

Trap nodded, fighting back the gnawing ache in his stomach. They situated the blanket roll that held Cora's body in a seated position next to a smoldering tree stump a few feet away.

"When was the other time?" O'Shannon stretched his back.

Clay was lost in thought, gazing up at the gray jumble of horse-sized rocks on the talus slop above them. "Huh?"

"You said there was another time that came to your mind when your were happy."

"I did at that." Clay nodded and turned to face his partner. There was a look of grim determination in his furrowed brow. His eyes sparkled the way they did when a battle was about to be joined. It was as if he'd suddenly been imbued with a double dose of swagger. He motioned toward the horses with a slight nod. Trap followed.

"If you take a gander over my left shoulder, you'll see a man workin' his way across the rocks up yonder. He's carryin' a long gun, but I'm bettin' he won't be close enough to have us in range for a little spell yet."

Trap looked up the slope. He could just make out a dark form slipping down through the jumble of rocks, a rifle in hand.

"I don't think I ever introduced you to my newest sweetheart," Clay said, sliding a long, bolt-action rifle out of the sheepskin leather boot on the off side of his saddle. Trap recognized the Mauser-style bolt action, but hadn't paid attention to what type of rifle Clay carried. While O'Shannon was perfectly happy with his 1881 Marlin—even loyal to it, any new firearm to hit the military or civilian market was likely to steal Clay Madsen's eye.

"She's what the U.S. government calls a 'Ball Cartridge, Caliber 30, Model of 19 Aught 6.' " Madsen smiled casually and rubbed his hand across the smooth steel barrel as if there were no sniper a few hundred yards away, possibly sighting in at that very moment. "Thirty-aught-six, for short. I just call her Ramona."

A bullet whined into the charred dust twenty yards in front of the horses. A short moment later, the report of the rifle popped in the distance, barely audible above the wind.

Clay shook his head. "He's trying to walk it into us, but in this storm, he's got a better chance of shooting himself. I bet he's still using an antique like you." Madsen nodded toward a downed tree and a small hummock of burned ground big enough for two men to hide behind if they lay flat. "Just the same, we best hunker down in case he gets lucky."

"Why Ramona?" Trap hesitated to ask, but he was too good a friend not to allow Clay time to make the explanation he sorely wanted to give. Madsen had had a habit of naming his firearms from the day Trap met him, and some of the reasons proved interesting.

"Remember that little Mexican whore down in Nogales?" Clay squinted down the barrel, then closed his eyes, feeling the wind. Both men were on their bellies. Trap acted as a spotter, watching the target while Clay worked out his aim. "She had that darlin' spot of a mole above her upper lip?" His words muffled into the polished wood of the rifle.

Trap grunted, though he didn't keep a catalog of whores in his brain like Clay did. If he said he didn't remember, Clay was liable to give him more of a description than he was up for.

"Well." Clay pressed his cheek against the walnut stock. "I heard tell Bill Cody named his Springfield needle-gun after Lucretia Borgia on account of her bein' so beautiful and deadly. Well, that Mexican whore, Ramona, was by far the most handsome thing I ever did see—and the most deadly—just like my aught-six here." Madsen aimed in earnest now. More reports echoed down from the rocks above, but the rounds still fell harmlessly, yards away.

"He don't have the patience it takes to get a good shot off," Trap observed when a bullet drove up a dust cloud ten yards in front of them. It was carried away immediately by the wind.

"Or the gun," Clay said, squeezing off a crisp shot

from Ramona. He worked the bolt and rolled half up on his side, a wry smile parting his lips. "Unless I miss my guess, Ramona just gave him a 150-grain lead kiss about where his left hand used to be. If it's Mr. Feak up there, I reckon that will be a lesson to him about cuttin' fingers and such off poor folks. What do you say we go talk to him before he bleeds to death?"

The two trackers approached through the rocks cautiously since Clay figured the sniper might still retain the use of his gun hand.

They needn't have worried.

Though still alive, Feak was a mess when they found him. Ramona's kiss had torn away the top two thirds of his left hand where he'd been holding the forearm of his rifle. Ironically, only his little finger was left, dangling by a bloody thread of flesh. Bits of wood from the demolished weapon had lodged in the outlaw's face and arms, flecking him with blood. Feak lay on his back behind a large rock, panting and staring up at the smoky sky. Bright swatches of blood marred the rocks where he'd thrashed about after the shot—until he'd grown so weak he could do nothing but lay back and wait to die.

Though he would have lost his hand and maybe part of the arm, the wound hadn't been a mortal one. A quick wrap of a tourniquet would have stemmed the flow of blood. But Feak was shot, and to some people being shot was as good as being dead. Trap was glad Blake didn't share the same thoughts on the matter. Trap himself had been shot several times, once not even realizing it for several minutes until he noticed a hole in his britches leg.

"Johannes Webber be damned to Hell," Feak groaned, a pallid sweat forming across his bald head.

Clay kicked Feak's pistol aside, just to be sure he didn't get a sudden burst of energy, and looked down at the dying man. "Funny you should say that, mister. You're readin' my mind. Did Mr. Webber say where he might be headed?"

Feak snorted, then winced. He squeezed above his shattered wrist with his right hand. His voice was pointed but weak. "You must be Madsen. He said you would be the mouthy one. It ain't really you he's after." Feak lifted his head to get a good look at Trap, then let it fall back to the rock. "It's O'Shannon he be lookin' for. He never told me why he had it in for you so bad. Just said it was personal." Feak's eyes fluttered and a wan smile crossed his fat lips. The pain was easing. He wouldn't last much longer.

Trap stooped down next to the outlaw to hear him more clearly. "Did Webber say where he was going, what he had planned?"

Feak shook his head. A small tear formed in the corner of his eye, then dried in the wind before it fell. "He plans to kill you—make you see those you care about die in front of your eyes—then kill you."

"Is the Kenworth girl still alive?" Trap didn't like thinking about the grudge Johannes still held for him. Too much guilt still festered in his heart about what had happened all those years ago.

"Last I saw of her she was. Damned little coyote nearly bit ol' Juan Caesar's arm off." Feak tried to chuckle, but the effort was too much for him. "Webber will be waitin' for you." The killer coughed like he'd been lung-shot. "He's a smart one, that Johannes is. I doubt you can take him."

"Where?" Trap raised his voice to get Lucius back on track. "Where's he taking the girl?"

"A canyon . . . west of here." Feak stammered pitifully, "You boys don't have any water, do you?"

Clay shook his head. "It's down with the horses. Which canyon?"

"Stone Canyon. It ain't far—he wants you to find him—all part of his plan." He clutched at Clay's arm with his blood-smeared right hand. "I'm dyin'."

Clay jerked away in disgust. "Feak, you blasted boob. There ain't no reason for you to die just yet unless you have a mind to. Show some backbone for pity's sake."

Trap rose. He now possessed the information he needed about Webber's whereabouts, and saw no further reason to listen to the dying outlaw's self-pity.

"I'll be meetin' my maker soon, boys." Feak seemed to be talking to someone who wasn't there. His eyes fluttered. His face and scalp grew pale. "I ain't long for this world now."

Clay shook his head and stood. "Well if you're bound and determined, go ahead on to Hell then. We'll be sendin' Johannes your way shortly."

"When was the other time?" Trap asked as they

mounted to move off down the trail again together.

"What do you mean?"

"You said there were two times that came to your mind when you were truly happy."

Clay smiled and twirled the thin leather reins in his hands. "I was just bein' a bawl baby."

"All right. If you don't want to talk about it." Trap knew there wasn't much chance of that.

Ten feet down the trail, Clay broke the short silence.

"It was when I saw you and Hezekiah on the road there yesterday and we was all back together again. I reckon most of the times back when we was younger, trackin' bandits and chasin' outlaws was the finest hours a man could ask for. I was just too young and knot-headed to realize it at the time.

"Hell, I'm even looking forward to burnin' to death along with Johannes. To tell the truth, I reckon I'm as happy as I can be right now."

CHAPTER 29

With a raging fire behind them and a bright smear of blood on the alder leaves ahead, Zelinski paused and held up an open hand to slow the column of men sloshing down ash-choked Ruby Creek in the narrow ravine. Something the trackers had told him earlier tugged at the corners of his mind. He'd been so concerned about the death of his friend George White and his crew that he hadn't taken the time to listen like he should have. The big Texan had said there were renegade Apache involved.

"Renegade Apache my hind end," the fire boss said under his breath as he drew his forty-four. For Horace Zelinski, a veteran of the Spanish American War and many furious battles with fire, to be faced with renegade Indians of any sort in 1910 seemed an outlandish notion and he didn't have time to fool with it.

"Ranger!" the familiar voice of Corporal Bandy Rollins hailed from a thick stand of alder bushes off a fork in Ruby Creek. "I brought you a lost sheep. Don't you be shootin' us now."

Zelinski let out his breath and watched as the gigantic soldier walked out of the gray cloud of smoke that poured out of the side ravine as thick as the plume from the top of a steam engine. The ranger recognized the wounded lawman.

"What happened to you? Renegade Apache?" Zelinski chuckled holstering his revolver.

Blake nodded and the ranger's smile vanished. "Corporal Rollins winged him, but he slipped away."

Zelinski gave the boy a once-over and shook his head. "Can you walk?"

Blake nodded. "With help."

"Good," the ranger said, waiving his ragtag troop of men forward. "We don't have the time for all this." He looked at Rollins and then at Daniel Rainwater. Worried about more trouble with Ox Monroe, Zelinski had entrusted the young Flathead with his rifle. "If either of you see a wounded Apache and he so much as looks cross-eyed at you, shoot him."

Both men nodded. The face of Brandice the beetle-man creased in worry, and it looked as if he might lose control of his bowels.

"There were two others with you," Zelinski panted to Blake as he half-trotted beside Rollins. It amazed him how the soldier could carry the wounded deputy at such a fast pace that some of the men were having trouble keeping up.

"Yes, sir, my father and Mr. Madsen. They went south after the missing girl." Blake spoke through clenched teeth from the jarring gate and Rollin's big arm around his middle.

Horace slowed enough at that news that Brandice, horrified at the prospect of being left behind, almost crashed into him.

"They went toward the fire?" Zelinski said.

Corporal Rollins's eyes caught Zelinski's and he nodded knowingly. "I tried to stop 'em, but they wouldn't pay me no heed at all. The little tracker just asked me to save his son here, so that's what I'm doin'."

The group had to slow to pass single file around a lumbering porcupine that scurried as fast as it could down the same drainage—fleeing the oncoming fire.

"Even the whistle-pigs are smart enough to run from this," Zelinski said to no one in particular. He turned to look back at his collection of panting, mud-soaked, bone-weary men.

Few of the others knew what was about to happen.

All had seen fire from a distance. They'd fought it and pushed it back, moved when it got too near or jumped the breaks—even Voss's group, who'd watched it devour their pack train, had no inkling of what was going to occur.

First the smoke would thicken, get so hot they might not be able to see more than a few inches. Then the crown fires would tear through the tops of the trees. Running before the wind and raining down flames, these horrible, screeching demons would suck up all the usable oxygen. What little useless air was left would be superheated enough to blind them and sear their lungs closed at every attempted breath. Even if they found a way to survive all that, the ground fire would bring up the rear, eating up the thick underbrush—an unstoppable, unquenchable fury consuming everything in its path.

"We're here, boys," Zelinski cried over the storm of dust and flying ash when they arrived at the tiny entrance to the mine adit. "Wet your blankets in the creek as best you can and move with speed into the tunnel."

"Mercy, would you look at that!" someone cried from the rear of the party. "It's dark enough the bats have come out." Indeed, the tiny black creatures flitted in and out of view in the swirling clouds of dark smoke. Some of them, confused or overwhelmed, flew directly into trees to be thrown to the group's feet by the wind.

The ravine opened up to about two hundred feet wide before them. The slanting walls rose over two hundred more on either side covered with thick stands of white pine.

A horrendous moan like the roar of a furious ocean storm tore down the ravine toward them. It grew too dark to see more than a dozen yards.

"I ain't goin' in there," Roan Taggart yelled over the wind. He stared at the yawning six-by-six mouth of the mine adit.

Brandice rushed past the red-bearded firefighter, happy to find some relative safety from the encroaching flames. Other men followed, their sodden wool blankets flapping wildly in the wind.

"Monroe!" Zelinski barked into the dark hole. "Get out here and get your friend into that mine shaft!"

As big as he was, Monroe poked his head out the adit entrance but would come no further. He looked back and forth from Taggart to the now-glowing ravine, but he dodged Zelinski's eye.

Flaming brands, as big as a man's arm, began to fall in earnest and a blast of superheated wind blew in behind them, taking Zelinski's breath away. He fought to keep his footing. He had everyone in now except Taggart.

Zelinski grabbed at his shoulder, but Roan tore away and turned to run at the oncoming fire. A monstrous orange glow ripped through the tree crowns on either side of the ravine high above, snapping and cracking like gunfire as it was pushed by the faster winds. Trees fifty to seventy feet tall snapped like matchsticks and spun in the whirling gale. Flaming brands two and three feet long exploded into showers of sparks as they collided with the ground. Countless fires sprang up along the mountainsides, ahead of the main blaze.

"Get back here!" Zelinski screamed above the melee. Taggart paid no attention. He seemed transfixed, staring at the orange glow up the steaming creek bed while fiery sparks spun around him like a swarm of angry wasps.

Then, with slow deliberation, as trees flew past and the whole world seemed to melt around him, Roan Taggart pulled the revolver from his belt and shot himself in the head.

With no time to mourn the man, Zelinski dove into the tunnel as a wave of flame engulfed the entire gorge.

Corporal Rollins handed him a waterlogged blanket and helped him beat at the support timbers around the door as they began to catch fire.

"Taggart . . ." Zelinski said, shaking his head.

"I saw." Rollins tried to hold his blanket up to block the door. Steam rose from the wet cloth and a flame caught along the bottom edge.

Men coughed and choked in the cramped, steaming darkness. Someone in the back whimpered for his mother. Others chattered nervously like children. Cyrus McGill, with his fine tenor voice, began to sing "Abide With Me" at the top of his lungs.

Thick smoke poured into the tunnel as the air rushed out.

Horace Zelinski saw the world outside the opening turn bright orange.

Then, everything went black.

CHAPTER 30

Angela pressed her back against the rough bark of the jack pine and cast her eyes back and forth looking for a way to run. The red dirt trail behind her led almost straight uphill. Above it marched the huge column of smoke and flame that would surely kill her. Webber was off his horse, cutting some sort of mark on the smooth red bark of an alder.

They were heading into a circular valley surrounded on all sides by high walls of rock and towering trees. It was difficult to see what awaited them on the valley floor, for smoke poured over the cliffs filling it like a deep bowl of smoky soup. The wind stirred it some, and Angela thought she could make out the thin trickle of a small stream amid the huge boulders and thick groves of dark green trees and scrub.

There was nowhere to go, nowhere to run without getting burned or killed. Still, it was not in Angela's nature to march quietly to her death.

Webber turned from his business with the knife and walked toward her. He didn't resheath the bone-handled knife. The long blade reflected dully in the dusky haze, and Angela could see blood on the brass finger guard.

"O'Shannon should find us soon." He held the knife between them, staring at the blade, but didn't threaten her with it. In fact, his tone was civil, almost friendly. His eyes were a different matter. They blazed with a fury Angela had never seen. She knew Webber had no more against her than the fire did, but it didn't matter in either case. Both would destroy her if she got in the way—without even a hint of remorse.

Trying to survive had overwhelmed Angela's thought processes since she'd been abducted. She'd always assumed it was about a ransom. She'd read stories about men who kidnapped rich people's children for money. But none of this made sense.

Sensing she was doomed no matter what, Angela was suddenly consumed by an overpowering urge to understand.

"Why?" Her voice still croaked from breathing around the rawhide gag. She wondered if it would ever come back—if she lived at all.

Webber smiled and drew the blade of the knife across the palm of his hand. He let the blood drip down on the stirrup fender of Angela's horse, then on the ground.

"Why indeed." He returned his knife to the sheath at his belt and wrapped a strip of cloth around his hand when he seemed satisfied with the amount of blood he'd left. "I suppose you are deserving of, if not entitled to, a few answers, my dear." He looked back to the west. "It looks like we have a moment." He looped the puddin'-footed horse's lead around the low branch and beckoned Angela to follow on foot with a flick of his hand.

It was not a request.

"The men that are following us are the best at what they do." Webber walked along without keeping to any sort of trail, expecting her to follow. Bunchgrass whipped in the wind at Angela's feet, and she stumbled to keep up.

"I used to work with them, called them my friends—until I was betrayed."

Webber stopped talking and Angela coaxed him. "How? What did they do to you to make you hate them so much?"

The madman stopped in his tracks and nodded, letting his head bob up and down while he took several deep breaths. "It was the little half-breed, O'Shannon. He's the one who's to blame. It was his fault, but the others backed him up. They were there and thus they bear some of the responsibility—but the bulk of the burden, the bulk of the guilt falls on Trap O'Shannon. I will show him he cannot play God with other people's lives."

"Why me? Why now?"

Johannes chuckled, his gaze softening some as he looked at her. "Because, my dear, you were handy. I'd not counted on this cursed fire, but it makes little difference. I didn't give myself much of a chance of survival anyway."

"What do you mean, I was handy?" Angela wanted to strangle him for not getting to the point.

"It was my nephew's idea really. Tom Ledbetter. I don't know if you ever got the chance to meet him, but he works for your father. The poor boy hid under the porch while he watched my dear sister butchered by a band of Cheyenne dog soldiers. He was nine. Had what you might call a thirst for Indian blood since that time . . . and who can blame the boy?"

Webber resumed his walking, brusquely, as if he had a particular destination in mind and it was not too far away.

"Poor Tom knew about the debt I owed O'Shannon. When it seemed your politically connected father was having you out west for a visit, we knew he would call on the best trackers around to find you. It was Tom's idea to have you ride in the coach and give you the 'Western experience' rather than your father's model T.

"All I really had to do was start things in motion. Natural momentum took care of the rest. You see, I know these men. I ate, drank, worked—and killed alongside them for years. A telegram here, a phone call there, it was really all too easy."

"How can you be sure this Trap O'Shannon won't kill you first, if he's as good as you say?"

"He's got to save you." Johannes shrugged, as if the fact was obvious. "You see, he feels enormous guilt."

Angela wanted to scream. She struggled to keep up through the brush-choked trail. "If he feels guilty, then why do you still want to see him dead?"

Johannes stopped and turned to face her. Leafy alder limbs whipped back and forth around him, adding their whispering whoosh to the moan of wind. "Guilt is not enough," he said through clenched teeth. "I feel guilt.

O'Shannon has to atone for what he did. I know him, Miss Kenworth. He'll come for me in order to save you. No fire will be able to stop him from trying."

"Then you plan to kill me. You want him to fail." Angela felt strangely calm to know her ordeal was almost at an end, one way or another.

Webber smiled serenely. "Don't think so much, Angela. It's not good for you." He turned and motioned for her to follow.

The trail flattened out into a wide valley of birch and towering cottonwood. Angela kept her head down and trudged along behind. She wondered how her end would come—a fire or at the hand of this lunatic? There were times the pain in her hand was so intense, she felt she would welcome death.

Webber suddenly stopped in the trail ahead of her and drew his knife. Angela had just enough time to make out the figures of two men through the smoke and swaying trees before he spun her around and locked her arm behind her back. He took an iron grip on her bad hand. Searing pain shot up through her elbow at the rough treatment. She didn't have the energy to resist.

A thick cottonwood tree stood between them and the two other men. Webber put the blade to Angela's throat and used his shoulder to pin her to the rough bark of the tree.

"Be still," he whispered. The wind was loud enough he could have yelled and the trackers would have had trouble hearing him.

One cheek pressed against the rough bark of the tree, Angela was able to catch glimpses of her would-be rescuers. There were two of them, leading animals across a small stream not thirty feet away.

"That's right, my old friend. Keep coming," Webber whispered as the two men moved cautiously in their direction. Angela could feel his muscles quiver with anticipation.

He tightened his grip around her and jammed her harder against the tree. His breath was hot against her neck. "Now," he hissed. "Go ahead and scream."

So this was it, Angela thought, and drew in a lungful of air. Before she could make a sound, the trackers stopped in mid-stream. The shorter of the two cocked his head to one side and looked hard in her direction. He dropped the reins of his mule and let his hand fall down to his pistol. The burly man next to him followed suit. He looked directly at her.

CHAPTER 31

"I can't even hear myself think over this damned wind," Clay barked as he sloshed into the ankle-deep stream. The bay gelding pulled at the reins behind him, trying to get enough slack to take a drink. Clay jerked its head up. "Stop it, you fool horse. This water'd kill you deader than a nail keg. You're gonna force me to ride a jackrabbit like O'Shannon if you don't watch yourself."

Hashkee, with plenty of slack, bent to sniff at the

water, but refused to drink any.

Trap studied the shoreline on the far edge of the creek. White-barked birch trees whipped in the wind, their limber trunks bending in great arcs with each dynamic gust. In the towering cottonwoods, leafy canopies as large as houses swished and sang on the shrieking gale. It was too dark to see into the trees more than a few yards.

Trap caught a familiar smell on the wind and stopped in his tracks. It was an odor he recognized from the massacre site: the smell of fear.

He looked at Clay, who for all his jabbering noticed it too and strained his eyes forward, searching the tree line.

"There!" Clay spit. "I see him." He started for the shore again, but Trap stopped him with a quick hand on his arm.

"Don't make it so easy for him," Trap said, stepping back behind his mule. "Let's settle in to this."

A shrill laugh carried toward them on the wind. "Go ahead, Clay. You can leave," Webber shouted. "I only want Trap today. You're free to go if you like."

"I'd only circle around from behind and kill you, Johnny. You know that." The wind was in his face and Clay had to yell to be heard.

"Together again, eh?"

"Yup," Clay said, not caring if Webber heard him or not.

"Madsen, you imbecile. You're still playing Damon to his Pythias—too foolish to realize you are the better man. You two were always much too close for your own good."

"Whatever you say, Johnny." Clay moved slowly toward his horse. "But the fact remains that I'm stayin'. I'd much rather look you in the face when I kill you than go sneakin' around like that boob Feak you counted on to take care of me."

The winds from the firestorm blew in such a fury, it was impossible to know if Johannes heard anything Madsen said. Trees groaned against the stress. Ash and dust choked the air, and caused Trap to squint as he strained to see Johannes through the whirling torrents of smoke and debris. Clay pulled something out of his saddlebags and turned, a wide smile pulling back the tight corners of his mouth.

"What have you got in mind?" Trap asked, risking a quick glance away from Webber. His jaw dropped at what he saw.

Amid a virtual tornado of fire and sparks, Clay Madsen held three sticks of Dupont dynamite. The Texan winked. "Thought this might come in handy someday, so I borrowed it from the jail when I was lookin' in on Maggie. I was thinking of usin' it to blast Johannes to Hell."

Trap swallowed hard. "You mean to tell me I been riding beside you through these fires and all this time you've been sittin' on a sack of explosive?"

Clay shrugged off the danger. "Dynamite don't explode unless you put a fuse to it. It just burns. You know that."

Trap tilted his head toward the sticks in Madsen's hand. "Those have got fuses in them already, in case you haven't noticed."

"I'll be damned." Clay chuckled. "I guess they do at that."

"Come get what you came for," Johannes shrieked. He threw the Kenworth girl to the ground in front of him. She landed on her knees at the base of the huge, swaying tree. "You and I have an appointment to keep, O'Shannon. Come to me and I'll let her go to Madsen."

Clay tucked the dynamite in his hip pocket. Both he and Trap started for the tree line—and Johannes.

"Both of you stop," Webber screamed. He dragged the sobbing girl back to her feet and put the point of his knife to her throat. "One more step, Madsen, and I kill her here and now. There is only one way for her to live through this."

Flames ate away at the trees behind Johannes. The furious wind howling ahead of the fire sent small rocks skittering across the scoured ground. The surface of the shallow creek rolled back from the force of it at the trackers' feet.

"He'll kill her anyway," Clay groaned to Trap. "I'm sick of playin' around. Pardon me while I go . . ."

A horrific groan from high above caused all the men to look up. Webber moved the knife a fraction of an inch and the girl fell away, just as a fearsome wind grabbed the towering cottonwood and slammed it to the ground. The tree landed with a reverberating crack, its huge branches snapping under its own weight.

For a moment both Webber and Angela were hidden from view by the leafy crown. Trap and Clay seized the opportunity and leapt forward. Angela crawled out of the branches to meet them.

The fire up the canyon swept through the trees toward them with the screaming cries of a banshee. It was less than a mile away now, and they had nowhere to run but the tiny creek behind them.

"Does Webber have a gun?" Trap yelled above the melee as Clay dragged the weakened girl into the shallow water between Hashkee and the gelding.

"I think so," she whimpered. Her words came on jagged breaths. "He . . . I . . . think the tree fell on him."

"Johannes, you all right?" Trap yelled toward the downed tree. There was no answer.

"We're still in the open if Johnny's got his gun handy." Clay gazed back in awe at the approaching firestorm. "But I reckon it won't make any difference for any of us in a minute or two." Orange and yellow flames surged on all sides of the valley now, pushed through the trees by the angry gale. The Texan pulled the trembling girl to his chest and patted her softly on the back to soothe her. "We got her back from Johannes, Trap, but a lot of good that does her now." He ducked his head toward the fire, squinting at the brightness and heat of it. "This sorry little pissant creek ain't gonna be no help at all."

Trap looked down at the shallow stream. Only inches deep, it barely covered Hashkee's fetlocks. "Maybe there's a hole further down." He grabbed the mule's reins and motioned for Clay to follow with Angela. "We have to try."

Madsen put out a hand to stop him and motioned up the canyon. "It's too late, old buddy. We gave it our best, but that blaze will be on us momentarily. I feel good about what we've done. At least we can rest easy knowing these fearsome winds will blast Johannes on to Hell in a . . ."

"How many sticks of dynamite do you have?" Trap dropped the mule's reins.

"Six, but I don't . . . wait a minute." Clay looked down at Angela and gave her an excited squeeze. "I think my little friend is gettin' one of his famous last-minute ideas."

"Six should be enough—I hope. Don't have much experience with this sort of thing." Trap slapped Hashkee on the rump to herd him out to the stream away from the approaching firestorm. "Give me all six and get the girl back behind those rocks."

Clay dug the rest of the dynamite out of his saddlebags and gave it all to O'Shannon.

"How long will fuses like this burn?" Trap yelled as Clay sloshed out of the creek with Angela.

Clay gave him a sheepish look. "I don't know, maybe a minute or so," he screamed back, though he was still only fifteen feet away. "They came that way."

A minute or so—Trap looked back at the approaching flames. He cringed at the growing intensity of the heat. Steam rose from the edge of the tiny stream. Falling branches sang and hissed as they flew into the water like flaming arrows. Two minutes and they'd all be cooked.

Trap estimated as best he could, and used his knife to cut the fuses in half.

Behind him, the branches of the downed cottonwood began to burst into flame—and Johannes Webber began to scream. Trap winced at the thought of the man, even one as bent on evil as Webber, trapped under the huge tree, burning alive. Grateful for a loud wind, he tried to push the sounds out of his mind as he worked to find a place to put the explosive. O'Shannon glanced for a moment in the direction of the screaming, but saw nothing. He was certain Johannes posed him little danger now.

Wasting precious seconds on a search, Trap finally found a small pile of rocks the size of musk melons located roughly in the center of the shallow current. Water swirled around the dynamite, but the fuses stayed dry, inches above the water. He kicked at the gravel bed, hoping it was loose enough for his plan to work.

Small fires burned everywhere, and it was no problem to find something to light the fuse with. Trap grabbed a burning length of pine at the water's edge and sloshed quickly back to the dynamite. He had to bend over and protect the fuses from the wind to get the fire to catch. When it did, he dropped the torch and ran, slogging for the rocks where Clay hid with Angela and the animals.

CHAPTER 32

The explosion knocked Trap off his feet as he stumbled behind the protection of the rocks. A muddy slurry of gravel and sand rained down in all directions. Rocks the size of his head slammed into the bank up and down the creek. Miraculously, none fell on the huddled group.

Clay helped him up and gave him an exuberant kiss on the top of his head. "You're a genius, O'Shannon."

"Is it working?" Trap mumbled to himself. Even his own voice was a muffled grunt inside his head. He couldn't hear a thing.

Clay chanced a peek around the boulders and slapped his friend on the back. O'Shannon looked up to read his lips. "Water's flowin' into your brand-new pond."

The ringing in Traps ears quieted some by the time the trio waded into the rising water. He estimated it would be four feet deep by the time it was full. He hoped that was deep enough.

"Throw this over you," Trap heard Clay cry above a rush of fiery wind as they led the animals into the water beside them. He was happy to see the creek already lapped at the mule's belly. Trap took the waterlogged blanket and ducked into the water beside his friend and the girl. He thought he could still hear Webber's screams as the molten gases engulfed the world around him.

• • •

Clay laughed as he sloshed out of the creek, the girl in his arms. His teeth chattered from almost an hour in the chilly, lifesaving water. "Ain't it amazing how things change? I never thought I'd look for another fire again as long as I lived when that demon was bearin' down on us like that. Now, I fear we'll all freeze to death if we don't get warm."

Trap looked at the smoldering remains of the huge cottonwood that had fallen on Johannes. The world was eerily quiet, with no more than the gurgle of the nearby creek and the telltale snap of burning embers. If not for Madsen's constant jabbering, Trap would have thought he was still deaf.

"You think he suffered bad?" The little tracker stood staring at the tree.

"He's been sufferin' a lot of years, Trap. Gone plumb loco—outta his mind."

"I guess we should still bury what's left of him," Trap muttered, his eyes locked on the pulsing embers along the thick cottonwood trunk.

Clay shook his head. "You stay here with Angela. I'll take care of that."

Moments later, Clay called out from the other side of the smoldering tree. "You're gonna want to see this."

Despite his fatigue, Trap trotted around the cottonwood. Angela, unwilling to be left alone, followed.

Johannes was gone. Madsen put his arm around a trembling Angela Kenworth and toed a shallow depression in the dirt. He shook his head and laughed out loud. “The son of a bitch cut his own arm off to get away.”

A chill ran up O’Shannon’s spine. He looked around at the blackened, ghostlike trees. The underbrush had been burned away for miles. There was no place to hide.

In the dirt, half hidden by the huge tree trunk, was a charred arm, the bone crushed, the flesh cut away just below the elbow. Beside the arm, in a small depression of earth, Trap found a gold pocket watch. It was still hot, and he used his bandanna to pick it up. He chewed on the inside of his cheek as he pushed the button to open the timepiece so he could look at the inscription.

He already knew what it said.

CHAPTER 33

“The boss is dead,” Horace Zelinski heard a muffled voice say. The ranger couldn’t move his arms or legs, but he felt the pistol, clutched in his hand, and assumed that if he truly had crossed over, the Good Lord would have had him check his firearm on the other side.

He had a splitting headache, and the longer he lay still, the more he became aware of the pain in his blistered hands and forearms. He reckoned the pain was a good sign, since it attested to the fact that he was alive.

“He died valiantly.” Horace felt the gentle prod of a boot toe and heard the pinched nasal voice of Milton Brandice. “He gave his life to save the rest of us.”

"I'm not dead yet, you patent-leather idiot!"

The beetle specialist squealed and jumped backward as Zelinski groaned and pushed himself upright.

Bandy Rollins gave a hearty laugh and yanked the ranger to his feet.

"Easy now, Corporal. You're gonna tear my wings off. I fear my flesh is a bit on the tender side after the fire."

"Forgive me, Mr. Z. I'm just tickled to count you among the livin'." Rollins pressed a damp rag to Zelinski's forehead. It dripped with cool water. "Hold that up against you there. It'll make you feel some better."

The moist rag helped immensely. As the pain in his head subsided, Horace slowly became aware of the men around him. Some lay on scorched ground around the tunnel opening, nursing their wounds and gasping for air like landed fish. Some wept with the relief of knowing they were alive. Daniel Rainwater sat against the mountainside with his cousin. Both of the Indian boys grinned openly when Zelinski looked at them.

"Did we lose anyone?"

Corporal Rollins cast his eyes at the ground. "You already know about Taggart."

"I remember that. Anyone else?"

"The Swede and Ox Monroe," Rollins said in one exhalation of breath.

Zelinski eyed the black trooper under a crooked brow.

Rollins raised his thick arms and shook his head. "Don't be so quick to jump, Mr. Z. I was busy lookin' after the wounded deputy. I didn't have time to do no wrestlin'. Turned out I didn't need to kill the fool anyway. Seems he was so all fired bent on savin' his own skin, he bullied his way to the back and passed out in a seep. He drowned right there in no more than a three-inch trickle of water oozin' in from the guts of the mountain."

It was easy for Zelinski to accept Monroe bullying himself to death. "And what about Peterson?"

Don't know for certain," Bandy said. "Heart seizure maybe. All of us was breathin' the same amount of smoke. That's for sure."

"How did the O'Shannon boy fare?"

"He's fine. Bleedin's stopped and he's restin' peaceful. He'll be up chasin' outlaws and gals in no time. I hope not in that order."

"Well and good then." Zelinski was ready to move on. The odds of any one of them surviving such a firestorm had been long in the first place. To lose only three men was nothing short of a miracle. He tossed the damp rag back to Rollins and turned to the survivors of his tired crew. "I don't know about the rest of you, but I'm ready to get into town for a meal and a bath."

A general buzz of excitement ran through the men.

"And," Horace added, a small tear in his eye, relief flooding his emotions, "if anyone is still alive down there to serve us, supper is on me."

CHAPTER 34

August 27

Clay let the pocket watch twirl in front of him, twisting and untwisting on the long golden chain. The weather had turned cooler and brought enough rain to stop the fires. An afternoon drizzle had beaten the dust back down, and the sun now shone bright yellow on the crest of the western mountains. The light reflected beautifully off the spinning watch.

Trap stood in the corral, rubbing the mule colt's ears but looking at his son, who sat on a stump, his leg in a splint courtesy of Doc Bruner. "Isn't it about time you filled me in on everything?" Blake asked. "I was a part of it, if you both care to recall."

"I'd be happy to, if I understood it myself, son." Trap shrugged and turned his attention back to the colt.

"He sure twisted off on us, didn't he, Trap?" Clay seemed hypnotized by the watch. "I mean, he put that young Kenworth girl through hell just to get back at you. That seems too wicked even for Johannes."

"His mind was gone, eaten up by revenge," Trap mused. "How's the girl doing?"

"Pretty well, considering what she's been through," Blake offered from the stump. He seemed more outspoken now that the ordeal was over, as if he'd passed some test of manhood and was now allowed to be a larger part of the conversation. "Telegraph and telephone lines are all down, so her mother can't get through to make her come home. She and her daddy are gettin' reacquainted. Old Man Kenworth told me he was startin' to think about bucking his wife and having the girl stay out here permanent. I don't know if he'll ever pay to get the lines fixed."

Clay cocked an eyebrow at Blake. "So, you been out to the Kenworth place checkin' in on the girl, have you? Good boy. You remind me of me."

Blake smirked. "I took her on a buggy ride yesterday evening, but all she could talk about was how handsome and brave that Mr. Madsen was." He threw a pine cone at Clay. "It's like you weren't even there, Pa. I don't know how you put up with that all these years."

"Wouldn't have bothered him unless your mama was involved." Clay let the watch twirl around his finger while he spoke. "And she never was, to my utter dismay."

"You think he's still out there?" Blake leaned forward on the stump, steadying himself on his homemade cane. He looked hard at both men.

"I don't know." Trap shrugged, dropping the colt's rear foot to stand up straight and face his son.

"Well, I know." Clay caught the watch in his palm and held it. "I know and so do you. Johannes ain't dead, and that's a fact. Any man bullheaded enough to dog after you all these years, patient enough to put together a plan like that, and tough enough to hack off his own arm to get away, didn't die in the fire. No, sir, I don't know how he escaped from that inferno, but I do know this: He damn sure didn't die."

"So." Blake leaned back again. He scanned the trees around him, as if a singed, one-armed Johannes Webber might come running out at any moment. "He's still out there somewhere, making another plan."

"Reckon so," Trap conceded. He bent to step through the fence rail to join Maggie, who'd come out of the house with a plate of fry bread and butter. He put his arm around her shoulders. The cooler weather over the last few days had made him a lot easier to get along with. One morning, they'd even awakened to an early dusting of snow. Maggie had been pleased. Trap had been ecstatic.

"Well, then." Blake looked at his mother while he spoke. "If Johannes Webber is still out there, just biding his time until he can try and kill you again, someone had better tell me the whole story."

"It's hard to understand," Trap said, repeating his earlier misgiving.

"Still." Clay held the watch out to Trap. "The boy's right. Johannes is bound and determined to hurt you, and by hurtin' you, he's likely to hurt all of us. Hard to understand or not, we got to try to figure out what's goin' on in that sick head of his. I say let's find the son of a bitch wherever he is and take the fight to him." The Texan grimaced and turned to Maggie. "Forgive the language, darlin'."

Maggie smiled and tapped the watch that was now in her husband's hand. "I think Blake is right. He needs to know what happened. We have to think about the future. Sometimes, the best way to do that is to rediscover the past. To understand Johannes, stop thinking about him as an enemy. Perhaps if you would reflect on the time when you gave him this gift, you could better understand his thoughts."

Trap depressed the golden stem at the top of the timepiece. The round face flicked open with a whisper.

"To: Johannes, a trusted companion," the inscription read. *"From: Trap, Ky, and Clay, 1881."*

Maggie closed the watch and Trap's fist in her own hands. "To catch this killer, you must remember when he was your friend."

EPILOGUE

The firestorm raged on through August 22nd, finally destroying over three million acres in Idaho and Montana alone. Entire mountainsides were reduced to ash. On the 23rd, much-needed rain, and later snow, finally slowed its relentless advance.

Scars from the fires are still visible today.

The towns of St. Regis, Saltese, DeBorgia, and Taft, Montana, along with Grand Forks, Idaho, were actual locations. All but St. Regis are now just dots on a map, destroyed by the great fires residents later came to call The Big Blowup.

AUTHOR'S NOTE

Every Boy Scout knows that with a little fuel, a little heat, and a little air you can have yourself a little fire. In the summer of 1910, the Rocky Mountain West saw giant helpings of all three ingredients—and a devastating inferno that destroyed three million acres in Montana and Idaho alone.

The United States Forest Service, still a fledgling agency, enlisted the aid of every able-bodied man they could find to join the battle against over 1500 fires that threatened to destroy western Montana, Idaho, and southern Canada. Loggers, skid-row bums, Native Americans, miners, and Army soldiers all united in the fight.

By mid-August, many of the fires appeared to be under control. Then, a low-pressure system moved into the West from the Pacific Ocean, spawning hurricane-force winds in the rolling grasslands of southeastern Washington. By late afternoon of August 20th, sustained gales of over seventy miles an hour roared into the northern Rocky Mountains.

Fanned by these fierce winds, sleeping fires sprang to life. Separate blazes rushed together engulfing each other and melding into a huge firestorm.

Some five hundred miles away, in Billings, the sun was completely obscured. At five P.M., eight hundred miles distant, a forty-two-mile-an-hour gale ripped through Denver, Colorado, bringing with it a swirling amber cloud of thick smoke that engulfed the entire city. The temperature fell by nineteen degrees in ten minutes. The next day, the sky was dark enough in the eastern United States that streetlights in Watertown, New York, stayed on all day.

Hundreds of settlers were blinded or permanently maimed. Official records show eighty-five—including seventy-nine firefighters—lost their lives in the inferno. No one truly knows the actual number of dead.

The characters here are works of fiction, and while they move in a historical setting, their adventures spring purely from my imagination. Though based on real locations, beyond the main roads and towns the geography is also fictionalized—out of respect for the brave souls who died along the various ridgetops, valleys, and creeks doing battle with the fires on August 20, 1910.

Center Point Publishing
600 Brooks Road • PO Box 1
Thorndike ME 04986-0001 USA

(207) 568-3717

US & Canada:
1 800 929-9108